An Orphan's Tale

An Orphan's Tale

by Jay Neugeboren

Holt, Rinehart and Winston
New York

Copyright © 1976 by Jay Neugeboren

Library of Congress Cataloging in Publication Data

Neugeboren, Jay.
   An orphan's tale.

   I. Title.
PZ4.N4840r   [PS3564.E844]   813'.5'4   75–24989
ISBN 0–03–015271–2

A section of this book was first published, in slightly different form, in *Moment* magazine.

The author is grateful to the National Endowment for the Arts for a fellowship given him while he was writing this novel.

First Edition

Designer: Robert Aulicino

Printed in the United States of America

10 9 8 7 6 5 4 3 2 1

for Peter Spackman and Donald Hutter

And thou shalt love the Lord thy God with all thy heart, and with all thy soul, and with all thy might. And these words, which I command thee this day, shall be upon thy heart; and thou shalt teach them diligently unto thy children, and shalt talk of them when thou sittest in thy house, and when thou walkest by the way, and when thou liest down, and when thou risest up. And thou shalt bind them for a sign upon thy hand, and they shall be for frontlets between thine eyes.

—DEUTERONOMY. VI. 5–9

What have I in common with the Jews, when I have scarcely anything in common with myself. . . .

—FRANZ KAFKA

I
The Home

One

Every year, just before the World Series began, Sol would leave his apartment in Brooklyn and go around the country by train to visit his old boys. He would arrange his trip so that he would arrive in Los Angeles in time for the Rose Bowl, and Charlie remembered, when he had been a boy at the Home, how he and Murray had followed the cross-country trip by tacking the postcards Sol sent them to a large wall map of the United States.

But where was Sol now? For two days and nights, using the list of names and telephone numbers Murray had given him, Charlie had been unable to find a trace of him. His failure only intensified his desire to go through with his plan —to buy the house for the two of them—but what he feared was that, just when he would get in touch with Sol and present the idea to him, the house would be sold out from under him.

In Mr. Plaut's jewelry store Charlie telephoned again, charging the long-distance call to his office phone, and when a woman answered, he explained that he had been trying to reach her husband for two days, that he had been given their number by Murray Mendelsohn, that he was trying to get in touch with Sol, and that—like her husband—he too had grown up in the Home. She replied that they had returned late the night before from a family camping trip to the Grand Tetons and that she knew nothing of Sol's whereabouts. He had not stayed with them for at least five years. She was certain, though, that her husband would want to reminisce with Charlie about Sol. Could she have his number?

"Forget it," Charlie said, and hung up.

He stood in front of the store window, his back to the jeweler, watching the children play inside the schoolyard across the street. He wasn't surprised that he couldn't discover Sol's whereabouts. In fact, he knew that his instinct about buying the small house had been connected somehow to his instinct about Sol's trips—to his sense that, except for Murray and one or two others, there were fewer and fewer boys who would take him in.

If he couldn't find Sol, he knew he would have to let the house go. He didn't want a whole house for himself. Who would take care of it? He looked across the street at the children and he tried to see himself as he was when he had been a boy, but he couldn't. He never could. He could see the faces of the others—Murray and Slats and Morty and Irving and Herman and Louie and Jerry and Stan—but he could never see his own, not even when he imagined photographs of himself. He saw Sol's face instead, and Sol was smiling at him. Sol was younger and wore a soft tan-and-gray-checked, tailor-made suit; he was standing in the courtyard of the Home waiting to take Charlie out for the day with some of the others. They were going to a restaurant and a Dodger game at Ebbets Field. Sol knew the reporters, the owners of the restaurants, the players. . . .

He had been Sol's favorite, though. He knew that. When he had told Murray about his idea, Murray had told him he was nuts, but Charlie tried not to care about what Murray said. Why shouldn't he and Sol live together if they wanted to? Charlie had thought of explaining his reasons to Murray—of trying to make him see that he wanted to do it not in order to pay Sol back, but because, simply, when he had come to the small two-bedroom house in the middle of the night, he had seen himself and Sol living in it together and enjoying it.

4

But how would Murray ever understand a thing like that? Murray always wanted reasons for things, and while Charlie could name the things he and Sol shared, what made him want to do it was, quite simply, that it was the kind of thing people told you you couldn't do. It was the kind of thing Murray called impossible.

I have dreams and needs too, Charlie thought, and he smiled, remembering the astonishment in Murray's eyes when he had used the same words in Murray's study two nights before. He checked his list, tried another number, but received no answer.

In the schoolyard the children were all packed to one side now, their faces pressed against the wire fence. They jeered and shouted as a group of boys walked past them along the sidewalk, struggling with an enormous king-size mattress. They carried it over their heads, their necks and backs bent, one boy at each corner, one fat boy in the middle where it sagged. A tall boy walked ahead of them carrying a long stick with nails in it, and he shook it at the children inside the schoolyard. They screeched back in Spanish.

Charlie turned to Mr. Plaut. "But listen," he said, "I was remembering just before when Murray held me by the ankles once, upside down into a sewer—that was down the street from the Home where they used to have a firehouse. You still live near there, right? I don't know what's there now. I haven't been back for years."

"Empty lots."

Charlie laughed. "I get pictures like that in my head sometimes, of myself as a boy, but do you know what?" he said. "I can never see my own face." He walked to the back of the store and sat down next to Mr. Plaut. Short and thin, with a smooth round head, Mr. Plaut worked a pair of silver tweezers inside the back of a small gold watch. His white shirt billowed lightly around his arms and shoulders. "I remember that Murray was holding me that way so I could get a hardball that had fallen in. I can see the sewer cover, the hole, the ball, even Murray's hands on my ankles— but I can't see my own face, or what it looked like down in there. Maybe it's because it was so dark. Tell me what you think."

"I think it's the first Monday of the month and you want your envelope, yes?"

"Sure," Charlie said. "But you can tell me what you think also."

Mr. Plaut removed the magnifying lens from his left eye and handed Charlie an envelope. "What do I think?" he said. "I think you're a good boy and that you should have a nicer job than working for Max Mittleman. I've told you before."

Charlie laughed again, easily, and patted Mr. Plaut on the back. "Don't worry about me, all right?" he said, standing. "I have a plan. This isn't forever."

They stood at the front door. "Max and I used to be good friends," Mr. Plaut said. "He was very good to me when I first came to America from Antwerp. . . ."

"I know the story by heart," Charlie said, and he stepped from the store onto the sidewalk.

Mr. Plaut had one hand cupped over his right ear, as if to protect himself from street noise. His bald head was freckled with sunspots. He held on to Charlie's wrist with his small soft fingers, but said nothing. Charlie told him that he'd tell him more about his plan the next time he saw him, if things worked out, and Mr. Plaut released him.

Charlie crossed the street and walked beside the empty schoolyard, running his fingers along the cold metal fencing. He looked up and, squinting, saw a Puerto Rican boy and girl sitting on the edge of the roof, kissing. A second boy—waiting his turn, Charlie imagined—sat several feet away from them, his feet dangling over the edge of the four-story building. He was tossing stones down into the schoolyard.

In the street, despite his irritation at not being able to reach Sol, Charlie felt good. The truth, which he didn't ask Mr. Plaut or anyone else to believe, was that he enjoyed his work. He enjoyed being away from Mittleman and the office; he enjoyed being in the city and walking in the old neighborhood; he enjoyed the pictures and sounds that would

fill his head when he went on his rounds; and—most of all—
he enjoyed handling the money.

He touched his inside jacket pocket, where the envelopes
bulged. Behind him, a young boy with straight sandy-col-
ored hair was staring into Mr. Plaut's window. Charlie wondered where the boys with the mattress were. At the corner,
in front of the BMT subway entrance, he pictured them
trying to bend and fold it so they could lug it down the
steps and through the turnstile.

He walked along the street, going from store to store, and
then from apartment building to apartment building, and the
boy followed him, a half-block behind. Charlie didn't look
back.

In the apartments of building superintendents he tried
numbers from Murray's list, but without success. He called
Mr. Mittleman at the office in New Jersey, and Mr. Mittleman told him that the house had not yet been sold. Mr.
Mittleman didn't ask him why he wanted the house for himself. Charlie imagined that he thought it was purely for the
bargain. It wasn't too often that you could take over somebody's mortgage at such a low rate. But the guy needed the
cash and Charlie had it.

"I'd get up in the middle of the night to take a listing,"
Charlie had said to Mr. Mittleman.

"It is the middle of the night," Mr. Mittleman had replied.

Charlie sat in the basement apartment, listening to the 70-
year-old superintendent tell him about his 91-year-old
mother, who lived with him. For the first time in years, she
had not been sitting on the stoop when Charlie had come
to the building. "The sun's no good for her eyes," the superintendent said. "She got big cataracts and got to stay in the
dark now."

"I'm thinking of buying a small house for myself," Charlie said.

The superintendent circled horses' names in *The Morning
Telegraph* and, in his head, Charlie saw the other guy, in

7

New Jersey, pacing the small living room, one cigarette in his mouth, one between his fingers. The man was exceptionally small and wiry, like a jockey, and when he wasn't smoking or talking, he ground his teeth against one another and cracked his knuckles. Charlie had seen his chance at once and had explained to him how long, given the high interest rates, he might have to wait for a buyer. And then—especially if it was FHA or GI—how much longer he might have to wait until the buyer could get a new mortgage approved.

The man said he'd paid twenty-four thousand for the house and was asking forty. He had bought it six years before at 6¾ percent interest. Charlie said that he might be able to offer to buy the house himself in a day or so—he could give him the difference in cash and take over the mortgage. They could close the deal within a week. The man said he'd take thirty-eight—he needed fourteen in cash —and Charlie said he'd let him know within a day. But he had been unable to get the guy to give him an exclusive listing, and, short of buying the house outright before he'd spoken with Sol, he had no way of keeping Mittleman—or some other realtor—from finding a customer.

He was confident that Sol would like the idea, but he couldn't take the chance alone. He didn't want to tie up that much cash—and the monthly payments—in a house. It wasn't the kind of investment he believed in. He heard Mr. Mittleman's voice, telling him that property ate three meals a day: principal for breakfast, interest for lunch, and taxes for supper.

He finished his rounds by early afternoon and walked back to his car, which he'd parked behind the school. He drew fresh air in through his nostrils. His pockets were full. He got into his car, and, driving toward the Brooklyn-Battery Tunnel, he thought of his money, expanding endlessly, and he wondered how much Sol had left.

Mrs. Mittleman had packed a corned beef sandwich for him, and Charlie ate it as he drove, to save time. He smiled, thinking of the loaves of unbaked bread in the bakery at the

Home. When he thought of his money he always thought of those loaves—he saw the pale oblongs of dough rising under damp cloths near the ovens. He remembered how much, as a boy, he'd looked forward to being on night shift—had even volunteered for it—just so he could have the chance to lift the corners of the cloths every half-hour and see the difference. His money grew that way.

He smiled, remembering once again the time, almost twenty-five years ago, when he and Irving, working the night shift, had plotted their famous adventure. It had taken them nearly two months just to save enough money from their weekly allowance of twenty cents—they had forgone snacks in the nearby luncheonette—to buy a bottle of cheap wine for the baker. Irving had been the salesman, convincing the old man that they were skilled enough to do the work by themselves and that when it was all done the director himself would praise him for having taken the initiative in designating responsibility.

While the old man had been drinking and sleeping on a stool behind the ovens, Charlie and Irving had twisted and carved the dough into the shapes of penises and vaginas and breasts and they had watched all night long—peeking under the cloths and into the ovens—as their creations swelled to magical proportions. When the breads were done, they had packed them into baskets and had delivered the baskets to the dining room tables, covering them with cloth napkins. Then, too excited to return to the dormitory for their usual two-hour nap before reveille sounded, they had waited on a bench, side by side, saying nothing.

When the three hundred boys tumbled into the dining room for breakfast that morning and discovered the breads, the place had gone wild. Charlie could still see Irving, standing on a table in the middle of the room and biting off huge chunks of bread as the others cheered him on. He saw Jerry and Herman leading a parade of bread-eaters across the tabletops—loaves in hands, like scepters—chanting: *Some like it hot . . . Some like it cold . . . Some like it in their mouths nine days old!"*

9

By the time the director and the counselors arrived, the boys had divided themselves into two camps and, with tables turned on their sides for barricades, they were flinging chunks of bread and pitchers of milk and juice across the room at each other. He and Irving had been banned from all evening activities for three months, he recalled, and their allowances had been docked for six months, but neither of them had ever really minded.

It was a story, Murray announced at the time, that would probably be passed down in the Home from one generation of boys to the next. He'd been right about that, and Charlie already had the item on his list: *tell Murray about KC + 2;* three of the guys he'd telephoned—including one in Kansas City he'd never met—had wanted to talk about it on the phone during the past two nights.

When Sol first heard the story, Charlie recalled, he'd agreed with Murray, but he had refused to intervene and ask the director to lift the punishments. "Character," he said then—and in his head Charlie saw Sol wink at him—"develops from loyalty to a cause. That's what your Uncle Sol believes."

*

Today I saw him. I recognized him from his pictures and I was glad he wasn't looking my way when I realized who he was because I must have been gaping. His hair is still black and curly and it crawls down the back of his neck and into his collar. I thought of Samson and how he went blind and I smiled.

This is what I thought: Now that I see him before me I know that everything will be all right and that I'll be able to get out of here.

Once he turned and smiled at me and when he did I stared into a store window and I don't think he was really paying any special attention to me. I think he likes to smile at everybody.

When I first awoke this morning before the others I

had the feeling that something would happen today that would change my life. I dressed quietly, checked the lock on my locker and I didn't put my shoes on until I was outside the dormitory. I went to the neighborhood where I lived until I was 7. I always go there when I want things to happen.

But what made him come on the same day?

A question: If I had the same feeling last week and had come then, would I have met him today or would he have been there last week also?

He looks the same as in his pictures, only older. He's 20 years older than when he left. When I came back I looked at his pictures on the walls. There are more pictures of him than of anybody else.

This is what I'll do tomorrow: Leave before breakfast again and try to see him before the stores open. But if it rains I'll stay here and rest and read and memorize things.

What will he do when I tell him where I come from? How will he look at me?

I know he'll be surprised at how much I know about him. When he walks on the street people turn to notice him. I had to hurry just to keep up with him and while he was inside stores and houses and I was outside waiting, this is what I thought about: Can anyone ever really know what goes on inside another person? If you talked to somebody you loved forever and he talked back to you forever, would you ever be able to tell one another everything you thought and felt, or would each new thing you told and heard change what you were up to that point so you could never finish?

I wonder what he would think if I asked him a question like that. He doesn't look like he ever thinks of things like that so it might mean that he does.

Here's Danny Ginsberg's brand new THEORY OF OPPOSITES: I am the opposite inside of what I seem to be outside!

Out of the difference I create the real me!

When he drove away I couldn't stop myself from taking a chance and waving to him, but he didn't see me from his rear view mirror. My heart is pounding now just like it was then.

The other boys are working on their secret room in the basement now but they didn't invite me to come.

Remember to look up: his address and phone number.

They're having movies in the dining room now so I'm in my bed writing with the lights on instead of by flashlight. When I hear noises I jump so that tells me how frightened I really am, but nobody misses me downstairs or cares.

When he knows, will he care?

I was there before the stores opened but he never came. I waited until 12:30 and followed the same route he took yesterday. I wish I had the courage to ask somebody he spoke to about him and when he might be coming back.

I got back here early but I didn't want to see anybody or go to Dr. Fogel's Hebrew class so I went to sleep. Somebody was touching my combination lock while I was gone and trying to read what I write.

> A SPECIAL MESSAGE TO WHOEVER
> MAY BE READING THIS:
> DANNY THE ORPHAN SAYS,
> "ALL ORPHANS ARE LIARS."

Because I'm an orphan my statement must be a lie. But if it's a lie then all orphans could not be liars. But if all orphans are not liars and I'm an orphan, then All Orphans Are Liars is a true statement. But it cannot be true because I am an orphan.

That's called an antinomy.

A COROLLARY: THE TRUTH IS THAT EVERYTHING I WRITE IN MY DIARY IS A LIE!

WEDNESDAY

Today I stayed here and asked if I could work in the office and Mr. Gitelman let me. They let me do anything I want here because they're grateful to have me in comparison with the others. Mr. Gitelman said he'd be in the maintenance shed working but he winked at me and he knew that I knew that he and Mr. Levine and George and Ernie would be playing cards.

I locked the door and looked him up.

His file is very thick, but even though nobody would ever know the difference I didn't remove anything or copy out anything. I like to read about what he was like when he was a boy before he got to my age. All the reports say he would have been a Leader others looked up to even if he wasn't such an athlete. When he was my age he was only an inch taller than me.

I went through the letters on Mr. Gitelman's desk and found out that the rumor about closing the Home is true. There was a letter from the Federation of Jewish Philanthropies to Mr. Gitelman giving the reason: *There aren't enough Jewish orphans anymore because of the new abortion laws!*

I remembered not to feel guilty about spying and this is what I imagined: If I was on an airplane and it was hijacked and if the hijackers asked all the Jews to stand up, I wouldn't do it. If they murdered all the Jews in front of my eyes and if the FBI came and killed the hijackers in a shoot-out and if I walked off the plane by myself I still wouldn't feel guilty!

Today Larry Silverberg came up to me and said I could come visit their clubhouse but that they voted not to give me a key. I told him what I knew about the Home closing and he smiled and squeezed my shoulder muscle, next to my neck, so that it hurt until I almost screamed. He whispered that they were making plans already. He said that if Mr. Gitelman found out they would know who the rat was.

What will Dr. Fogel do if the Home closes? Where will he go? From the photos he's been here since before Charlie or his group. The 1st photo of Dr. Fogel is from 1932 but he might have been here before that. Even though his face was softer then it looks the same as now, with his skin being full of folds like a bulldog's. 1935 is the 1st year with him in the pictures with the football teams.

1 3

I worked in Mr. Gitelman's office again in the morning. I told him he could have the day off and he laughed to hear a sentence like that from a boy like me. I'm a mystery to him.

I typed out names and addresses I need and I tried some letters, giving the reasons I'm being transferred. I liked writing about myself. I made up different life stories for myself and I thought: I could make up my whole life's story before it happens and present it to Charlie and he could see how beautifully our life would turn out together!

At 11 o'clock Larry and Marty came into the office carrying Steve between them and screaming that he was having a heart attack. I telephoned to the shed and told Mr. Gitelman that Steve was having another fit and he came and took care of things.

Mr. Gitelman and I stood in the hallway together after looking at the photos of former orphans which go all the way down the corridor. There are photos from as far back as 1904. There are photos of all the Home's football, baseball and basketball teams. There are photos of members of the Board of Directors and officers of the Maccabee Clubs and Bar Kochba Clubs and the Thespian Society, and there are signed photos of great Jewish athletes sending their best wishes to us. There are 5 locked glass cases with trophies and cups and medals.

Above the exit to the courtyard is a sign which says

 BENNY LEONARD HAS DONE MORE
TO CONQUER ANTI-SEMITISM
THAN A THOUSAND TEXTBOOKS!

Mr. Gitelman saw me staring at photos of former orphans and this is what I said to him then: "They don't make orphans like they used to."

He laughed so hard he was almost crying, but I didn't smile.

Mr. Gitelman calls us an Army of Defectives.

14

Mr. Levine calls us retards and retreads.

Even though we don't have enough boys to have teams anymore, on the 1st day of the school year each of us is required to choose a famous Jewish athlete after whom we're supposed to model ourselves. It's something they've been doing here for over 40 years. Mr. Levine the gym teacher calls it a tradition. Dr. Fogel laughs at him!

These are the athletes I have chosen since I'm here: Johnny Kling, Herman Barron, Dolly Stark, Jackie "Kid" Berg. This year Mr. Levine told me to be Moe Berg, the major league catcher who could speak 6 languages and was on a radio program called "Information Please."

People think I'm smarter than I am just because I don't say so much out loud.

After Mr. Gitelman left I decided that my favorite photo of Charlie is the small one where he has his arms around the shoulders of 2 other boys. They're in the country with their shirts off and 2 other boys are sitting on the grass in front of them. Next to the boys is an elderly man in a suit. He's very handsome, with skin that shines, and he's wearing a straw hat and holding a football under one arm. Under the photo it says, "Uncle Sol and His Boys. Spring Valley, 1947."

What I think Charlie was thinking when the photo was taken: He wishes he could know all the people in history who will ever be seeing him in this photo of this single moment! When I think of the photo now I see light coming from his eyes.

In the photo of him with the football team when he was 12 years old he didn't have any scar on his bottom lip. Then when he was 13 years old you can see a new scar running sideways even though the photo of his face in the picture is as small as a dime. Then the next year the scar is almost gone. But in the photo I like best, when he's smiling, it makes the scar show again!

I saw a page in LIFE magazine of a man who took a photo with his daughter and himself in front of his house, standing in the exact same position every year for about 40 years from the time she was a little girl until he was an old man and she had grown children of her own.

15

After supper it was my turn to work in the kitchen. I like to watch the trays of glasses go through the suds machine. I like the noise of pots and silverware, and I like to be inside the steam. I laid out all the leftover bread on trays and covered the trays with damp towels. I filled the salt shakers and sugar bowls and ketchup containers. I sorted silverware and stacked dishes.

At supper I counted. There are 14 of us left now, and counting the Puerto Ricans who work in the kitchen and clean the buildings there are 19 staff members.

*

The courtyard, with connected two-story buildings on three sides and a brick wall and wide iron gate on the fourth, was a rectangle of dirt, 230 feet wide and 160 feet long. A boy stood on top of the brick wall that was beside the gate and, in the dull yellow light that came from the lamp-posts beyond the Home, he gestured frantically to somebody on the street below. Suddenly—Danny felt his heart stop—the boy turned and leapt from the wall, rolled in the dust, then scampered to the iron gate and pulled it open.

Three boys came through the entrance, carrying a large stuffed sofa, upside down, above their heads. "Turn around," Steve said. Danny turned and faced the building from which he'd come. All lights were out. Steve tied a handkerchief around Danny's eyes and, one hand on his shoulder, Danny followed him across the courtyard and into one of the un-used buildings. He heard the other boys grunt and curse as they bumped the sofa down the metal staircase ahead of him. They passed through two rooms, then went down a second staircase and along a dirt-floored corridor before they stopped. Another door opened.

When the blindfold was removed, Danny saw eleven boys sitting on the floor, in a circle. They were all dressed in street clothes, and, the only one in pajamas and slippers, Danny could not keep from shivering.

Larry Silverberg put an arm around his shoulder and told him they expected to come across a good electric heater in the next few days. He told Danny they had invited him down because they thought he might be able to help them with strategy. Larry gestured to the room. "Not bad, huh?"

Danny said nothing. He looked around at the calendars and posters on the walls—naked girls with large breasts, horses pulling sleighs through snow-covered landscapes, sailboats dipping in peaceful waters—and he tried to smile back at Larry. The walls were paneled in a golden-colored wood, and there was a double porcelain sink built into one wall, with glass-doored cabinets above and below it. A large pink water-stained mattress took up about a third of the floor space. There were wooden chairs, three stand-up lamps, the sofa he had seen in the courtyard, an oval Formica table, and cartons of paperback books and comics.

As always, the others said nothing to Danny, and he said nothing to them. Larry sat at one end of the circle and talked about making plans. He announced that Danny had heard from Mr. Gitelman that the Home was definitely going to close and that all of them would be separated and shipped out to different institutions. He told Danny to tell them that what he said was true and Danny nodded, but he did not move toward the circle.

While Larry talked about battle plans and defenses and assignments, Danny tried to see pictures of Charlie in his head, but instead he saw a supermarket in Charlie's neighborhood, where he had stopped two days before, and he saw himself in one of the antitheft mirrors on the ceiling, watching an old Jewish man stuff cans of food into his coat pocket. Danny had looked away at once—had felt, somehow, as if *he* had done something wrong. When he was in supermarkets, he played a game he called "shopping for Jews" —he tried to guess which customers were Jews by how they looked and what they bought. Women and men who bought no meat were Jews. Those who turned cans around in their hands, looking for a Kosher ⓤ, were Jews. . . .

Two boys rolled around on the mattress, punching and cursing, and Larry yanked one of them by the hair. He glanced at Danny and talked about how the Jews had been

17

outnumbered one hundred to one by the Arabs and had defeated them because they were smarter. He talked about recruiting the Puerto Ricans from the neighborhood to help them when the time came in exchange for letting the Puerto Ricans sneak into the clubhouse as a place to take their girl friends in the winter.

"But I thought we got this place ready so we could hold out here when the spics attack *us!*" Steve yelled.

Larry slapped him on the side of the head.

"Burn the jerk, Larry!" a boy yelled, offering a cigarette. "C'mon, let's burn the jerk!"

Then—Danny had not even seen them shift from their positions—Larry was punching and shouting and grabbing, trying to get the boys back under control. Three of them held Steve down on the mattress, threatening to burn his bared stomach with a lit cigarette. Two boys slouched around the room, their right arms swinging limply from their sides, mimicking Dr. Fogel. Two of the younger boys were on top of each other on the new couch, moaning and giggling, a calendar of a naked girl between them. Danny backed to the door and waited. "I didn't want you to see them like this," Larry said to him. "It always ends up this way."

He wrapped a beer-soaked handkerchief around Danny's eyes and Danny squirmed slightly, but stopped the instant Larry put pressure on the back of his neck.

When they were outside in the courtyard Larry spoke to him again. "You're a real smart boy," he said. "You tell me what you would do if you were me, okay? You think about that."

They walked across the courtyard, then up the stairs, and the stone steps were colder under Danny's feet than the dirt had been outside. Marty stood guard at the hallway window outside the dormitory. "Nothing to report," he said.

"You think about what I said and give me a good answer tomorrow," Larry whispered to Danny.

Danny went into the dormitory and got into his bed. There were pillows and rolled-up bundles of clothes under the blankets in the other beds, but it didn't really matter, he knew. The night watchman, an elderly black man who worked full-time at the Post Office during the day, spent his shift sleeping in Mr. Gitelman's office. Danny waited awhile. Then, when he was warm again, he tiptoed to the other end of the room, out into the corridor, and unlocked his metal locker. He sat on the stone floor and wrote by flashlight.

*

Continued:
I just got back from seeing their secret clubhouse. I'm not sure exactly where it is because they blindfolded me to take me there, but it's a room that was probably once used for special meetings of trustees or alumni, with beautiful wood walls and sinks and cabinets and counters for serving drinks.

Larry Silverberg wants me to help him plan what to do to stop the Home from sending us away but I couldn't say anything to him!

All the others didn't have the patience to make plans with him and they went crazy the way they always do, wrestling and imitating boys and girls making love to each other. They have beer and wine hidden in their room.

What I kept telling myself: I can't get involved in their plan because it will get in the way of mine!

I just kept saying nothing and trying to show nothing in my face and that kept Larry from getting angry with me. I'm the only boy here he's never really tried to hurt but I have to remember not to trust anyone, whether it's him or Mr. Gitelman or even Dr. Fogel!

I hear some of them coming back across the courtyard now, trying to keep their voices low. I'll tell you more tomorrow.

FRIDAY
In the morning Mr. Gitelman asked me why I didn't go out to public school since I was the only boy from the Home with the right to go and I told him that a group of Puerto Rican boys there had threatened to beat me up because I was a Jew.

19

I didn't have to say anything else. Mr. Gitelman's children are in private schools. He used to be a public school teacher.

But this is what really happens: When I go to the school they leave me alone. I'm in all the special classes and the teachers always give me a lot of attention, but what I like to do most is just sit in the school library and memorize things. Most people leave me alone most of the time. When groups of blacks go through the subways and gang up on people they never choose me. I can look at you in a way that doesn't make you feel anything.

They can take me out of the school or send me away from the Home or change teachers on me or transfer me to a different school, but they can't take away the words I have inside me! When you have enough facts and know when to use them people believe you're strong. That's why the boys don't bother Dr. Fogel the way they do the other teachers who come here, even though he's an old man who's smaller than I am, and has a right hand and arm which are no good.

I went to his class in the afternoon and there were 3 other boys there. Dr. Fogel sat in the front with his head on his good hand, resting his eyes. I chanted the Haftorah for my Bar Mitzvah and he listened without saying if I was good or bad.

Then he sent the other boys away and asked me if I wanted to chant the Maftir also on my Bar Mitzvah day. The Maftir is the portion from the Torah that comes just before the Haftorah. I said yes.

I followed him from the room and across the courtyard. Larry Silverberg was sitting with his back against a wall, carving a pointed stick, and he waved to me. We walked down 3 steps and Dr. Fogel went into the Shul. The room is small and the only time we ever use it anymore is when one of us is Bar Mitzvahed.

My Haftorah is אחרי מת from Ezekiel and it lists the sins of the Children of Israel and how they murdered and committed adultery and incest and did not observe the Sabbath.

Why I believe Dr. Fogel likes it: because of what Ezekiel makes God say about his own hand.

20

This is what it says: "Thou has greedily gained of thy neighbors by oppression and has forgotten Me, saith the Lord God. Behold, therefore I have smitten My hand at the dishonest gain which thou hast made and at thy blood which hath been in the midst of thee."

I helped Dr. Fogel take a Torah from the Ark. He took off the velvet cover and rolled the scroll from one side to the other until he found my portion.

A question I thought of that I didn't ask: If God believes He is the only God why is He always jealous of other Gods who don't exist?

Dr. Fogel unlocked the door next to the Ark and we went into a small dark room called the GENIZAH. The smell there was beautiful, from the dust and old leather. Dr. Fogel explained to me that old prayer books, because they contain the name of God, can never be destroyed. When a Torah is too mutilated to be used anymore it's buried in the ground like a man, wrapped in a Talis.

I wanted to ask him to tell me everything he remembered about Charlie, but I didn't. He might get suspicious.

There were old Tephillin bags piled in boxes and he gave me one, and also a white and black Talis that still has some silver threads in it. He gave me a copy of PIRKAY AVOS which has the Hebrew and the English and I told him it was my favorite book, but he didn't react. Even though I'm the only real student he has left I don't believe he really cares about me.

We walked back to the classroom and I told him about the Home being closed and that they're going to use our buildings as a halfway house for Jewish mental patients. I gave him the reason I saw in the letter, about the supply of Jewish orphans drying up and he only laughed. He got angry and said that the real reason was always the same: the lack of religious observance. The Home was failing because it was failing God. Our kitchens were no longer Kosher, our Shul was unused, our boys received no real Jewish upbringing.

He said that the Home was like the state of Israel because its real purpose was to lead the Jewish people away from religion and God!

I never saw him speak with so much passion before

21

and I wondered if Charlie ever heard him speak like this. He stood in front of the blackboard and waved his good hand in circles above his head. He said the Zionists were willing to sell all of Jewish history for a nationalist "mess of pottage."

He said that Zionism represented the greatest heresy of all time. He looked at me with great anger and told me to remember his words because nobody else would ever tell me the truth. I didn't say anything but I concentrated as hard as I could.

This was what he said: "ZIONISM IS AN ATTEMPT TO ESTABLISH A JEWISH KINGDOM ON EARTH WHICH WAS AND ALWAYS WILL BE THE PRIVILEGE OF THE MESSIAH ALONE."

He got so excited that he began to choke and his face turned from red to gray but I still didn't say anything or move from my desk. Marty and a 10 year old boy named Norman were peeking through the window with their eyes bulging. Dr. Fogel punched his own chest with his fist and his color began to come back. He gave me a piece of paper and told me to write out a receipt for the Talis and Tephillin and book.

Larry Silverberg was very friendly to me today but he forgot to ask me for my answer.

What I want to know: more about Israel and its history, so I can refute Dr. Fogel!

SATURDAY

Today was visiting day so I went into the Shul with my new book and stayed there all day, memorizing and sleeping.

This is what I told myself: The Sabbath is a day of rest and a day of study and I am doing both!

I stood in front of the Ark and chanted my Haftorah. I opened the Ark but I was afraid that if I tried to lift a Torah out by myself I would drop it.

There were only 6 boys at supper, and the Puerto Rican cooks and dishwashers ate with us and talked in Spanish about baseball players. After supper I took out my Tephillin and sat on my bed and unwound the leather

22

straps. I wondered if the boy who once used the Tephillin was still alive somewhere and if he had a son who was putting on Tephillin.

When the lights were out and time had gone by the guys got into each other's beds and whispered about things they would do to girls and movie stars when they had the chance.

To remember to do before leaving:

> buy new batteries for my flashlight
> withdraw money from bank
> telephone Charlie's home
> buy sack for carrying notebooks and Tephillin +
> put aside extra set of clean underwear

A question: Is there an orphanage anywhere for Jewish girls?

*

The narrow line of colored glass that ran along the top of each section of the wall shimmered in the sun. Danny sat on a chair by the window, his *tephillin* bag in his lap, and watched the courtyard below. When the police car had appeared fifteen minutes before, Danny had been surprised to see Mr. Gitelman step out of it, but he had not, he realized, been afraid.

The boys stood huddled in a group, at a safe distance, watching Larry Silverberg being handcuffed. Danny felt nothing, except relief: he would not have to give him an answer.

A group of Puerto Rican boys stood on the other side of the street, outside the gate, watching. Larry Silverberg stepped toward the car, then raised his handcuffed hands above his head and looked up toward Danny. Danny moved away from the window, put his book and *tephillin* in his locker, and took out some of his money.

When he came to the window again, the police car was gone and only three boys were left in the courtyard. They played catch with a football. Danny left the dormitory, walked

23

downstairs and along the main corridor. Mr. Gitelman's office door was open.

Danny went in and, nobody there, he telephoned Charlie's home in New Jersey. A woman answered and said that he would be back later in the day. Danny left his name and said he was from the Maimonides Home for Jewish Boys.

Then he walked from the building, showed his pass to the guard at the gate, and stepped onto the sidewalk. He stared back through the iron bars at the boys left inside the courtyard, and he wondered what—not being friends with any of the boys he himself had been growing up with—he would have to share with Charlie when they were together. What stories of the Home could he bring to him?

He looked at the bronze plaque on the wall next to the gate and wondered if Charlie would remember it.

THE MAIMONIDES HOME FOR JEWISH BOYS

 Founded: 1897
"Give me Friendship or Give me Death."

Moses Maimonides
1135–1204

He took the IRT subway to Grand Army Plaza and went into the public library, to look things up. Afterward he walked in Prospect Park and thought about what he'd read. He wondered what Charlie and his friends had done evenings in the Home years before, and decided that having had more boys then made the difference. In the year Charlie had left the Home there had been 326 boys enrolled.

He took the bus to the neighborhood in which he'd seen Charlie, and he walked along the streets. Most of the stores were closed, but in a used-clothing store he bought a green cloth sack for $3.49, and in a drugstore he bought batteries and candy bars. He returned to the Home in time for supper and he listened to the boys at his table compare things Larry had done to them. Steve was proudest because he still had large purple marks on his arms and legs. They talked about running away and hiding out in movie theaters and getting jobs as delivery boys. One of them said he knew where a summer cottage his aunt and uncle owned was, and the boys became excited about going there. Danny didn't ask them if the cottage was heated for the winter.

Mr. Gitelman came into the dining room while they were eating and announced that Larry was going to have to go to court because the mothers of two young boys had brought charges against him. He had been forcing the boys to steal things for him by doing things to them that Mr. Gitelman would not mention. He warned all the boys to be careful and to report to him personally if they wanted to tell him anything. They would never get in trouble for telling him things, he said. "You don't know how good you have it here until you get sent to the kinds of places he's been in," he added. "Believe me."

Danny left the room while the boys were eating dessert, went upstairs, and wrote.

*

This morning the police came and took Larry Silverberg away. Now they'll have nobody to rally them when the time comes. I think I was glad that he was gone because it makes it easier for me to get ready to leave.

I went to the library this afternoon and read about Zionism.

The word Zionism was first used in 1892. In Europe at that time there was still a head tax on "Jews and cattle" that moved from town to town.

There have *always* been Jews living in Jerusalem! Jews tried to create a state there in the 16th century and at other times too!

A saying I found for Dr. Fogel: "It is better to dwell in the deserts of Palestine than in palaces abroad."

A question I thought of for him: If we had a place to call our own in 1941 would 6 million of us have died?

I looked at pictures of Jewish children frozen to death in the snow in the Warsaw Ghetto and I was surprised because instead of making me cry the pictures made my body go stiff. A girl sitting near me saw the way my fists were clenched with anger and she moved to another table.

A question for Danny Ginsberg: Why do I care so much about a Jewish Homeland? Is it because I never had a real Jewish home of my own, or is it because it's really something worth caring about?

Here are the last words of my Haftorah: "Thus saith the Lord God, Because ye are all become dross therefore behold I will gather you into the midst of Jerusalem."

I read a story about a great Zionist named Michael Halpern who was being mocked by a group of Arabs at a circus, so he entered the lion's cage unarmed and sang the "Hatikvah."

What that proves, according to Danny Ginsberg: True strength comes from imagination.

*

Danny handed Dr. Fogel his *tephillin* and Dr. Fogel told Steve to come to the front desk and show Danny how to put it on. Steve did as he was told. He made the blessing for the box and strap which go on the arm and he slipped the leather loop over his elbow and onto his biceps, so that the small black box containing the *Shema* faced in toward his heart.

He wrapped the strap that came from the box around his forearm seven times, for the seven blessings. He rolled the end of the strap around his palm and held it there while he picked up the second *tephillin* box. He kissed the top, said a prayer, and placed the leather loop that came from the bottom of the box around the crown of his head and under his *yamulka*. Danny thought that the box looked like a miniature square hat with a narrow black rim. Two leather straps hung down from the nape of Steve's neck to either side of his shoulders, and Marty and Heshy giggled, watching.

Dr. Fogel glared at them and pulled open the drawer to his desk. Inside, Danny knew, there were nipples for baby bottles, and even though it was silly, it scared the boys to think of Dr. Fogel handing them one to suck on.

Steve unwound the strap from his left palm and drew it through the spaces between his fingers, three times, so that on the back of his hand the straps looked like the letter "shin," representing the name of God.

Dr. Fogel told him to take the *tephillin* off and he did, winding the straps carefully around the black rims of the boxes and kissing the tops of the boxes lightly before putting them back into the bag.

Danny realized that, except for playing ball, putting on *tephillin* was the only thing Steve knew how to do.

Dr. Fogel asked Danny to come to the front of the room, and he asked him what the meaning of Bar Mitzvah was.

"Son of Commandment," Danny said.

Dr. Fogel asked him how he would be different after his thirteenth birthday and Danny said that in the eyes of the Jewish people he would be a man.

"In what ways?" Dr. Fogel asked, smiling.

"I can be counted among the ten men necessary for a *minyan* without which a service cannot be held and mourner's *Kaddish* cannot be said," Danny recited. "I will be considered responsible as an adult for all my actions. I will put on *tephillin* every morning. I will—"

"Yes, yes," Dr. Fogel interrupted. "But in what way will you be a *man?*"

Behind him, the boys had their heads on their desks, hands over mouths, to keep from laughing out loud. Dr. Fogel kept his eyes on Danny. Danny said what came into his head: "I'll be a man by taking care of Jewish orphans."

Dr. Fogel smiled. "Very good," he said. "That is a very good answer."

Danny saw Dr. Fogel's smile, and it seemed unnaturally large, so that he could not see the man's eyes above the smile. He felt confident suddenly. "What I want to do is be a doctor on a kibbutz in Israel," he went on. "So I can take care of Jewish children whose parents have died for God."

"For land," Dr. Fogel corrected. "For land."

*

I couldn't write anything last night about what happened yesterday because Mr. Gitelman made the night watchman check on us every 15 minutes. He must know we all know about the Home closing and the boys whispered in bed about being afraid he'll find their hideout.

Yesterday in Hebrew class Dr. Fogel made Steve show me how to put on Tephillin and he asked me questions about being Bar Mitzvahed and I answered him. Since the class ended the boys look at me in a new way because I'm the only one of them who ever spoke back to Dr. Fogel.

They might ask me to take Larry Silverberg's place but I won't do it in the way they think!

Now it's just getting light outside and I see the gate open for delivery trucks the way it is every morning. I went to the savings bank yesterday morning and closed my account. With the money left in my locker I have $72.54. When you become Bar Mitzvahed they give you a $25 Savings Bond but I won't wait for that.

I followed Dr. Fogel from the Home in the afternoon so I could see where he lives if I ever need him. He walks quickly and it doesn't bother him at all when dogs bark at him. I think the Puerto Rican boys in the neighborhood don't make fun of him because they're afraid of his arm.

When we came to a street where a group of Chasidic Jews were standing around a mobile van, he crossed to the other side. Chasidic Jews try to make Jews more Jewish by taking them into their vans and teaching them things about Judaism, but Dr. Fogel told us to beware of them. He said they were like gypsies who love to steal children! He said they worship their Rebbes more than God.

But I like to watch them move around and talk to each other anyway. When women go by the Chasidic Jews look the other way. Dr. Fogel calls them cowboys because of their big black hats and their long beards.

From where I was almost a block away I could see their eyes sparkling in their faces and I wondered what they talked about to each other when they weren't talking about God and Torah. I wanted to get near them just so I could touch their long black silk coats.

By the time I made myself stop staring at them Dr. Fogel was gone and I couldn't find him again so I came back here.

What I was thinking last night before I fell asleep: that my mind contains tunnels, boxes, corridors, caverns, mazes, layers, webs, and grids. In one second I can think something more complicated than my words can ever show, even if I had all the time in the world and I could write out all the details and relationships.

But if my mind is as complicated as I believe it is, why do I write so simply?

A good answer: My words are the other self to my thoughts!

After I took my money out I worried that the bank might telephone the Home to tell them and that Mr. Gitelman will tell everybody to be on the lookout.

I'll know tomorrow if they let me out the gate without stopping me!

*

Danny was surprised at how gently Dr. Fogel was treating him. Dr. Fogel had told the others to go outside and play and he had taken Danny to the *shul* again. He touched Danny's shoulder lightly with his good hand and asked him to put on his *tephillin,* and when Danny did things in the wrong order, Dr. Fogel did not get angry.

Danny remembered that Orthodox Jews did everything in an order, even to the point of putting the left foot out of bed in the morning before the right foot.

After Danny removed his *tephillin* and put the boxes away in his *tephillin* bag, he chanted his *Haftorah* for Dr. Fogel. Then they took out the Torah and went over the

Maftir portion several times. Dr. Fogel told him he was doing very well, and Danny wondered if Dr. Fogel was changing because of his knowledge about the Home's closing.

When they had returned the Torah to the ark, Dr. Fogel told Danny that he was a very wealthy man.

Danny wanted to please him, so he recited from the *Pirkay Avos:* "Who is the wealthy man? He who is content with his portion."

Dr. Fogel sat down. "No," he said softly. "I have land. Do you know how much?"

Danny shrugged.

"Guess."

"An acre?"

Dr. Fogel laughed. "Guess again," he said. "You're a bright boy. Guess again—I have land enough for Leviathan."

Danny stood in front of the ark, facing Dr. Fogel, and he imagined that he was a rabbi and that Dr. Fogel was the only other Jew left in the world. He told himself that he could say anything he wanted because, after the next day, he would never see him again.

"A hundred acres."

Dr. Fogel clucked inside his mouth. "I have over three thousand acres," he said, and smiled. Danny said nothing. "Do you want to know how I come to have so much land?"

"Do you want to tell me?" Danny answered.

Dr. Fogel patted the chair to his left with the palm of his hand. "Come. Sit next to me and I'll tell you the story."

Danny sat next to Dr. Fogel and Dr. Fogel, his good hand touching Danny's arm occasionally, started telling him about his father, who had escaped from Poland as a boy in order to settle in Palestine. But the man to whom he had given his money had tricked him, and at the age of thirteen and a half Dr. Fogel's father had awakened one morning to find that he had arrived in America.

Danny asked no questions. He wondered if Dr. Fogel was telling him of his father's trip because he knew of Danny's own plan. And if he knows, Danny wondered, does he want me to escape or does he want to keep me here with him?

Danny felt dizzy. He pressed his fingers tightly against the seat of his wooden chair, between his knees. He did not hear everything Dr. Fogel said, but he saw Dr. Fogel's hands moving toward his own, the limp fingers of the man's right hand kneading the good fingers of the left. Danny jerked his hands upward and let them rest in his lap. Dr. Fogel was talking about a Jewish settlement his father had established on one of two large tracts of land. The settlements existed to train Jews who wanted to go to Palestine.

Danny tried to make his own mind go backward, so he could hear again about what Dr. Fogel's father had done in New York to earn enough money to buy the land, but he couldn't recapture the words. Danny thought that it had to do with buying and selling notes, and that the notes represented money. Dr. Fogel said that his father would search out wealthy Jews from New York who had come from his city in Poland—his *landsleit*—and would get them to donate money to him for his settlement.

He said his father could talk anyone into anything but that he had never been able to talk his own son into believing in the settlement. Dr. Fogel's voice remained gentle even as he insisted with his eyes that Danny pay full attention. Danny stared at Dr. Fogel's right hand and he believed that Dr. Fogel wanted him to touch it. Dr. Fogel was saying that he was certain a bright boy like Danny knew the words to the psalm: How shall we sing the Lord's song in a strange land? If I forget thee, O Jerusalem, let my right hand forget her cunning. . . .

Dr. Fogel laughed to himself, gurgling slightly, and said that he had disobeyed his father and run away when he was nineteen, but that his father had, in his bitterness, willed the land to him anyway. It was his joke, Dr. Fogel said. Danny thought that the fingers on Dr. Fogel's right hand were growing red and scaly, but he knew it was all in his imagination and so he concentrated on Charlie's face and imagined himself telling him who he was and where he had come from. He saw Charlie smiling the way he had when Danny had been looking into the store windows.

Danny looked up. Dr. Fogel was no longer sitting next to him. "Come," Dr. Fogel said, standing at the door. "Enough. I shouldn't bother you with such tales. Come."

Danny wanted to stand but he couldn't. Dr. Fogel asked Danny if he knew that the great Theodor Herzl, the father of Zionism, had wanted to buy land in Argentina or Uganda for his Jewish Homeland? Did Danny know that Herzl had advocated having all Jewish children baptized?

"Why?" Danny asked.

Dr. Fogel turned away without answering.

"What will happen to your land when you die?" Danny asked.

Dr. Fogel's back passed through the doorway as Danny spoke and Danny thought Dr. Fogel felt bad because he had told more of his story than he had planned to, even though Danny didn't believe he had done anything to force him to.

He sat for a while, looking at the faded blue velvet curtains that covered the ark. How much, he wondered, would he need to know to be able to feel completely what it would have been like to have been Dr. Fogel's father when he was just past thirteen being smuggled on the wrong ship across the Atlantic Ocean?

*

WEDNESDAY (MORNING)

I never slept last night.

I thought about the end of the world.

I read in the library that the end of the world will come not from war or starvation or radiation or overpopulation but because man's creation of energy will add too much heat to the earth's atmosphere.

If you were the only Jew left on the face of the earth would you contain in your genes the entire history of all the Jews who ever lived, and if you found one Jewish woman and started all over would you be able to repeat all of past history? But if you could, wouldn't it mean that because the past is finite and you were multiplying into the future based on the past that the future would be finite also?

I spent my last evening in the Home watching TV with the other boys. Years from now will I become somebody so that they'll want to say they knew me now? Will they remember what I looked like today?

Nobody will be able to explain me.

DANIEL GINSBERG HEREBY DECLARES THAT THE MAIMONIDES HOME FOR JEWISH BOYS IS NOT RESPONSIBLE FOR HIS ACTIONS. ANYTHING WHICH MAY BEFALL HIM, GOOD OR ILL, IS DUE TO THE EXERCISE OF HIS OWN FREE WILL.

I am grateful to the Home for having fed, clothed, and educated me for the past 5½ years of my life.

Possessions left in my locker if and when it is opened shall be divided among the other boys with 100% orphans getting 1st choice and those with 1 living parent 2nd choice.

I forgive my mother.

Yesterday Dr. Fogel told me about land he inherited from his father who was a Zionist. He said that he and his father agreed on only one thing about land, that it was the only thing God wasn't creating more of!

What I'd like to do: learn to play a musical instrument, either the flute or the violin. I don't think I'm too old to start. Years ago they used to have bands in the Home but I didn't see Charlie's picture in any of their photos.

I was born near the spot where I 1st saw him but I've never been outside of New York City in my entire life as far as I know.

Remember to look up: Herzl and baptism.

Now that I'm leaving I can say what my great desire is someday: to have friends who will be like brothers! Since my stay here was only temporary and the Home itself will soon be gone, it's a good thing I didn't become attached to anyone here who I might not see again for years and years. It got easier to say nothing to them as the years went by.

If I was a real genius it wouldn't be so hard for me to memorize things.

It's easy for me to figure out why I want friends like brothers, but the reasons don't matter to me. I believe that my chance will come soon and that when it does I will have a great deal more to offer another person because of the way I've been saving myself.

DANNY GINSBERG WILL SAY NOW THIS 1 TRUTH THAT EVERYTHING HE TELLS YOU IS A LIE.

Two

From where the boy sat, on the hill above the playing fields, the grass appeared to be black. There was, he knew, a physical explanation: the sun, setting in the west, was in his eyes so that he squinted, and the breeze, coming from behind him, was blowing the blades of grass away, in shadows, all down the slope of the hill. The soft blackness, coming after lush green, comforted him.

Beyond the playing fields, upon which boys were working out in football uniforms and girls were playing field hockey, the school itself seemed cold and beautiful to him. There were no turrets, no towers, no old stone, no shadowy recesses: it was all rectangular and shining, and this pleased him. He imagined that he was sitting just inside the rim of an enormous plastic dome, his back grazed by its hard smoothness; the frantic yelling of the girls and the chants of the boys, rising to him, were buffered by the enclosure so that, reaching his ears, the sharpness of each isolated cry was gone. The dome seemed to be protecting them all from harm.

He thought he could hear the panting and feel the warm breath of each individual girl. They wore blue skirts and white blouses; those who sat on the sidelines, or watched the boys practicing, wore blue blazers with red and silver emblems on the left breast pockets.

Some of the boys were pushing blocking tackles, grunting like cattle. Other boys stood along the sidelines, and on the edges of the fields, away from the games, he saw boys and girls with each other, lounging on the grass. He wondered if they would kiss in front of their teachers.

He heard a rustling and his heart thumped. He didn't want to be caught or questioned before he had done things his way. He stood and lifted his green sack, shielding his eyes with his left hand. He saw her skirt first, and then her thigh—the knee was lifted and bent slightly. She had her back against a thick birch tree and the boy held on to the tree with both hands as he pressed into her. Their blazers were folded into one another like rich drapery, and he saw the boy's hand move underneath her school emblem. Behind the calf her ankle gripped the boy's leg. Their schoolbooks were scattered around them among the ferns.

He watched them for a while, mesmerized by the rotating motion of their heads as they kissed one another. His heartbeats came more slowly, and he felt calm again. He didn't, he realized, even feel jealous of them. They seemed to kiss so quietly that he actually felt that he wanted to be able to tell them how happy he was for them. . . .

He moved to his left, along the ridge where he had been sitting; the sun, molten orange, was now below the tree line and he could see more easily. The shadows on the playing field were longer, the colors, in the afterlight of the bright sun, more intense. The green of the lawns was more profound, more lush, and the trees seemed larger. The glass windows of the school buildings, without any reflections, were black, and he could now see beyond the buildings themselves to what looked like formal gardens: hedgerows, mazes, clusters of color among the green rows, geometric shapes along borders. There were flashes of reds and yellows along trellises, and more delicate pinks and purples and blues within the rows. He realized that he knew nothing about trees and flowers, not even their names.

The students seemed to have such easy ways with one another! He watched them shout and wave, touch briefly, and then move off. He imagined this: that the girls were, as they ran across the field chasing one another, swimming in clear green water. Their motions were fluid. He was unaware of their shrieks. The sunlight, coming through the trees at a low slanting angle now, tempered the driving bull-like movements of the boys. Their drills were mechanical, yet graceful. The football spiraled through the air soundlessly. He had never, he felt, seen any scene that was so peaceful —as if, he thought, the boys and girls were *about* to do things. As if, really, they were not even there and what he was seeing was an empty field, and images that they were watching with him—images that they would, when they played on the field itself, imitate with perfection.

He thought of a story he knew about a king, Frederick II, who ruled Italy in the thirteenth century, and who had wanted to know what language was the true language of mankind. He had therefore placed a group of newborn infants in a room together in the remote part of his castle and raised them so that they were clothed, fed, and nurtured without ever hearing the sound of an adult voice. His philosophers observed them. In this way the king believed he would discover what the true universal language of man was.

There were women who fondled and kissed and played with and loved the children, and the children seemed normal in all ways: they ate, they crawled, they cried, they laughed, they walked, they played—all without ever hearing the sound of a human voice.

Then, one morning, when the servants opened the door they found that the children had, during the night, all died. The oldest child was not yet four and the youngest just past three. The king grieved, for he had loved the children.

It was a story, Danny thought, that would have appealed to Dr. Fogel.

He saw the girls running together, their hockey sticks in the air, toward the buildings. The boys lined up in rows and were racing in groups, as hard as they could, toward the far sideline. They ran with their helmets off and they swallowed air in giant gulps. Boys in blazers collected the balls and equipment.

Danny felt hungry. He had not eaten since nine that morning, when he had had two Hershey bars and a Coke. He felt his stomach flutter, and he hurried down the hill, digging his heels into the sod for balance. His palms were moist and his throat dry. His thighs quivered slightly, as if his pores were about to open and allow the sweat to rush out over his skin. Under his arms, the soft hairs were already drenched.

He breathed slowly and deeply and walked to the man with the megaphone and clipboard. In their uniforms, with shoulder pads and hip pads under the red jerseys and blue pants, the players seemed monstrous to him. Their faces, framed above the red and blue bulges of fabric, seemed absurdly young. Some of them were his own age, though most seemed older.

When he spoke, his voice was stronger than he had expected it to be. He had planned to recite the Home's motto first, so that he would be able to see Charlie's eyes sparkle with illumination, but now that he was in the midst of the actual situation he found that he felt so totally disconnected that he could recover only by speaking to the point.

"My name is Danny Ginsberg," he said, "and I come from the Home. I came here to tell you that it's going to close soon. You have to save it."

"What?"

Charlie turned, the megaphone moving sideways in an arc, and he looked down into the boy's face. *"Next—ready—go—!"* he yelled to the last row of boys, and they sprinted across the field, helmets cradled under arms or swinging by their sides. "Move your fat sissy ass, Hills!" he called, and, winking at Danny, he started out across the field himself. He caught up to the players before they were halfway to the other side, and he whacked the clipboard against their rear ends, one after the other. Then he veered to the left and yelled for all the boys to follow him.

They ran around the field three times, and Danny, inside

the circle, turned slowly to watch their progress. Charlie drifted among the runners, now taking the lead, now dropping back to force stragglers toward the front of the group. On their fourth time around he led them through the goalposts and yelled to them to sprint to the building. Danny felt cold, watching them.

Charlie trotted to him, smiling, then leaned over, hands on thighs, chest heaving, and he thought, if I make it to forty, I'll make it to fifty. He pressed his hand against his chest, on his blue nylon windbreaker, and he felt his heart pumping hard and fast. The tones were strong. He touched his fingertips to his wrist and watched the second hand move on his watch. Seventeen months to go.

"Come on," he said, impatiently. "Tell me again. Talk to me. Talk to me—"

Danny shivered. He watched the sweat pour off Charlie's face, and he saw, where Charlie had been pressing his hand against his chest, a moist dark handprint. Danny stared.

"Come on," Charlie said again, sucking in air and taking his pulse a second time. His rate was dropping fast. He noticed the boy's hazel eyes. "Come on. Talk to me—"

"My name is Danny Ginsberg and I come from the Home. I came here to tell you that it's going to close soon. You have to save it."

"Haven't we met somewhere before?" Charlie asked, and laughed at the line. He put his arm around the boy's shoulders. "Listen, Danny—that's what you said your name was, right?—you eat steak and drink lots of milk and work with the weights and then try us again next year, okay?"

"But I'm from the *Home!*" Danny cried, and he pulled away. "I saw you in the city—in Brooklyn—and I recognized you from your photos. I'll prove it—I'll give you facts."

Charlie squatted, so that he was just below the boy's eye level. The boy's hair, with slanting rays of light filtering through from behind, seemed to float just above his head in golden puffs. In his head, Charlie was making lists of things to do for the evening and for the next day. "Listen," he said, laughing at himself. "Do you know what I do sometimes?—If I finish something that wasn't on a list I made, I write the thing down anyway just so I can cross it out." He clapped Danny on the shoulder. "What do you make of that?"

"You're not listening to me," Danny said. "I saw you in the city. I come from there—from the Home—and I need a place to stay. *Please*. Would you let me stay with you for a while?"

Charlie brushed a picture of Sol from his head. "Let you *what?*"

"I can prove things," Danny said. "Dr. Fogel was the coach. The laundry room used to be behind the boiler room in the West Wing. Dr. Fogel gave out nipples if you acted like—"

"Hold on, hold on—" Charlie bent down again, let his clipboard and megaphone drop, and took the boy's hands in his own. "You mean you came from there *today?*"

He watched the boy nod, and he saw the tears in the boy's eyes.

"And you told me that they're going to close it and that you ran away to come stay with me, right?"

The boy nodded his head again, but did not speak.

"Christ!" Charlie said, and then Danny saw the light in Charlie's eyes that he had dreamt of seeing.

Charlie shook his head, half laughing, half helpless. "What do you make of that?—I mean, what do you make of it?"

"I won't be a bother," Danny said. "I have some money. I could help you learn to read. I—"

"You know about that, huh?" Charlie ran his tongue along his lower gums, searching for something sweet. He let go of the boy's hands and stood. He heard screaming and cursing from inside the building, and in his head he could see the boys snapping towels at one another and grabbing balls. "I mean, you have to see that this interferes with my life, right?"

"Yes," Danny said, and he could see the sentence that

40

he'd memorized, as if the words were hanging in front of him: "But this is what I figured out that made me come— if they close the Home, then when you die and I die there'll be no living memory of what we were like when we were boys."

Charlie blinked. "How old did you say you were?" he asked.

"I'll be thirteen soon." Danny showed Charlie his green sack. "I have my *talis* and *tephillin* with me. Dr. Fogel taught me how to put them on."

"And what you're looking for," Charlie said, amused at the words that had occurred to him, "is a home away from the Home, right?"

Danny nodded, and, as Charlie smiled, he saw the slender white scar appear on Charlie's lower lip. Charlie put his arm around the boy's shoulders. "We'll try to work something out, all right? Here—" He handed him the clipboard and used one of Sol's lines: "Do something for your country. Carry this."

They walked across the lawn, in silence. Charlie liked these autumn evenings, after a good workout. He needed the silence to fill up on. He held the door open, so that Danny passed inside, under his arm. "But listen," he said, "why'd you pick me?"

Danny shrugged. "I liked the way you looked in the pictures on the walls there. . . ." The lights were off in the corridor, and the change, from the daylight, made it seem black, with spots flickering in a funnel shape toward the far end. "And then when I saw you in the street last week I just . . ." Danny stopped. "I don't know. It seemed right."

"I want you to meet Murray—Murray Mendelsohn. I'll shower first and then we'll see if he's still in his office. He's from the Home too—you knew that, didn't you? He got me the job here—he's the headmaster."

"I saw his pictures on the walls," Danny said. "But I never looked him up. I didn't know he was here."

"He'll be glad to meet you," Charlie said. They walked

41

down the hallway. The sound of Charlie's cleats, metal on tile, was like rain; the only light came from the windows to classrooms. Charlie said that Murray took a great interest in the Home—in its history, in what happened to all the boys. He told Danny that Murray had once organized an alumni association.

Inside an enormous gymnasium Danny saw braided climbing ropes, with mats underneath. He thought of Dr. Fogel, and when he did he knew why—he could see coils of rope on the sea-blown deck of the ship Dr. Fogel's father had come on. He followed Charlie into the locker room. All the players were gone.

Charlie started to undress, and Danny sat on a bench in front of the lockers, the clipboard on his lap, waiting. Danny looked down at the diagrams of football plays—circles and X's and arrows and broken lines. "The truth is," Charlie said, "you said the right things to get what you wanted from me and that's something I like in people. It's a quality I look for."

As they drove up the driveway, the car lights illuminating two rows of rhododendrons that led to the garage, two small lights moved toward them, from the left. Danny thought he was hearing the sound of subway trains. The lights continued toward them, growing larger, up a slope, then onto a level even with the driveway.

Danny got out of the car and stood by Charlie's side. He smelled wood smoke, sweet and pungent. In the open doorway of an enormous white house he saw faces of children, one above the other. The two lights, from the left, were almost upon them and they blinded him momentarily, so that he looked away, surprised to find himself frightened.

The machine—orange and black, with wide grooved wheels—stopped a few feet in front of them. The grinding and chugging noises were gone. Danny looked at the stars, through the leaves of the high trees that surrounded them, and he found himself wishing that the lawnmower were a tractor, the house a barracks, and the stars those looking down on a border settlement in Israel. There, he felt, sharing danger among Jewish boys and girls who had grown up with one another, away from their real parents, he would never need to have explanations ready for anybody.

Murray walked toward them, through an opening in the rhododendrons. He wore a blue blazer with the red and white school emblem on its left breast pocket, and he was smoking a pipe. Danny recognized the face from the photos—a series of circles, pinched together in the middle of a round, pock-marked face. Small rimless glasses magnified a pair of small round eyes. He was only an inch or two taller than Danny, if that, and despite the round lips and bulbous nose he was very thin.

Charlie was saying something about interrupting Murray in his oblivion and Murray was shaking Charlie's hand and telling him how glad he was that he'd come by. He told Charlie that he had good news. Charlie said he would have time for one drink, and when he glanced at Danny, Danny put his hand forward, believing Murray wanted to shake it.

"My name is Danny Ginsberg and I come from the Home," he said. "I recognize you from your pictures."

Murray did not take Danny's hand. He was touching the steering wheel of his mower and joking about it. He said his mower was the only thing his wife was jealous of. "It's the free time, I suppose, that she'd like to have with me for doing nothing. Anita is gifted that way," he said to Charlie. "She's not like you and me. She can enjoy doing nothing."

"Hey!" Charlie said, squeezing Murray's arm above the elbow. "Shut up and listen to somebody else for a change. The kid told you he's from the Home—from *our* Home."

"They're going to close it," Danny said.

Murray looked toward the house, gesturing to his children to come forward and join him. "I'm very sorry," he said. "We'll have to talk about that, won't we?"

Danny stepped back and he thought: *Murray can call Mr. Gitelman and they'll make me go back!*

Three children ran up the walkway yelling Charlie's name —calling him "Uncle Charlie"—and asking if he were going to stay for dinner. Charlie lifted the three of them at once, in a bear hug. Then he swung the youngest girl around and asked for a kiss. "Okay," he said, setting her down. "Here's the question of the day—are you ready?" They nodded, all eyes. "What's the difference between a duck?"

"It's a problem," Murray was saying. "I keep in touch, you know. A Mr. Gitelman—I've had correspondence with him. I know things have been going downhill."

"His left hind foot is both the same!" the children squealed. "His left hind foot is both the same!"

A woman emerged from the house, wiping her hands on an apron. Two older children, a boy and a girl, were with her. Danny wished he could laugh with the children. Why had they found Charlie's riddle so funny? Why did he feel so incapable of laughing at silliness? It was something he had always been afraid of at the Home—his inability to enjoy nonsense or horsing around—and yet he did not want to change, he knew, not even for Charlie.

He watched Murray's wife kiss Charlie, and this made him feel better—less fearful somehow that Charlie would want to return him. Danny took the woman's hand when she offered it to him. "I'm Anita," she said. "And these are our children."

They were lined up in front of him, and when they each stepped forward and shook his hand, they gave him their names and ages: Ephraim—fifteen, Hannah—fourteen, Dov —eight, Rivka—six, and Eli—four.

Anita took Charlie's arm and led him toward the house. "I'm sorry you didn't get in touch with Sol in time," she said. "Murray told me about your plan falling through."

"Good lord," Murray said. "Are you going to encourage him—?"

"Have you heard from him at all?" she asked.

Charlie said he hadn't, but that it was probably just as well. Dov and Rivka grabbed Murray's sleeves and yanked, asking him when Uncle Sol was coming to stay with them. "When your Uncle Charlie finally grows up," Murray answered, and he walked into the house.

Charlie laughed. Danny followed him inside, into an enormous kitchen. In the center of the room a large oval table was already set for supper. White cloth napkins, beside each plate, were rolled inside silver rings. The table was made of oak, and Danny saw that its pedestal was carved in the shape of lions' paws. The room reminded him of rooms he'd seen at the Brooklyn Museum, next to the library—of one of the reproductions of a genuine colonial home. There were wood beams in the ceiling, copper pots and saucepans hanging above the stove, and painted plates —with flowers and butterflies in swirling colors—hung on the walls. The floor was made of wide, smooth pine boards. Danny remembered how he had, at the museum, imagined that he was the guard, and how he saw himself, at night, when the museum was empty, taking out his lunch bag and entering one of the old dining rooms and eating there, at a table set with silver.

He wanted to tell Anita how beautiful her kitchen was, but when he spoke he said something else: "All your children have Hebrew names."

"That's right," Murray said. "It's interesting that you should have noticed that, isn't it?"

"He's a sharp kid," Charlie said. "Dr. Fogel's been teaching him things."

"He's from the Home," Murray explained to Anita, "and he told Charlie that they're going to close it."

Anita looked up from the oven, where she was basting a roast with a syringe. "But you knew that already, didn't you?"

"Not officially," Murray said.

Charlie put his arm around Danny's shoulders, and Danny found himself stiffening. The children moved quietly around the room, getting things ready, as if, Danny thought, by prearranged signals. He watched Ephraim set two new places and rearrange the place mats around the table. He didn't want Charlie to tell Murray anything else, but he had no way of saying so. "Danny's the reason I can wait to get in touch with Sol," Charlie said. "Danny's going to be living with me for a while."

Murray started to say something, but checked himself and sighed: "And what am I supposed to say to that?" he asked.

"Nothing," Charlie said. "I didn't go out and find the kid—he came to me."

"Did I ask you for an explanation?"

"You said you had good news," Charlie said, sharply, and he walked away from Danny. Danny saw Anita smiling, her cheeks flushed. "I've heard so much about Dr. Fogel," she commented. "Except for Sol, I think you talk more about him than anyone else."

Murray removed three glasses from a small three-shelf oak cabinet next to the pantry. On the top shelf, behind the glass door, Danny saw a silver spice box—a *tsumin* box— that was used for making *Havdalah* when *Shabbos* was over. There was a blue and white braided candle next to the box. Danny stepped toward the cabinet. He had never seen a real *tsumin* box before, except in photos. The box, about eight inches high, looked like a tiny minaret, and Danny wanted to touch it, to tinkle its bells, to open the door on the side and sniff the spices. He felt Charlie's eyes on him, and he stopped. Why would a man like Charlie—the thought was in his head for the first time—want to let him stay?

Murray poured sherry into three glasses. "He's an interesting man. I'll admit that." He held his pipe by its bowl, pointing the stem toward Charlie. "What I mean is—I've said it before—he's the kind of man you remember. Like Sol. He stands out. Even now—and I haven't seen him for at least ten years—I can hear his voice, his sayings."

At the peak of the minaret was a silver flag. Danny forced himself to look away from the *tsumin* box, and he now noticed other things—a brass *menorah,* with lions of Judah on either side of a Star of David, above the fireplace; a *mezuzah* on the doorpost; a silver *Kiddush* cup and a stack of *yamulkas* on a table by the door; a United Jewish Appeal poster tacked up inside the pantry. These things should have made him more comfortable, he thought, yet they didn't. They seemed out of place to him in the large house, and because he felt that they did, he also felt, to his surprise, ashamed somehow.

Ephraim spoke: "Was he the one who gave out the nipples?"

Murray laughed. "That's right." He handed Charlie a glass. "He knew what things make impressions on children. I think about him a lot at school, you know. Children remember people who say things that are different—and who keep repeating them."

"It must be why they cling to you," Anita said to Charlie. She filled a tray with pale yellow buns and put it in the oven.

"We really can't stay for dinner," Charlie said. "I want to get us set up at home." He smiled at Anita, and spoke for Murray's benefit: "And I want to start looking for another place, right?" He counted on his fingers. "If Danny stays there and then Sol comes too, that's two deductions right off. Then you could set up an alumni room in the basement, we could have one room for an office—maybe Danny could bring in some more friends and before you knew it, with all the write-offs, I'd wind up with a profit."

"I know when you're teasing me," Murray said, without smiling. "But I also know that in part of you you're serious about a scheme like that, aren't you?"

Charlie laughed easily. "Could be," he said.

Danny felt faint. He backed to the door. The fragrance of the spices, he knew, was supposed to represent the sweetness of the Sabbath—a sweetness intended to linger all week long. "Please," Anita said. "Murray needs to relax, to unwind—if you go away he'll spend the evening in his study, finding work. When he finishes mowing, that is." She sipped her sherry. "My husband mows by moonlight."

"Mower power to him," Charlie said, and Anita frowned, though her eyes smiled.

"Do you remember the saying Fogel had that used to get us all upset?" Murray asked. "That money can buy everything in life but a mother, father, and brains?"

"It never upset me," Charlie said. "It's true."

Anita pretended to shiver. "I don't like that saying," she said.

The fragrance of the roast and the buns filled Danny's nostrils. He wanted to touch the *tsumin* box, to press its cold silver against his cheek. Hannah poured water into glasses. The three younger children were gone. "Ephraim," Anita said, "why don't you show Danny your room?"

"No," Charlie said. "Just give us your news and we'll head out. Your husband's workday may be over, but mine is just starting." He smiled at Ephraim. "You know what Charlie always says—for everyone who drinks the wine, there's one who stomps the grapes, right?"

"See what I mean?" Murray said. "I've heard countless students repeat those very words."

Charlie shrugged, uninterested. "What's your news?" he asked. Anita removed the buns from the oven and painted their tops with a brush. Charlie saw her look away, briefly, and then Danny saw the happiness appear in Charlie's eyes. "Again?" Charlie asked.

Murray nodded and Charlie embraced him, then hugged and kissed Anita also. "How far along?"

"Third month," Anita said. "At least that's what Dr. Shapiro says—for all doctors ever know about these things."

Danny heard somebody practicing scales on a piano. Then he heard the sound of a flute. Murray took Hannah to him and smoothed her blond hair as she leaned against him. Danny watched her breasts move underneath her white blouse. "Hannah has been studying ecology at school," Murray stated, "and did a report on the world population explosion, so we had to have quite a discussion, didn't we?"

Hannah nodded.

"I explained to her that, as Jews, while we do not of course have any special dispensation, we do have certain unique obligations, to our people and to our past. I put it this way

—and only for people who already feel the way we do—" he paused for effect, "I say this: we're not overpopulating, we're replacing."

Danny felt gooseflesh rise on his arms, and, at the same time, he realized that he was wishing Murray had not given Charlie the news. He didn't want Charlie to be distracted.

"You breed good news," Charlie said.

Murray sighed, as if relaxing, and, putting his arm around Charlie's shoulders, he walked with him from the house. "Anita's right, you know. We need more time together—we see each other at school, on weekends, but when do we sit and do nothing? How often do we drink things in and appreciate what's become of our lives—our children, our friends, our careers, our home. . . ."

Outside, in the darkness, Danny felt as if he could breathe again.

"You know what I'd like to see?" Charlie asked. "Most of all?"

"What?" Murray asked.

"I'd like to see you out here some beautiful spring day, mowing your lawn, with your kids grown up and a bunch of grandchildren all around. I'd be sitting under a tree with Anita and she'd be knitting, and there'd be a great big shit-eating grin on your face as you drove by, your grandchildren waving at you—and then suddenly Anita would jump up and yell, and—pipe and all—you'd ride right over the edge and into your pool—!"

Murray laughed and swung at Charlie's shoulder with his fist, but Charlie caught his fist and squeezed until Murray cried out in pain.

"I've warned him," Anita said. "I've told him not to mow at night. The pool is still full."

"But he's Murray the Mower," Charlie said.

From the doorway the children chanted in singsong: *"Mur-ray the Mow-er . . . Mur-ray the Mow-er . . ."*

"There's no point in draining it yet," Murray argued. "Why did we pay to get a heated pool if we don't use it at this time of year?"

Charlie sat in the car. Anita held Danny back slightly, by the arm, and whispered to him to take care of Charlie, to promise to see that he didn't work so hard.

Charlie looked past Danny, out the car window, into the blackness, and, in his head, he saw the tables in the main dining room, set with white linen cloths and the Home's special Passover plates and silverware. It was black outside the dining room windows also, and most of the boys were swaying from side to side and flopping into each other, to prove how much wine they'd had to drink.

Dr. Fogel sat at the head table, on two huge white pillows. Murray sat next to him on a single pillow, helping him run the Seder. The director, the counselors, and several guests—former orphans who had become successful doctors or lawyers or businessmen but who, like Sol, had no families of their own, sat with them.

Charlie wondered: am I still the simplest son? He remembered the story they had read, about the four sons—the wise son, the wicked son, the simple son, and the son-who-doesn't-know-how-to-ask. The wise son asked for the meaning of the Passover laws. The wicked son asked, "What do you mean by this Seder?" and by using the word "you" he did not include himself. The simple son asked what it was all about. But the simplest son said nothing—and Charlie could see Murray calling upon him to read the part from the Passover Haggadah. Even now, more than twenty years later, Charlie felt, all over again, slightly nauseated with helplessness. He heard the silence as the three hundred boys waited for him to read and then, realizing that they made the connection—Murray had chosen him because everyone knew he had trouble reading—he heard their raucous laughter fill the room and he saw Murray smile at him triumphantly.

Charlie saw Dr. Fogel stand and point to the cup of wine that had been set out for the prophet Elijah. It was much later and the Seder was almost over. Some of the boys were sleeping with their heads on the tables. The dishes—all but the wineglasses—had been cleared.

Charlie heard Dr. Fogel say that the coming of Elijah would herald the coming of the Messiah. The Jewish People had been chosen to be a blessing unto all nations, and all nations would, in the time of the Messiah, know why. The joy and freedom of the Seder—the singing and drinking and being allowed to eat as one wished, sitting or reclining—was but a small taste of the *Olam Habah*—the world to come. They would open the door for Elijah, Dr. Fogel said, and they would pray to God and ask Him to pour out His wrath upon the heathen who did not know His name. They would ask Him to destroy those who had destroyed the House of Jacob. . . .

The room was absolutely still. Charlie heard Dr. Fogel speak again. "We will now open the door so that Elijah may come in and join us. Let the stranger and the homeless—let all those who are hungry and poor—let the widowed and the orphaned—let them enter also!"

Charlie saw the back of his own head as he turned to face the doorway. A group of boys raced to it, fighting with each other for the honor, and when they had shoved it open, there was Sol, a big grin on his face. The boys all gasped—and then they cheered. Dr. Fogel began chanting the prayer, looked up, and stopped. Sol stepped into the room, laughing and waving. Charlie remembered how his own heart had leapt, how he had run from his chair and tried to get through the pack of boys surrounding Sol. *"It's Elijah! It's Elijah!"* they had all screamed, and Charlie had joined with them.

When Sol had reached the head table, and was shaking hands with the other men, Dr. Fogel was gone.

Charlie wondered what Dr. Fogel would do when the Home closed. He smiled to himself, thinking of telling Murray that he'd take him in also, and let Fogel and Sol fight it out for the leadership of his new Home! He heard Murray lecturing him about trying to turn everything into a joke, but he knew, at the same time, that he was really worried about Sol. Did Murray know that? Did Murray understand that taking Danny in was more than a crazy scheme? Charlie admitted that, like Sol, he liked being the center of attention, he liked thinking of people laughing and repeating stories of things he'd done. The story of Sol coming through the door had become a Home legend within days, and, at his own Seders, Murray would now tell the story to his children every year. But Charlie also believed in the things he did and the schemes he thought up.

He reached across the back of the front car seat with his right hand and patted Danny's head. He answered the boy's question and told him that it was true, Dr. Fogel had really been the coach, and he added that he had been the best coach because he'd never played himself and didn't know how to. He told Danny that if he'd learned one thing in all his years at the Home it had been the thing Dr. Fogel had taught him—that desire is everything. Dr. Fogel had wanted to know how to do something he would never be able to do.

Danny shrugged and said that Charlie *was* a great athlete and now he was a coach too, and Charlie was surprised—pleased—by the boy's sharpness. "Sure," he said, "I was a natural—but it's what made me work even harder, don't you see? I can never know what it's like to desire things I already have."

Danny laughed. "Everything is upside down sometimes, isn't it?"

They drove in silence on dark winding roads where the houses were set far back, behind walls or trees or hedges. Charlie was glad to see the boy more relaxed than he'd been in Murray's house. He listened to the boy tell him that Dr. Fogel had given him a book, and that he tried to memorize something from the book every day. Danny recited something in Hebrew, but Charlie didn't pay attention. "I can remember when it used to be romantic to be an orphan," he said. "I got a lot of mileage with girls when I was younger, being an orphan." He looked at Danny. "But who gives a shit about orphans anymore, right?"

Danny nodded. "We're an endangered species," he said.

"A what?" Charlie asked, but before Danny could repeat

himself, Charlie was laughing and telling Danny that he'd have to remember the line for Murray.

Danny saw a sign in the front window, a red neon light: *Mittleman Realty.* "I think I'm very hungry," he said. He looked down at his legs, at the cloth sack on his lap. "But —but I'm not sure I can get out of the car."

Charlie was trying to make the boy understand. "Don't get me wrong about what I said before," he said. "Don't think I'm one of those guys who'll keep going forever, never satisfied. I have a plan, right? When I get to forty, I stop— whether I've made my bundle or not."

"And then?" Danny asked.

"Then—? Then I'll become a rabbi."

Danny felt his heart jerk. *"Really?"* he asked.

"Sure," Charlie said, and he laughed in a way that made Danny feel uncomfortable. He got out of the car and walked around to Danny's side. When he reached in for him, Danny shook his head sideways, leaned on the seat, pushed himself up, and stepped out. His legs were cold.

"I didn't have to say it—that I felt as if I couldn't move, did I?" Danny asked.

They walked up the front steps and into the house. A woman called and asked if it was Charlie and he called back that it was and that he had someone with him.

"Rabbi Akiba started out from home when he was forty," Danny said. "And he didn't even know how to read and write. When he returned to his village six years later he was already the most famous scholar in the land of Israel."

Charlie patted Danny on the shoulder. "I had him in mind," he said.

Charlie embraced Mrs. Mittleman. "How's my sweetheart tonight?" he asked.

Danny watched the woman's eyes, over Charlie's shoulder. They were slate gray, and they stared at him coldly. "I'm Danny Ginsberg," he said. "I telephoned you two days ago."

"Of course," Mrs. Mittleman said, stepping away from

53

Charlie. "I would have thought you were older—on the telephone your voice was much older—but come. Max is already showing his movies. You'll enjoy them. Are you hungry?" She smiled. "You must be."

She left them. Charlie hung his jacket in the hall closet and spoke to Danny, softly. "It goes against what most people think, my living here, but it's the very thing people resist too much. Just relax with her if she seems jealous. She likes to think of me as her only child, if you know what I mean. That's desire too, right? They never had a son, I never had parents. We fill one another's needs. It's what lets things work out."

Danny took his jacket off but held on to his sack. "How much will you tell her?" he asked.

He followed Charlie through a dark room where there were desks and file cabinets. The neon light flashed red on the inside walls. "Like with you," Charlie went on. "I mean, my wanting you to stay with me. We know the reasons, right? So why fight them?"

"Sometimes you don't answer my questions."

"Come on now," Charlie said, taking Danny and pressing him to his side. "What are you so scared of? Let's put it this way—I always wanted a kid brother and you probably wanted an older one like me, right?"

They were in the living room and Mrs. Mittleman stood in front of them, blocking images on a movie screen, plates in her hands. "I don't think so," Danny said to Charlie. "Not really."

"We'll work on it then."

Mrs. Mittleman led Danny to a metal folding chair and he sat. She set up a TV tray in front of him and put a sandwich and a glass of milk on it. "This will hold you while the chicken warms," she said.

Mr. Mittleman, sitting on a three-legged stool next to a movie projector, grunted slightly, acknowledging Charlie's presence. Charlie sat on the couch, his arm along the back, Mrs. Mittleman's head resting on his arm. He balanced a plate on his lap. Danny bit into his sandwich and looked at Mr. Mittleman. He was a thin man with a large round head. He wore a jacket, a white shirt, and a tie, and he was smoking a cigar. Without looking at any of them, and without removing the cigar from his mouth, he spoke to Charlie. "Here's a new one—what's the difference between a Jew and a pizza?"

"I give up," Charlie said. "What's the difference between a Jew and a pizza?"

Mr. Mittleman's voice was even and dry, and his lips did not seem to move when he spoke. "When you put a pizza in the oven, it doesn't scream."

Nobody laughed.

"Danny's going to be staying here with me for a while," Charlie said to Mrs. Mittleman. "If that's okay with you—"

"Of course," she said.

"It's my house too," Mr. Mittleman said. "I pay the bills and tell the jokes."

On the screen, in black and white, a boy and girl were in a bathtub together, the boy spilling water on the girl's head. "Max has home movies of his whole family," Charlie explained to Danny. "It's his hobby. He has films going way back—"

"To 1933, the year we were married," Mr. Mittleman said.

The film fluttered. Mr. Mittleman rested his hand lightly on the reel, the sprockets caught, and a man was wrapping the boy in a towel. Then the boy was being tossed up and down toward the ceiling.

"Danny's from the Home," Charlie said. "Where I grew up."

"Yes," Mrs. Mittleman said. "I know."

Mr. Mittleman looked toward Danny for the first time. "You know something?" he said. "He looks like an orphan." Then his eyes were on the screen again. "But Shirley will fatten him up."

Danny dug his fingers into the side of his sack and he

could feel the ridges of the *tephillin* boxes. He tried to concentrate on a passage from the *Pirkay Avos* that he had memorized, about love. He was aware that Charlie was telling the Mittlemans about Murray's news and that Mr. Mittleman was telling a story about a Jewish man who had tried every form of birth control and had ten hungry children. The doctor recommended orange juice. " 'Before or after?' the husband asked. 'Instead of,' the doctor said."

Charlie was saying that he was happy for Murray and Anita. He said that Murray seemed cold about things, because of his theories, but that it wasn't so. Mr. Mittleman, on the screen, twenty pounds heavier and twenty or thirty years younger, puffed smoke into the camera. "I was once a young man," Mr. Mittleman said.

"I like Murray and Anita," Mrs. Mittleman said. "I think their family has a beautiful image."

"My wife thought the Kennedy family had a beautiful image," Mr. Mittleman said.

Charlie asked Mrs. Mittleman if he'd ever told her that even before he'd come to live with them, he'd often seen movies in his head. Danny smiled.

"If his brother had lived to become President I don't think his image would have been as good as John's, do you?" Mrs. Mittleman asked. "He was too emotional."

Charlie looked at the film, in color now, of a boy jumping up and down in a wading pool. Mrs. Mittleman and her brother Oscar and Oscar's wife sat in wicker chairs watching, and Charlie realized that he had, again, been seeing pictures of Sol. Sol was with Jerry the waiter, who worked in the Catskills in the summer and spent his winters in Florida, and Charlie saw them sitting in a box together at Hialeah racetrack. "They're thinking of closing the Home," Charlie said. "But we'll see what we can do. Danny and I are going to work on it."

"It's the new abortion laws," Danny stated. "They can't find enough orphans anymore—especially Jewish orphans."

"There must be an angle for us there, Max, don't you

think?" Charlie said. "I mean, in getting into the adoption business. If there's a shortage of something there's money to be made, right?"

"We knew people who were in the business," Mrs. Mittleman said. "As a matter of fact, we were once offered a good black-market baby but—"

"Shush," Mr. Mittleman said.

"Jewish parents want Jewish kids, right?" Charlie said. "So if we—"

"It's not funny," Mr. Mittleman said. "We shouldn't make jokes with the boy sitting here."

Charlie looked at the screen more intently, trying to see himself as a boy. He remembered Adoption Day, when they'd all act as crazy as they could, so nobody would take them. He had always appeared with different color socks, his pants inside out, his fly open. Murray would stuff food in his mouth at breakfast and save it there until it was time—and then let it drool out. Charlie laughed, seeing Irving, slowly unbuckling his belt in front of some of the "buyers," as they'd called them, to show he was a genuine Jewish boy.

"We used to act nuts on Adoption Day," he said aloud. "We didn't want to leave one another. Nobody ever took any of us home, from our group."

"There are only twelve boys left, without me," Danny said. "We haven't had a new boy for over two years."

Mr. Mittleman turned to Danny. "Tell me," he said. "Just from looking at me, how much money would you say I'm worth?"

"The very young kids got taken fast," Charlie went on, "but once you got past five or six you were safe."

"Poor boys," Mrs. Mittleman said.

Charlie shook his head and smiled at Danny. "No," he said. "That's where you're wrong. We loved it there. You know what Murray always says—the Home ruined all of us for life in the world. We had everything we needed back there, is his theory—all the things families don't give to people anymore."

57

"I'm not worth anything," Mr. Mittleman said to Danny.

A small girl ran across the screen, chasing bubbles. "Don't believe everything Max tells you," Charlie said to Danny.

Danny smiled. I wish Charlie was the father of Murray's children, he thought.

On the screen the camera zoomed in on Oscar's father. He was sitting on a wooden chair, sideways, showing no interest in his grandson. Danny recognized him as having the face of the young man who had thrown the boy toward the ceiling. He was very old and he wore round silver sunglasses and a khaki windbreaker. The collar was turned up and buttoned across his throat. On one side of his neck there was a bulge of skin—a goiter like a hand grenade—and Danny gagged on his milk, felt some of it come through his nose.

"He looks like death," Mrs. Mittleman said. "I asked you not to take his picture." She handed Danny another napkin and left the room.

"Here's your answer," Mr. Mittleman said. "I'm not worth anything until I sell."

Charlie imagined a movie about the Home, with Sol going around the country to see all his old boys. The movie could tell the story of his last trip. Charlie saw Sol calling each of his boys, but they all gave excuses. There would be flashbacks to the boys when they'd been kids at the Home, and when they'd been starting out in life with their families and jobs and Sol had helped them.

Charlie imagined the film playing in theaters, with the proceeds going to save the Home. There could be a kid in the movie with a camera who turned out to be the guy who decided to make the movie about the Home in order to raise the funds to save it. But Jerry the waiter would be the only one who would agree to see Sol. The flashbacks and cross-country scenes and scenes of the Home could alternate with the nine races at Hialeah, and at the end of the ninth race—Charlie leaned forward—when Sol and Jerry were laughing at what a good time they'd had, and in the middle of a big crowd pressing to the payoff windows, Sol would be struck down with a heart attack.

"What?" Charlie said, aloud, and he stood. The camera was moving up and away and Charlie couldn't find Sol's face in the crowd. He stood next to Danny and touched the boy's hair, lightly.

"The boy thinks you're special," Mr. Mittleman said. "You shouldn't disappoint him."

The lights were on and Danny felt dizzy. He remembered how good he had felt on the hill a few hours before, when things were beginning. "I told you to come have your chicken," Mrs. Mittleman said. "It's warm." Mr. Mittleman unhooked the screen, then put the projector away in a closet and told Charlie he was going back to work. When he was gone Mrs. Mittleman sighed and said he'd be up all night. She asked Charlie what she should do about him.

When Danny opened his eyes he heard ringing and smelled smoke. He thought of Larry and the other boys puffing cigarettes in their secret hideout. The inside of his mouth was dry from the chicken. Mr. Mittleman sat at a desk across the room, looking directly at him.

"Good morning," Mr. Mittleman said.

Charlie was on the telephone, telling a man that he knew what a big step it was to buy a house. "But let me put it this way," he said. "If I came up to you in the street and handed you a five-thousand-dollar bill, would you tell me you needed time to think it over?"

Danny rested in a corner of the easy chair. His back was damp from perspiration. The last thing he remembered hearing was a discussion between Mr. Mittleman and Charlie about a piece of property. Charlie had asked Danny to pay attention—to memorize Mittleman's words.

Mr. Mittleman picked up the phone on his desk. "Abe, this is Max. Listen to my boy Charlie. He's giving you the deal of a lifetime."

Mr. Mittleman hung up. Danny stared at a wall of photos

—houses, with prices, tacked to corkboard. He went over the things Mr. Mittleman had explained.

Charlie was listening, then smiling. He told the man to come in the next day and settle the details with Mr. Mittleman.

"I don't know why we bother with the houses," Mr. Mittleman said when Charlie had hung up. "They take up so much time, and for what? It's all cats and dogs."

Charlie looked at Danny. "You feel okay?" he asked.

"I'm all right," Danny said, and found that he was saying something he'd been half thinking when he awoke. "I wish you were still married."

"Me too," Charlie said.

"Wonderful," Mr. Mittleman said to Danny. "Tell me, when you grow up, what do you want to be—a Jewish mother?"

"Lay off," Charlie said. "He's had a long day, coming all the way from the city to find me."

Mr. Mittleman shrugged. Danny stared at the photo of John and Jacqueline Kennedy on the desk. "In all our years of marriage," Mr. Mittleman said, "the most important thing that ever happened to us was John F. Kennedy's death."

"Come on," Charlie said, starting to pull Danny from the chair. "We'll get you to sleep."

Danny pushed Charlie away. "I'm okay. Leave me alone."

"It was an experience we could share," Mr. Mittleman said. "We made a scrapbook together."

"You look so tired," Charlie said to Danny.

Danny glared at Mr. Mittleman. "High borrowing reduces cash flow," he recited. "Depreciation not only develops a cash flow which is not taxable but it helps develop losses to offset other income. The important thing is to enhance proceeds and postpone taxes. Rabbi Akiba said, 'The more flesh, the more worms. The more possessions, the more worry. . . . ' "

"Hey!" Charlie shouted, the tip of his nose in Danny's face. *"Hey!"*

"I'm sorry," Danny said, blinking.

Mr. Mittleman seemed puzzled. "Tell me—how old did you say you were?"

"I'll be thirteen soon."

"I don't believe you."

"I told you to lay off," Charlie said.

"We should go over this before you sleep," Mr. Mittleman said, opening a book. "We have a good profit on the property, but if we sell, we want to avoid tax, right? What to do—we mortgage the property and sell it subject to the mortgage, taking back a second mortgage for you for the remainder of the purchase price. You don't mind, do you? You'll have the cash from the first mortgage in your pocket and you can take installment reporting to avoid having cash this year."

"Whatever you say," Charlie said.

Mr. Mittleman closed the book, put it aside, and picked up a folder. "You shouldn't worry, young man. It's very Jewish to be a landlord. It's a tradition."

Then Charlie and Mr. Mittleman talked about the project Danny remembered hearing them talk about earlier—buying land for a shopping center, near the George Washington Bridge. Mr. Mittleman said the property was zoned residential now, but that he had assurances, and that it would cost Charlie eight thousand to pay for the assurances. Mr. Mittleman looked at Danny and spoke for his benefit. "Where land is bought at residential prices and rezoned for commercial purposes," he said, "the benefits are extraordinary. Your friend is into a good thing. The land costs are low in relation to the cost of improvements, so that we have wonderful depreciation built right in—" He turned a looseleaf book around, for Charlie to look at. "Here are the figures."

Charlie waved him away and spoke to Danny. "Come on."

"You should look at them," Mr. Mittleman said.

Charlie winked at Danny. "What for? I told you a hundred times—I'm a counter, not an accountant."

"So?"

61

"I believe in money, not figures. You know that." He went to the door, and Danny followed him. "I keep all my money tied up in cash."

"It's one way to do business," Mr. Mittleman conceded.

Charlie switched on the light at the top of the stairs and entered the room. From the other side of a large double bed Danny heard a metallic sound, then saw a head rise up. "It's only me, darling," Mrs. Mittleman said. She wore a pink flannel nightgown. "I heard you coming and I remembered that I forgot to see if the cot was underneath your bed. It must be in the cellar."

"Forget it," Charlie said. "We'll sleep together—like old times at the Home, right?"

"But wouldn't you both be more comfortable—? I can get it myself. It won't be a bother. . . ."

The room impressed Danny as having been decorated not for a son but for a daughter. The bedspread was robin's-egg blue, and the curtains, at the far end of the room, were white with blue trim. The furniture was made of shiny blond wood, and the only item that seemed meant especially for Charlie was a modern black leather easy chair. Charlie opened a closet and took out a bridge chair, unfolding it and setting it beside the bed. "Danny can use this for his clothes tonight. We'll get him some new ones soon. I'll make room." He went to his desk, marked the item on a list.

"But it won't be any trouble."

"Just leave us be, all right?" Charlie said sharply, and Mrs. Mittleman backed toward the door. "I told you before that I didn't like you nosing around in here. I take care of things."

"I didn't mean to interfere," she said. "Wouldn't I do the same if my son brought a friend home?"

"You don't have a son."

"I just wanted you and—" she hesitated, then spoke coldly "—your friend to be comfortable."

"You meant well," Charlie said. "You always do."

Mrs. Mittleman left, and Charlie cursed. "Shit," he said, "why does she get to me? Why do I let her—?"

62

Danny sat on the chair, unlacing his shoes. "What's depreciation?" he asked.

"I'll explain tomorrow—it'll be easier when we can look at real buildings." He sat at his desk. "I have some things to do first, so you get to sleep now."

Danny slipped out of his shirt and climbed into bed. The sheets were cold and smooth. He pulled the cover to his chin. He dozed, then woke, and he watched Charlie at his desk, writing. He was glad he hadn't fallen asleep completely; he remembered now to say the *Shema* to himself: *Hear O Israel the Lord Our God the Lord is One.* . . . Then he reviewed the things he'd learned. He wanted to be able to keep all the sayings he'd memorized in his head at once, but he wondered if there would, after a while, be enough room. He thought of getting out of bed and writing in his notebook, but he decided that it might scare Charlie if he did.

When the lights were out and Charlie was in bed, Danny spoke. "I'm glad I was right—that you do buy and sell land. I think I can help you."

"I'll bet you can," Charlie said, but he was drifting off to sleep.

"I think I know how you can get a lot of money."

"You impressed Max with what you memorized—that's something."

"I mean it. But you have to swear to me first that you won't send me back." Danny laughed.

Charlie smiled. "Sure," he said. "No deposit, no return, right?"

Danny propped himself up on an elbow. Charlie's half of the bed sloped downward, from his weight. Charlie was turned away from him, on his side. "I mean it," Danny said. "Swear it to me."

"Let me sleep, okay?"

"Swear it. *Please.*"

"Okay, okay. I swear."

"All right," Danny said, and he lay back down, smiling. "I know something and it's this: Dr. Fogel has over three thousand acres of land."

Three

Today was the 1st day we were apart and even though I know he won't be home until after practice I keep going to the window and looking out for him. I'm afraid something will happen to him in the city but I don't want to telephone the school because I don't want him to see how much I worry about him.

Why I'm writing in my notebook again: 1. To help myself imagine that he's here with me. 2. To record this precious period of my life in writing.

I've been with him for 3 weeks and 6 days now and he never mentions my going anywhere else. We're together all the time: in the city, at the school, in the office, and in his car. I stayed here today because he said he might have time to stop at the Home.

What I feel: that more has happened to me during these few weeks than in my entire life up until now! Charlie can tell how happy I am. He always smiles at me and roughs up my hair and this is what he says: When you're in love, Danny, the whole world is Jewish!

A question: Is Charlie thinking about me while he's away, and if he is and he misses being with me the way I miss being with him, when he comes back will he say so, or will he be angry because I've made him become attached to me and will this make him give me back to Mr. Gitelman?

64

Mrs. Mittleman came up before and brought me cookies and a glass of milk. She asked me to call her Shirley but I won't. She saw my notebook and she told me not to throw away education. There was a sign in her school when she was a girl which said

AN EDUCATION ENABLES YOU TO EARN MORE THAN AN EDUCATOR.

While she kept talking I worked on my memorizing. Two days ago I found the saying in PIRKAY AVOS that our motto comes from but guess what? *The motto part isn't even from Maimonides!* He was quoting somebody else's saying! Here's the way the whole thing really goes:

AS THE SAGES USED TO SAY, "GIVE ME FRIENDSHIP OR GIVE ME DEATH." AND IF A PERSON CANNOT EASILY FIND A FRIEND HE MUST STRIVE WITH ALL HIS HEART TO DO SO, EVEN IF HE HAS TO GO SO FAR AS TO COMPEL THE PERSON TO LOVE HIM, EVEN IF HE HAS TO BUY HIS LOVE AND FRIENDSHIP.

Mrs. Mittleman looked out the window and said she was worried about Charlie being knifed or mugged. I told her I was doing special work for him and needed to be left alone.

Every morning at breakfast Mr. Mittleman pinches my arm to see if I'm fattening up.

Here are some of the things Charlie does in the city:

1. He collects rents for Mr. Mittleman. Some of the rents are his but most of them belong to Mr. Mittleman and buildings he manages. Charlie gets extra money for the stores and apartments in the black and Puerto Rican sections. He calls this "combat pay."

2. He checks to see that the buildings are running right and he calls plumbers and electricians to fix things. Sometimes he fixes things himself and shows the supers what to do.

3. Every morning at 9:30 he calls his stockbroker. He says stocks are good because they're liquid. Other things he

65

keeps his money in are land, bank accounts, Treasury notes, and options. He buys and sells options on land and stocks. He says he learned that from Mr. Mittleman. It's a way to spread your money.

4. We look at buildings and vacant lots and houses Charlie is thinking of buying, but when he asks me if I like a house I don't know what to say because I wonder if he's thinking of buying it for us now, the way he wanted to do for him and Sol.

5. He talks a lot about Sol with me and says that Sol never works at all and never did, as far as he knows. He told me that Sol's father was a very wealthy Jew from upstate New York who owned a company that made uniforms for athletic teams, and that Sol saved sample uniforms of old teams that are gone like the Brooklyn Robins and the Boston Pilgrims and St. Louis Browns and original Baltimore Orioles. Once a year in the spring Sol would bring his uniforms to the Home in a trunk, along with famous souvenirs of signed bats and gloves and balls.

The reason Charlie's worried about Sol's money is because Sol's father sold the uniform business when Sol was a young man and Charlie thinks that maybe most of the money Sol got then is used up now. He told me that Sol's father was a founder of the Home. He says people always enjoyed doing things for Sol. He says that's the most important thing: to make other people want to please you.

He talks to me like that all the time, making sure I learn things, and here are some of the things he taught me so far:

1. The 3 most important things to consider in buying any piece of property are 1. location, 2. location, and 3. location.

2. Always use other people's money! You can buy things with small percentages and when you sell you get the whole profit after you pay back the loan. He calls this LEVERAGE. In Murray's house Dov always wants him to crack walnuts in his fingers and when Charlie does Dov shouts "That's leverage!" and it makes Charlie laugh.

Will Charlie really speak with Dr. Fogel? What will Dr. Fogel feel when he sees him after all these years? If Dr. Fogel finds out how Charlie found out about the land will they get together and try to make me go back?

I'm only afraid of that when he's not with me but I'm not afraid of Murray anymore. Now that he thinks I'm so smart the way he was he tells everybody in the school I'm a special exchange student from the orphanage he grew up in. Also because he really loves Charlie! When Charlie was 1st put into the Home Murray was older and used to rock him to sleep in his arms every night.

I watched practice with Murray yesterday and he even put his arm around me. I told him how I thought he looked the same as he did when he was a boy in the photos except thinner and he told me about the heart attack he had 4 years ago and how he's lost 35 pounds. He told me about Charlie visiting him in the hospital every day and what Charlie said to him, through the oxygen tent: "Get well for yourself and nobody else." Charlie told him that people forget very quickly and Murray said he was right. Charlie said that if Murray died, Anita would remarry, his kids would grow up and have lives of their own, and for everybody else he would only be a memory and "a conversation piece."

This is how Murray runs his school: The students march from room to room, even the ones who are 18 years old. If you don't wear a school uniform you get sent home. Smoking, hand holding, and talking are not allowed in the halls. The students have to stand whenever an adult enters a room. All adults are called Mr. Mrs. Sir or Ma'am. Every student must practice a musical instrument 1 hour a day. Every student must study either Greek, Latin, or Hebrew. Every student must play on an athletic team. Murray is allowed to enter a classroom at any time and test students or check homework.

If a student doesn't like the way he's treated he can have a 15 minute interview with Murray, but Murray's decision is final, and there are things he won't discuss. If students or parents are displeased, they can leave the school.

What surprised me: How happy the students seem to be!

Also: The girls have to keep their arms covered at all times, and the men teachers have to wear jackets and ties.

Murray runs the school this way because he says democracy isn't everything. He believes that True Freedom comes from developing resources and skills in yourself that you can use for the rest of your life!

What Charlie says: Murray's happy because he's the boss.

When they were boys Murray was allowed out of the Home like me to go to a regular public school because he was so smart but Charlie wasn't. They had teachers come to the Home the way we do for regular subjects, but going to a public school gives you a better chance to get into college.

Every time I ask Charlie if he wants me to help him learn to read he ignores me. In the school library I read about what Charlie has. It's called DYSLEXIA and it comes because the hemispheres of the brain didn't establish the right "dominance" when you were young. I read about ways it can be cured with hormones and vitamins and training.

Some dyslexiacs read from right to left, but it doesn't make them Jews. I asked Charlie and he told me that things switch on him sometimes.

Words I thought of that would be fun if I had mirror vision like him: LIVE would be EVIL. LIVED is DEVIL. WAS is SAW. PAL is LAP.

A Palindrome is a sentence or word that's the same backward as forward, like MADAM I'M ADAM or DEIFIED.

I told Charlie I thought it would be exciting to be that way so that things could turn inside out at any moment of your life and you might discover something new, but he wouldn't talk about it.

LATER

It's pitch black out but he's still not home. I already had some supper with Mr. and Mrs. Mittleman but I didn't

6 8

eat much. Mrs. Mittleman said that Charlie might be late because he was having a date with a woman. She said it was normal for a grown man to want to be alone with a woman and she looked at me when she said it but I didn't show anything. I wondered if Charlie would visit Dr. Fogel in his home to talk about buying his land.

In the afternoon before supper I turned on the shower so they wouldn't hear me and I practiced my Haftorah and Maftir. Then I got into bed and played with myself. I have as much hair as some of the players on the team at Charlie's school. I do exercises and run with them sometimes but I don't get into a uniform. I'm better coordinated than I used to think I was. I thought of how Charlie and Murray were laughing 3 nights ago because Murray recited what the Director used to lecture to them at their Assemblies. This is what he said: MASTURBATION SHOULD NEVER BE ALLOWED TO GET OUT OF HAND.

We eat at Murray's house at least one night every week, and Murray and Charlie like to argue with each other while Anita watches. Charlie says he's worried about Sol because nobody's heard from him, but Murray says he's really worried about himself. He says that's the reason Charlie took me in—because he wants somebody to take care of him when he gets old the way he wants to take care of Sol because Sol took care of him when he was a boy! Murray says that he went through a crisis also when he was getting close to 40 about growing old, but Charlie says it has nothing to do with Murray's theories.

After I played with myself I slept for a while and while I was sleeping I dreamt that I was Charlie. When I woke up I couldn't tell at first if I was Danny Ginsberg who had just dreamed that he was Charlie or if I was now Charlie dreaming that I was Danny Ginsberg.

WEDNESDAY

It's nighttime now and the room is hushed with quiet. Charlie's at his desk, hunched over and adding things up, and I'm sitting in his black chair with my shirt off so I can feel the soft leather against my back. I have my feet up and my socks off.

I was sleeping when he got home last night but he woke me up to tell me he stopped at the Home. He said the place looked so empty it scared him and that he only stayed a few minutes and didn't speak to the Director or try to see Dr. Fogel. He said that as soon as he saw the way the Home is now he decided not to save it. "Let's just work on saving you, OK?"

I acted as if I was drowsy from being woken up and I said, "Save the Home!"

"But there are no more orphans," he said. "What do you want to do—import them?"

I told him that was a pretty good idea. There are poor Jews in other places in the world where they don't have so much birth control. There are Jews in India and China and Poland and Russia and even in Egypt and Syria. I told him that when men and women soldiers in Israel were killed by Arabs and their children made into orphans we could bring them here until they reached the age when they could go back. That way we could save the state of Israel the expense of raising them and training them.

He scratched his head and laughed at the way my brain works and said it would be cheaper to take in black and Puerto Rican kids from the city and teach them to be Jews but I said Jews weren't allowed to proselytize.

I was glad I didn't try to force him to promise me anything more because it might have made the shock of seeing the Home worse. He was relaxed today. We walked in my old neighborhood where I first saw him and I told him about my mother and he told me about his. He said he remembers his mother as being the most beautiful woman he ever saw. He remembers her when she was almost gone and weighed less than 70 pounds, but he said her face still glowed and that she had a look in her eyes which he said would last him forever.

I told him that my mother was very beautiful too, with sandy-blond hair like mine and hazel eyes and that after my father died people told me she wasn't the same as she was before and that a doctor told her it's better if we don't see each other very often. I said she had a lot of money and lived in an enormous old house with a lookout room on the roof like a crow's nest on a ship from where you can see for miles and miles.

Neither of us remembered our fathers.

He took me to the building where Sol lived with his brother. Sol's brother died a long time ago and was a bachelor too. It was only 2 stories high and I was surprised that it was so plain. It had fire escapes on the front side and big red brick stoops where you could sit on either side of the door. Charlie said Sol was gone so much he only needed it as a place to sleep in and store his things. I asked him where Sol lived now and Charlie said that was why he was worried. He doesn't know! He spoke to the super of the building and the super took us down to the basement and showed us a bin with Sol's trunks and dressers in it, but Sol's apartment was rented to somebody else.

Charlie told me the story of how when he was a young boy he snuck out of the Home 1 time after Sol brought them back from a game and followed Sol all the way to this house. He said he remembered seeing Sol on the street, teasing young children who were riding tricycles in a group by not letting them get by him. He could tell the children loved to have Sol tease them. He said the children went into Sol's apartment and he watched through the window while Sol gave them graham crackers and milk. He said he was surprised the place was so small and didn't have any decorations on the walls.

He laughed, remembering how angry Sol was when he spotted him peering in over the windowsill. He remembered feeling that Sol would have whipped him with a strap if he could have! Sol's brother took Charlie back to the Home in a taxi and they never mentioned the incident again.

Charlie said he would have another surprise trip for me in a few days!

Here are some other things Charlie does: He takes listings on new houses. He calls banks and insurance companies and mortgage brokers to get money for himself and other people. In the evenings he shows houses and telephones people. He doesn't have a realtor's license because he's afraid to take the test, so Mrs. Mittleman does all his paper work.

71

In the mornings sometimes we go over the birth and obituary columns in the local papers. People with more children need bigger homes. Widows and widowers want to move to smaller homes.

In the afternoon he coaches the team. They play 6 man football in a league with 7 other private schools and they've won the championship every year since Charlie was coach.

Every night Mr. Mittleman shows his movies and they talk business after.

I like to drive into the city with Charlie when the light is just beginning before most people wake up. The city looks beautiful from the bridge. What I think about is how they get enough food into it every day, day after day, to feed 8 million people plus commuters.

I said this to Charlie this morning and he told me he thinks about the exact same thing sometimes and that his conclusion is that it proves the city isn't dying the way people say it is. He said if he still had his own family he would bring his children up in the city.

Do you think about your daughter a lot? I asked.

No, he said.

But don't you think about how she keeps changing and you're not there to see the changes?

He said he still sees her sometimes if he's in her neighborhood and that he used to wonder about himself because he didn't miss her, but he says he stopped wondering a few years ago. He sends money to his ex-wife every month and he'll pay for college if Sandy goes there.

The only thing I think about sometimes, he said, is that after she gets away from home and gets married and has a family, that maybe then we'll be able to be pretty good friends. He asked me if I thought that sounded funny and I said it didn't. He said he sees the scene in his head sometimes, of him visiting her and her husband and her children and of them having nice evenings together.

Coming home he told me that Dr. Fogel used to make fun of him and ask him when he was going to learn to read. Who do you think you are—Rabbi Akiba? Dr. Fogel

72

would say. He used to send him out of the classroom and tell him to return when he was 40 years old.

What I imagined Dr. Fogel saying to him at the Home yesterday if Charlie walked into his classroom: GO HOME. YOU'RE 17 MONTHS EARLY!

Charlie said a boy at the Home told him Dr. Fogel hasn't been there for 4 weeks!

I see Charlie yawning. A good place to stop. The end of a good day!

Today we went to lunch for the 2nd time with the man from the city about Charlie's big project. The man didn't like me being with them but Charlie told him not to worry, that I was an orphan and didn't understand things. The man looked at me and I gave him my blank look and then they talked business.

What they're going to do: Charlie has an option on residential land which will be rezoned so they can build a factory. He'll sell the land to the city for an Industrial Renewal Project in a Model Cities Area. Then he'll take the profits from the land and put it into the building at special low interest rates and the result will be what Charlie calls "a windfall."

Afterward Charlie told me that when it's over the workers could go back on welfare or unemployment and the building could be used for something else or it could be torn down and they could start again. He said that the economy would collapse without projects like this.

A question: Am I writing this only for myself or so that Charlie will find it and want to read it? Whenever he sees me writing he asks me what I'm making up for my storybook today!

After supper tonight we watched movies of Mrs. Mittleman and her brother Oscar and his wife and some friends taken during World War II. They were in the country where they each had rooms in a house and shared a big kitchen, and they were playing games on a Saturday night like musical chairs and break the balloon and steal the baloney and they looked like they were having a wonder-

73

ful time. "Grown people don't play games like that any-more," Mr. Mittleman said.

When Charlie came into the room just before, I re-cited for him what Maimonides said about buying friend-ship and he said, That makes sense. I asked him why but he didn't answer me.

I have 2 books on my lap under my notebook: PIRKAY AVOS and a book Mr. Mittleman gave me called REAL ESTATE INVESTMENT STRATEGY. We'll see how smart you are, he said. In a month I'm giving a test.

*

When Charlie opened his eyes Danny was standing next to the bed, his *tephillin* boxes in his hands. He asked Charlie to tell him if he was putting them on the right way. "How would I know?" Charlie said. "Ask Murray. Religion is his department."

"But you're a Jew too," Danny said.

"Sure," Charlie replied. "But that doesn't mean I have to do anything about it, does it? If I do or if I don't I'm still a Jew, right?" He turned away, sat up, and began putting on his socks. "So until I get to forty, leave me be. . . ."

Danny did not move away and—while Charlie dressed and Danny put on his *tephillin*—Charlie tried not to show how pleased he was by the defiant look in the boy's eyes.

"Tell me this," Charlie said, when Danny was done. "Why do you care so much about being a Jew?"

"Because I am a Jew," Danny replied.

Charlie sighed. "But that's the point," he said. "If you do a little or a lot, you're still a Jew, so why do you care so *much?* It's not natural."

Charlie waited, but the boy said nothing. Charlie saw that Danny didn't realize he was being playful with him. "You weren't even brought up in an Orthodox Home," Charlie went on. "I bet you never even went to *shul* with your father or saw him put on *tephillin* in the mornings—am I right?"

Then Danny smiled. "Desire is everything," he said.

Charlie laughed and brushed the boy's hair. "You have me there," he said.

At breakfast Mrs. Mittleman read to them from a brochure about the John F. Kennedy Peace Forest in Israel, to which she was sending a contribution. The trees would be planted on the same slopes where two thousand years before Bar Kochba had fought his last battle against the legions of Rome. Charlie remembered hearing the story of Bar Kochba from Dr. Fogel. Mrs. Mittleman told him that her dream in life would be to go to Israel someday and visit the forest with her husband.

Charlie winked at Danny. "Good luck," he said.

Mrs. Mittleman bent over and kissed Charlie on the forehead. "But he's very good to me in his way," she said. "Sometimes people don't know everything."

Driving into the city, and thinking of what Danny had said to him, Charlie told Danny that the thing he'd always wanted in the world was the thing he could never have. He said he knew it was silly, but it was what he wanted: to stand with his father in his own home for his son's *bris,* and to imagine himself while the *mohel* was performing the circumcision as being at his own grandson's *bris* with his son imagining the same thing he had imagined a generation before. He said he saw it all, except for his own face. "Sometimes I try to see how many groups of three I can keep straight in my head at once, and how many hundreds of years backward and forward I can go, in equal amounts—do you follow?"

Danny seemed slightly puzzled. "I think you'd make a good rabbi," he said. "People look up to you."

"Sure," Charlie said, smiling. "The rabbi gets the fees, right? —But it's the *mohel* who gets the tips."

Charlie parked the car on Bedford Avenue, not far from Brooklyn College, in a section of expensive private homes. He pointed to a house that looked like a Mexican villa to

Danny, with a tile roof, wooden trellises over the porch, and stucco walls. "This is the house I told you about," Charlie said. "It's the surprise—"

Danny tried to keep himself from believing anything at all. He got out of the car and walked up the steps, behind Charlie. "Don't be scared," Charlie said, and, one hand on Danny's arm, he rang the bell. When the door opened and Danny saw Dr. Fogel standing there, he gasped and pulled away from Charlie, angry that Charlie had caught him by surprise.

Dr. Fogel was wearing a *yamulka,* and instead of his old brown suit, a bright orange and blue sportshirt. His skin, where he had just shaved, seemed to shine as if it had been pulled tight over his cheeks and jaws, and his eyes showed Danny how happy he was to see them. "I was expecting you," he said. "Please. Come in."

Danny followed him through the doorway and Dr. Fogel asked them both to go back and kiss the *mezuzah* on the doorpost. He gave them *yamulkas* to wear, but he did not speak harshly.

They sat in Dr. Fogel's living room, around a glass table through which Danny looked at gleaming chrome legs. The living room was large, with wall-to-wall green carpeting and lustrous mahogany furniture. One wall was totally covered with books, and a ladder was leaning against the books, for getting to the high shelves. The opposite wall was, from one end to the other, a mirror, and Dr. Fogel sat in front of it, facing them.

Danny waited for Dr. Fogel to say something about their both having been away from the Home, but he only smiled and took a cigarette from a silver box. He had never seen Dr. Fogel smoke before, and once Dr. Fogel let the smoke drift upward from his mouth, he seemed even more relaxed than he had been. "Well," he said. "I was wondering what had become of you, Chaim. I've thought about you often through the years."

Charlie stiffened when Dr. Fogel called him by his Hebrew name. "I think about you too," he said.

"I'm glad to see you looking so well," Dr. Fogel said.

"I'm a coach," Charlie said, as if he were answering questions. "I coach football. The headmaster of the school I coach for is Murray Mendelsohn—do you remember him?"

Danny saw how dazed Charlie seemed and he wanted to take him by the hand and run from the house with him. He stared into Charlie's face, hoping Charlie would look his way. "The last I heard was when he had a heart attack," Dr. Fogel said. "Mr. Gitelman told me. He's all right now, I take it."

Charlie nodded. "I'm not married anymore," he said. "My daughter's sixteen. I'm in the real estate business. . . ."

Dr. Fogel smiled at Charlie in a way that scared Danny. He seemed so relaxed, leaning back into a big plush, cream-colored couch, that Danny thought that perhaps he was a different Dr. Fogel. "You were the best player I ever had," Dr. Fogel said. "But you knew that. I never had a boy with as much natural talent as you had."

"I still can't read," Charlie said.

Dr. Fogel closed his eyes and laughed. "I remember the joke you always used to make," he said, "about waiting until you were forty years old, like the great Rabbi Akiba."

"No," Charlie said, shaking his head. "You were the one who said that."

"Was I?" Dr. Fogel asked, but he waved Charlie's objections away with his good hand. "Would you like a drink—?"

"I don't have the time," Charlie said, looking at his watch. "Danny and I have to be back at our school in time for practice."

Dr. Fogel looked at Danny, and then spoke to Charlie. "You came because of my land, didn't you?" he said. "That's what you said on the phone."

"That's right," Charlie said.

"Well," Dr. Fogel said, smiling. "I'll tell you this—you're a person I could do business with, yes? I've been waiting a long time for somebody like you. Come."

They walked from the living room, down a hallway whose walls were covered with paintings in large gold frames. Charlie held Danny back for a second, and whispered to him that if he bought Dr. Fogel's land, Danny would be entitled to a commission. Charlie called it a finder's fee. "Stop making jokes out of everything," Danny hissed back, but Charlie walked away from him.

They entered a large room paneled in dark-grained wood and filled with modern office equipment. There were file cabinets, swivel chairs, large desk lamps, electronic calculators, an electric typewriter, leather-bound books on real estate and investment, and an enormous oak rolltop desk, with dozens of compartments. The only item in the office that would have told anyone the home belonged to a Jew was a small black and white framed photo of an old synagogue, on the wall next to the light switch. A father and son, in long black winter coats, stood on the bottom step. There was snow on the ground. Danny thought of the secret hideout in the cellar of the Home.

Dr. Fogel unrolled surveyor's maps on his desk, and, his eyes bright with happiness, he showed them to Charlie and he talked. There were two parcels of land—a smaller one of approximately thirteen hundred acres, on the North Shore of Long Island just above the Suffolk County border, and a larger one of approximately eighteen hundred acres in Rockland County, New York, near Suffern. Danny thought of Dr. Fogel in the *shul,* unrolling the Torah scrolls, and he remembered what he'd said to him about dying. Danny sat in one of the chairs and swiveled from side to side.

Dr. Fogel was pointing out the areas where cabins had been, and areas where his father had planned to enlarge the settlements. No cabins had ever been built on the Long Island parcel. Charlie and Dr. Fogel talked about access routes and drainage and water tables and zoning laws, and Danny saw that Charlie was becoming more and more relaxed. Charlie was proud that he could show Dr. Fogel he understood how to read surveyor's maps.

Even while he seemed happy and relaxed, though, Danny imagined that inside his head he was counting his money. Danny remembered the story Charlie had told him about the bread war in the dining room. He thought of trying to warn Charlie about Dr. Fogel, but how could he? He felt, swaying from side to side and hearing the sounds of their words, extraordinarily calm even when the worst thought came into his head—that he was secretly glad to feel so helpless because he now wanted Charlie to be disappointed!

Danny followed them back into the living room; when they were sitting around the table, Dr. Fogel said that he had one question to ask Charlie and that if Charlie answered it correctly the money part of their transaction would be no trouble.

If my mind contains caverns, boxes, webs, mazes, corridors, and tunnels, Danny wondered, then what does Charlie's mind contain?

"It's only this," Dr. Fogel said to Charlie. "But tell me your true opinion. Do you think Israel is a land of the past or of the future?"

Danny gasped. "The future," Charlie said, quickly.

Dr. Fogel clucked inside his mouth. "I'm very sorry then," he said, standing. "You're wrong. Our discussion is over, yes? I'm sorry. . . ."

"What do you mean—over?" Charlie said. His face was red. "Just like that? That's *all?*"

Dr. Fogel turned to Danny. "I had thought you would have been a better influence on your friend."

"You leave the kid alone," Charlie said. "You just lay off and speak with me." He stepped toward Dr. Fogel and raised his hands, as if he were going to lift the tiny man and shake him. "I don't get it," he said. He forced himself to speak more calmly. "I mean, you haven't even given me a chance to come up with an offer. It's not fair, your leading me along like that and then closing the door in my face. . . ."

"It's my land," Dr. Fogel said.

"Okay," Charlie said, sighing. "If you want to play games I can play too, right? Ask me another question then. I'll do better."

Dr. Fogel chuckled. "I like your attitude, Chaim. I always did. So I will give you another chance, yes? Answer me this question—do you put on *tephillin* every morning?"

"No."

"Do you observe the Sabbath?"

"No."

"Are you kosher?"

"No."

"See?" Dr. Fogel said. "You would do well in Israel. You should think of going there to live—what do you need with my land and my father's land here in America?"

Charlie turned to Danny and rolled his eyes. "Let's go," he said. "I've had enough for one day."

They stood on the front porch together, under the trellis, and Danny wondered if Charlie would turn on him and blame him for what was happening. "It is a good thing to die in Israel," Dr. Fogel said, "but it is not such a good thing to live there now." He took one of Charlie's hands in his own. "You think about our conversation and come back and talk with me again sometime."

Charlie didn't say anything. "You're both smart boys," Dr. Fogel said. "So tell me: of what use to God is yet another earthly nation in which His children's blood is spilled?"

He walked down the steps, ahead of them, past his lawn. They all stood together beside Charlie's car. "God likes jokes also," Dr. Fogel went on, "and do you know what his favorite joke is? The joke he played on the Zionists! They worked and they worked and they worked, but in the end, why did the world give them the State of Israel? Because of all their work?" He spat, then answered his own question: "Because of the six million, that's why. Who can believe there ever would have been an Israel if not for the six million? Who? Don't you see what God is saying to us—?"

"No," Charlie said.

Dr. Fogel relaxed at once, the passion leaving his voice. "Tell me," he said, his hand on Charlie's arm. "What do you think of my house?"

"It's okay," Charlie said. "If you want to sell, I have a buyer."

Danny wanted to argue—to tell Dr. Fogel that he didn't make sense—the Zionists had not *wanted* to pay such a price for the state of Israel. . . .

Dr. Fogel was laughing with Charlie. "It's been good having you visit me. *Please*—you'll think things over and you will come back, yes?"

Charlie nodded, indicating he would, and when he did, Danny spoke for the first time: *"Mitzvat Yishuv Eretz Yisroel!"* he recited.

"Very good," Dr. Fogel said, patting Danny's arm. "Of course. But there are other commandments, equally important, yes?"

*

FRIDAY

WE SAW DR. FOGEL
WE SAW DR. FOGEL
WE SAW DR. FOGEL.

I want to write that sentence again and again because it contains everything, and since we saw him this afternoon Charlie hasn't been the same.

He's downstairs now fighting with Mr. Mittleman and screaming that he wants his accountant to look at Mr. Mittleman's books to make sure he's been getting the right commissions. He's learning not to trust anybody.

Is that what Dr. Fogel wanted to teach him today?

I have to write fast because he'll be up in a few minutes for us to go to Murray, so this is the way it happened: I thought we were going to look at a big house Charlie was thinking of buying but it turned out to be Dr. Fogel's.

He was glad to see Charlie at 1st but when he called Charlie by his Hebrew name he scared him and Charlie froze. Later Charlie relaxed when they talked about the land but it didn't fool me. Dr. Fogel was just setting him up. HE MADE CHARLIE BELIEVE THEY COULD HAVE AN AGREEMENT AND THEN HE KILLED CHARLIE'S HOPE!

8 1

He asked Charlie if Israel was a land of the past or the future and said that if Charlie answered that right they could come to terms. I knew the answer he wanted and I tried to think the words into Charlie's head but they never got there. Charlie said The Future and Dr. Fogel told him he was wrong! That was when Charlie started getting angry and he hasn't stopped yet.

Dr. Fogel also asked him about putting on Tephillin and being Kosher and observing Shabbos and he held out more hope to Charlie because when Charlie was truthful with him about not being a good Jew, Dr. Fogel told him to come back and talk some more!

This is what Charlie said to me in the car, right after we left Dr. Fogel: "If Maimonides said it was OK to pay money for a friend, wouldn't it be OK to become religious for money?"

This is what I think his mind contains: arrows, muscles, spices, knots, glass, and salty tears!

Dr. Fogel said things against Israel again and I quoted to him what the Rabbis say about it being the duty of every Believer to settle in Israel, but my words meant nothing to him. This is why you can't argue with him: BECAUSE HE THINKS HE CAN UNDERSTAND GOD'S BITTER-NESS.

Charlie kept asking me to explain Dr. Fogel to him, but he talked so much I never had a chance. When I said something to him about taking it easy, this is what he said back: "I have two speeds—stop and go."

I've never known anyone like him! His moods change so fast I'm afraid to speak sometimes and just when I'm thinking he's so depressed I need to find a joke for him, he'll turn around and make one to me.

He liked the joke I made this morning in Mr. Plaut's jewelry store. He told Mr. Plaut I was his trainee and I told him he could deduct me as a business expense. But he said I wasn't an expense, I was an investment.

Then I drew a line across the middle of my body, right above my waist, and I said: I'm amortized up to here! He laughed a lot at that and Mr. Plaut did also, but the minute I said it I was thinking of the Chasidic Jews who tie

82

belts around the middle of their bodies to separate the holy parts from the profane. I didn't tell Charlie I thought that.

On the way home he was talking as crazy as Dr. Fogel. He talked all about his money. He said that he always felt disconnected and that money made him feel connected. Money brought him closer to Murray again, money brought him to Mr. and Mrs. Mittleman, money made him able to help me, money would let him help Sol, and money would let him do what he wanted after he was 40.

These are the things he feels disconnected from, in Danny Ginsberg's opinion: his childhood, his mother and father, his not having real brothers and sisters, his separating from the boys he grew up with, his not living in the Home, his not living in the city.

Also: being Jewish but not practicing Judaism, having had a family but not having one now, doing business with people he doesn't really know personally, being in a business in which people come to him because they're moving from place to place.

He got very emotional trying to figure out why Dr. Fogel deceived him and he took my hand and told me he really meant it about becoming a Rabbi after 40. He said it was a feeling he couldn't explain but that he always believed, since he was a boy, that when he became 40 his life would change.

After lunch Charlie met with a black man who's a dentist and he talked about selling the man one of Mr. Mittleman's apartment houses. The black dentist works with a Jewish dentist in an office on Atlantic Avenue and he bragged about how much money they made in only 3 years. They have 6 chairs between them and they work on welfare and Medicaid people. They pull teeth.

These were his words: You can always find 2 teeth to pull in somebody's mouth.

Mr. Mittleman wants to sell as many of his old buildings as possible and put the money into low income housing. You can get a special 60 month fast write-off on low income housing and if you reinvest the net proceeds of sales in more low income housing you can avoid the recapture rule on depreciation. Mr. Mittleman calls this the quick way to build A Tax Free Empire.

He's on the stairs.

TO BE CONTINUED

*

Murray asked Ephraim to lead the *bentshing* that followed the meal, and Charlie was happy to see Danny, sharing a prayer book with Hannah, join in the singing.

What he needed to do, he decided, was to surprise Dr. Fogel.

In Murray's study, Anita and Hannah sat in front of the fireplace on their knees. Charlie saw Hannah smile at Danny even while Danny was staring at her breasts. When Murray spoke about the Home, Anita held his hand. Her eyes, from the firelight, appeared to be violet.

Once a month Charlie, Murray, and the other guys from their group at the Home got together, usually for a touch football game in Brooklyn, and Charlie had promised to take Danny to their game on Sunday. Murray was talking about the games and about what he felt every month after the reunions. "We're not right," he said. "That's what I keep feeling. Don't you see it?"

"No," Charlie said.

"Whenever I go outside the boundaries of the life I've cut out for myself here in Mill River," Murray said, "I feel like a helpless child somehow—and I'm not ashamed to admit it." Murray looked at Charlie. "Don't you ever feel the same?"

"No," Charlie said again.

Murray was silent for a few seconds; then he pointed to Danny with his pipe. "I think the boy's a lot like me—I think he has the same craving for roots and continuity."

"Who doesn't?" Charlie said quickly, and laughed. "But what the hell kind of roots and continuity can you have out here in Mill River where you're the only Jew in the whole place?"

"Ah," Murray said. "But that's just the point, isn't it?

8 4

Being the only Jew makes me understand more intensely what it means to be Jewish—as if I'm alone in the wilderness. As if—"

"Oh come on," Charlie said. "How can anyone think of suburban New Jersey as the wilderness?" He sighed, annoyed with himself for having been trapped into an argument he wanted no part of. "Look," he said. "I'll repeat for you what I said to the kid this morning—if I can't help being a Jew then whatever I do, that's Jewish too, right? So not being kosher and not putting on *tephillin* is as Jewish as being a rabbi. That's the way I figure it."

"Very interesting," Murray said. He turned to Danny again. "And what do you think of that?"

Danny smiled. "Rabbis are Jews too," he said.

Murray laughed. "Very good—I'll have to remember that." He puffed on his pipe, and then Charlie heard the familiar words flow—Murray talked about how bringing into his life rituals that had been practiced for thousands of years by other Jewish men and families gave him a sense of being part of the Jewish people, especially in a time when people were always moving to new places and everyone's values were shifting.

Charlie hardly listened. He saw that Danny was wide-eyed, drinking the words in, but he figured it was all personal—these were things that made Murray happy and that was all there was to it. Maybe, he thought, I can send Murray to talk with Dr. Fogel in my place.

"Being a Jew means being part of a special history," Murray said, his eyes demanding Charlie's attention. "And the less Jews practice Judaism, the more that history is lost!"

Charlie smiled but said nothing. He remembered what he'd said to Danny after he'd visited the Home, about letting dying things die, but if he said something like that to Murray—if he told him he shouldn't resist things that were natural—he imagined that Murray would reply that the craving for roots and continuity was natural too. . . .

When he looked at Danny he was surprised to see the boy smiling with him, as if he were reading Charlie's thoughts.

Charlie blinked. *I don't believe you,* he could hear Danny say. *I don't believe you because of what you said to me about the groups of three!*

Charlie saw Dr. Fogel standing in front of the classroom, and, from behind, he saw himself raise his hand and stand. *If the Torah says that God said an eye for an eye and a tooth for a tooth,* Dr. Fogel asked, *then how can we know the rabbis are right to say that God means something else— that He wants a different kind of punishment?*

He saw his own body tip to one side and he saw his shoulders lift slightly in a shrug. Dr. Fogel had taught them that God's laws had to apply to all men for all times. Charlie answered the question with a question: *Then what can you do to a blind man who pokes out somebody's eye?*

The class had giggled, but Dr. Fogel had silenced them by telling them that Charlie was right. After class, he recalled, Dr. Fogel made him remain behind and had praised him in a way he never had for anything else. It was the one time Charlie had surprised him.

Murray was laughing and telling another story about one of his children. They were in the kitchen, and, half asleep, Danny was staring into the flickering lights of the *Shabbos* candles. Murray said that last Friday he had promised to take Eli to the school football game, saying, "Tomorrow I'll take you to the game," and that when Eli had awakened on Saturday morning he had been terribly excited and had kept asking, "Is today tomorrow? Is today tomorrow?"

Murray said that he was going to put those three words on an index card and tape the card to his office door. He looked around the table for approval. "Don't you think it will encourage too much freedom?" Anita asked.

Charlie nudged Danny with his elbow. "Come on," he said.

"It's late," Murray said, refusing to respond directly to Anita's sarcasm. "And my wife—to whose question I would reply: perhaps, but my students are happy and creative— wants to talk about how severe Murray Mendelsohn is."

Murray tried to put an arm around Anita, but she pulled away. "Their happiness takes place in a vacuum," she said sharply. "They're culturally deprived."

"Ah," Murray said. "And what do you propose—that we import blacks and Puerto Ricans from the city?"

"It's not a bad idea," she said.

"It's late," Charlie said, and he kissed Anita on the cheek. Her skin was warm. "Thanks."

"Don't *you* see it?" Anita asked, barring the door with her body so that Charlie and Danny had to wait. "Don't you see that Murray's right—that there is something wrong with him?" She stepped aside. "But it doesn't have anything to do with being an orphan," she said quietly. "He can't use that crutch forever."

"It's not a crutch," Murray replied. "It's a ladder."

"Tell him, Charlie," Anita pleaded. "Once. *Please?*"

Then she left the room. Murray walked outside with Charlie and Danny. "She gets this way when she's pregnant," Murray said. "It's complicated—she wants the children and she wants her freedom too. She blames me for wanting them and then she feels guilty for blaming me and doesn't realize it, so she attacks me in front of you. And you—"

"I know the whole story," Charlie said, patting Murray on the shoulder. "Thank her for us again, okay?"

"It was brewing before you got here," he said. "The truth is, I believe in cultivating my own garden." He laughed. "I was explaining it to her while we got ready for *Shabbos* and I made a joke about planting Jewish seeds and tried to pat her stomach, and she froze on me." Murray shrugged. "I'll see you tomorrow, I guess."

In the car, Danny slept with his head against Charlie's shoulder.

*

SATURDAY

At our game today we won 34 to 6 and Charlie yelled the whole time. He hardly ever smiles at games. It's the way he gets the boys to work for him: He saves up his smiles and uses them only when it really matters!

I asked him once if Dr. Fogel shouted the way he does and he said Dr. Fogel was so good he never had to raise his voice. Because I've never really played sports Charlie thinks I can be a great coach someday like Dr. Fogel. But I don't have the kind of brain which can plan things far ahead.

For example: at the Home I tried learning chess a few times but I was no good at it.

Murray stood next to me at the game and told me that Charlie could have been better than Sid Luckman or Bennie Friedman or Marshall Goldberg if he'd played football. And if he'd played baseball he could have been another Al Rosen or Hank Greenberg. Murray said he could have been the greatest Jewish athlete of all time, but he decided to get married instead! Sol got him a tryout with the Brooklyn Dodgers when he was only 16 and they offered him a contract but he turned it down. He was married by 17.

There are a lot of married players, I said.

But Murray said that Charlie refused to do anything that would make him leave his wife overnight. Everyone pleaded with him INCLUDING SOL but Charlie wouldn't listen to anybody.

Anita was wearing a beautiful orange and black plaid wool coat at the game with a big collar that turned up and made her hair look red and soft inside it. I looked at her stomach when her coat was open but it didn't look any bigger.

She's in her 4th month now which means the baby already has everything a baby has, including all the internal organs and fingernails and hair. She's having the baby by natural childbirth the way she had her last 3 and Murray will be in the delivery room with her. Last night he talked about the last time and how hard the contractions were and this is what Charlie said: If they get too bad again tell her to subcontract!

I saw the way the mothers of some of the players looked at Charlie. I was glad when the game was over and we were back in his car. He asked me what Murray was chewing my ear off about this time and I told him about what Murray said about giving up his sports career for a wife and he said that was bullshit.

He told me he played semi-pro ball and he knew just how good he really was—good enough to make the major leagues but not good enough to make it big. He said he had more money now than he ever would have had if he had fulfilled Murray's dream.

Last night we spent Shabbos with Murray and his family but Charlie didn't say anything about our visit to Dr. Fogel. Murray and Charlie argued about being Jewish and I agreed more with Murray who says that if Jews don't practice Judaism then Judaism will die. Charlie tried to act as if he didn't care and I hated him for doing that! But then I remembered what he told me he felt about imagining himself and his son at his grandson's Bris and I felt better.

He said that if I saw Murray at Eli's Bris 4 years ago I would see that he really felt the things he spoke about. Charlie said he never saw a human being more proud and excited than Murray was on that day.

He told me Murray used to be very different. He said that 10 years ago Murray was very active in civil rights and he and Anita spent summers together teaching at black schools in Alabama. He was once beaten unconscious during a march.

While we were coming home from the game Charlie said there was one thing that stopped him when he thought about becoming a Rabbi.

What is it? I said.

That I'll never be able to eat lobster again, he said.

I never had lobster, I said.

He thought I was kidding and asked me if I wanted to try and I said I thought he had to get back to the office since it was Saturday, but he smiled and we went to a restaurant.

It was the 1st time I ever ate in a restaurant where waiters came and served you! There were red checkered tablecloths on the tables and the waiter and the owner wanted to please Charlie. They asked him about Sol and Charlie told them Sol was fine and would be visiting him soon after his cross country trip. I had to wear a plastic bib when I ate the lobster and Charlie showed me what to do and how to crack the claws with a nutcracker. I saw how expensive lobster was and I asked Charlie if he could afford it.

This was his answer: I save money faster than I can spend it.

I can still taste the lobster now. I never tasted anything so beautiful and tender. I ate every piece I could, even in the thinnest claws!

When we got home and Charlie told Mr. Mittleman where we were this is what he said: A ship in the ocean was caught in a great storm and all the passengers were screaming. The waves were coming overboard and women were tearing their hair out and praying to God to save them. Only a little old Jewish man sat quietly without screaming. Don't you care what happens to the ship? a fellow passenger asked. Is it my ship? the Jew replied.

Why I hate Mr. Mittleman: because when Charlie was in the bathroom for a minute and we were alone in the office, he smiled at me and said: Tell me—how do you know you're really Jewish?

He called Charlie crazy for giving up Saturdays and Sundays for sports when those are the big selling days but this is what Charlie said back to him: Living well is the best revenge!

I told Charlie that when it came to lobster he might be wrong about desire. It would be easier to become a Rabbi if you'd never had any at all!

SUNDAY

In the morning we went into the city with Murray and I met their friends from the Home. I met Irving and Louie and Slats and Herman and Stan and Morty and I saw how they still look up to Charlie as a hero. I even played some football with them and caught a pass from Charlie 2 times. Murray and Charlie made up to say I was from the Home and that Murray had me on loan for his school as an exchange student. They asked me things about Dr. Fogel and if certain other teachers were still there and how many of us there are left and things like that.

BUT THE MOST IMPORTANT THING WAS NOT WHAT HAPPENED WHEN I WAS WITH THEM BUT WHAT HAPPENED AFTER!

When we got home and I was here in our room reading he came in and picked up my real estate book and started reading out loud like a normal reader!

Do you know why I can do it? he asked me.

Because you're happy, I said.

He told me I wasn't paying attention. I told you once that I read better when I'm excited, he said, and then he said he was excited not because he had a good time with his friends but because ALL DAY LONG FROM THE TIME THEY FIRST MET IN THE MORNING HE'D BEEN IMAGINING HIMSELF DEAD!

It's what I do whenever I'm with them, he told me. I try to feel what each of them would feel at different points—when they'd get the news about me, when they'd first see each other, when they'd see me in the coffin, and when they'd shovel earth on top of me.

I'm getting gooseflesh again, hearing his voice in my head saying that! I told him he was trying to scare me and he told me that I couldn't deny how well he was reading. There's hope for me too, he said, and he went downstairs to fight with Mr. Mittleman.

I don't know what to do when he does things like that. He makes me feel very helpless.

LATER

We didn't talk about Dr. Fogel all day.

The man I liked most from their group was Irving, who's a Professor. I liked him because he didn't ask me any questions.

Just before I came up, when Mrs. Mittleman asked about Anita, Mr. Mittleman said: Maybe Murray and Anita are so talented, they'll give birth to an orphan.

They were watching movies of Mrs. Mittleman and her sister in a boat on the 1000 Islands in Canada. Mr. Mit-

91

tleman asked him what was the difference between a Rabbi and a prostitute and when Charlie said he didn't know, Mr. Mittleman said that a Rabbi sends bills.

His voice never changes. I hate him more because he's a Jew!

I said I had a stomachache and I came up here to write.

Herman kidded me and asked if I was a member of Murray's Alumni Association and if I had a membership card and I got scared for a minute, thinking he knew I ran away, but from the way they talked I found out that Murray once tried to have a meeting of Alumni from over 50 years and rented a big ballroom but less than 30 men came and they stayed in groups and only talked with people from their own years at the Home who they knew already.

I think Anita's jealous of the time Murray and Charlie spend together and of all the years they had together before she met them!

MONDAY

I have to be ready to go shopping with him in 5 minutes because he says I have no winter clothes. Does this mean he's going to let me stay with him all through the cold and the snow? Even though it's been harder living with him since our visit to Dr. Fogel I don't want to leave. I'd rather live with him worried than any other man relaxed!

When I woke this morning I found him looking at my Tephillin but I didn't let him know I saw.

At school he and Murray made jokes about cultivating Murray's garden. Murray said he was fertilizing his lawn with chicken fat and Charlie asked Murray if he could plant him a TSURIS TREE.

They joked about sitting under it together and letting their worries seep into the ground and feed the tree.

I have to hurry. When we do things he won't let me use any of my own money. He gives me some money for errands I do for him and for writing things down for him, but I keep that money separate. I think he pays Mrs. Mittleman for my meals.

I need to save my money because later I'll need it to buy a new suit for my Bar Mitzvah.

A girl sat next to me in the school library and asked me if I was the boy who was living with Mr. Sapistein and she said that Murray spoke about me to her class and told them how much I accomplished in my life even though I never stayed in a real school.

She didn't interest me. I told her I was busy with things to study and she went away.

I read in a book about Zionism and I read about the Fernald Tracing Method against dyslexia and I studied for Mr. Mittleman's test.

It's true about Theodor Herzl wanting to let Jewish children be baptized, but he changed his opinion later on. When he was young and for his whole life he really only loved blond and blue-eyed little girls! Also: He was once in favor of intermarriage so Jews would be better looking! This is what he wanted written on his gravestone: HE HAD TOO GOOD AN OPINION OF THE JEWS.

What else I discovered: The King Frederick who locked all the children in the room without words crowned himself King of Jerusalem in 1229.

The best thing that happened today: I found this saying in PIRKAY AVOS and wrote it out in Hebrew and in English for Charlie:

"LET A MAN DEVOTE HIMSELF TO THE STUDY OF TORAH AND TO THE COMMANDMENTS EVEN FOR AN ULTERIOR PURPOSE, BECAUSE FROM AN ULTERIOR PURPOSE HE WILL EVENTU-ALLY ARRIVE AT THE REAL PURPOSE."

He thought about that for a while and then he said: I was right then, wasn't I? What do you make of that?

He said he would try to memorize it and he put it on his list: Memorize Danny's Saying.

TUESDAY

He came up and stopped me from writing any more last night. It's morning time now and I'm up before he is. When we got home last night there was a message from Murray saying he got a postcard from Uncle Sol.

After we finished shopping last night we went to a beautiful white house with a long circular driveway. It was past 10 o'clock when we got there and a tall woman came to the door and spoke with an accent. Her husband came to meet us in a red silk bathrobe.

Charlie introduced me to them. Their names are Mr. and Mrs. Szondi. Mr. Szondi is Charlie's stockbroker. They escaped from Hungary in 1956. Charlie didn't waste any time. Before they sat down he was yelling at Mr. Szondi and asking him why he paid him good money. Mr. Szondi told him he expected the market to turn and Charlie said he didn't depend on miracles, that there was as much money to be made in bad markets as good. Mrs. Szondi sat very stiffly in a high velvet chair and her eyes seemed to burn. I couldn't tell how old she was.

The room was beautiful with lamps and teacups everywhere. The walls were made of wallpaper like velvet with curlicues in reds and pinks. Mr. Szondi tried to explain things to Charlie but Charlie wouldn't listen. He said he paid Mr. Szondi to do his thinking for him. Mr. Szondi told Charlie he knew about a merger and pension funds that would buy into the new company. The pension funds have been staying away from the market recently. Mr. Szondi said that if things went well Charlie could buy and sell within 60 days for a good profit but that would mean taxes.

Charlie said he never worried about taxes. That was his accountant's department. Mr. Szondi asked who I was and Charlie said I was a smart Jewish boy.

When we were leaving he asked Mrs. Szondi how she liked living in their house.

This is what she said: The hills are very beautiful but they are not mine.

Charlie made me promise to study a book on the stock market after finishing the real estate one. He said he played dumber than he was and I said he didn't have to tell me that. He seemed happy after we left and he said that Murray followed the daily ups and downs of things too much. Charlie called that death.

He explained to me what an overlay is and he said that's what he always invests in. An overlay is if a horse

94

is a 2 to 1 favorite in the morning but the crowd makes him 5 to 1. An overlay in land is when it can be developed in 5 years when everybody else thinks 10. If you only bet on overlays you can't go wrong!

I took a chance when he seemed in a better mood. I said this: If you don't let me help you learn to read I'll leave you.

And go where? he asked.

Lots of people could use a smart Jewish boy, I said.

I'll think about it, he said.

You're afraid, I said.

You're right, he said, but that doesn't mean I'm going to do anything about it.

I told him I could wait a little longer. The saying I gave him about an ulterior purpose is a good start.

He's waking up now. He always seems happiest to me when he's just coming out of his sleep.

Four

In the car, leaning halfway across the back of the front seat while Murray drove, Charlie tried to reassure Danny —that he was, despite what Mr. Mittleman had said, Jewish—and even as he was trying to comfort the boy, he wondered: how much of me shows?

Danny was pale, his head resting against the line that separated the back seat from the door, and Charlie, trying still to find a way to snap the boy to, told a joke Mr. Mittleman had once told him. A Jewish boy, going to a whorehouse for the first time, meets his father in the waiting room. The boy is speechless. The father shrugs and says, in Yiddish, "For fifty cents, why should I bother Momma?"

When neither Danny nor Murray laughed, Charlie turned and looked out the front window. If either of them had been clients, he knew, he could have made them laugh. Where was the difference? He wasn't, like Max, a joke teller, and yet, in his work, he made people laugh and Max never did.

He trusted his instincts and they told him that it was his desire to have money which brought the money. But where, he wondered, was that desire now, when he seemed to be, except for his sneakers and sweatshirt, the same man he had been the day before when he'd been selling houses. The difference fascinated him, and it reassured him; in fifteen months, when he reached forty, he would surprise everybody and turn his joke into reality. He would never work again.

At the George Washington Bridge, handing the girl in the booth the toll money, Murray stopped talking about Anita's moods and spoke instead of King David and the Angel of Death. "Last night," he said, "just before I went to sleep, I was reading that on the day when King David was destined to die, the Angel of Death stood before him, but could not prevail. . . ."

Charlie tried to see himself as a boy, in a sweatshirt and sneakers, playing football in the Home's courtyard. Looking back, he wondered, could people see that the boy he was then would have become the man he was now? Except with Murray, he remembered himself as having been an exceptionally quiet boy. The reason seemed clear enough: with the adulation of the others he'd never had need for words. His athletic abilities and good looks had done all his work for him. But when there had been no words issuing from him, what, he wanted to know, had been going on inside?

"The rabbis ask why the Angel of Death could not prevail, and they answer that it was because learning did not cease from David's mouth." Murray licked his lips. "Finally, the Angel went outside and climbed the trees in the garden that surrounded the royal palace and began to beat the boughs all about. When David heard the noise it disturbed him from his studies so that he went out into the garden to discover the cause. As he was climbing a ladder to find out what was happening in the topmost branches, the ladder collapsed and it was in this way that he died—do you see?"

Charlie's nose itched, and when he rubbed it he remembered how he and Lillian had touched the first time in the candy store. He'd thought of stopping to see her after the game—he wanted Danny to meet her and Sandy—but he was fearful: he didn't want Murray explaining his motives to him all the way back to New Jersey.

When Charlie wanted to think of Lillian he always thought of the way she'd held his hand that first time. He saw her face, looking down at the table, as if ashamed. Her

9 7

cheeks were flushed. He had to exhale, remembering. Oh how soft she was then! He had seen her hand on the seat next to him in the booth, and he'd let her think his own hand had fallen next to hers accidentally. He saw the hands only now, as if a camera had moved in on them silently, and he saw his small finger rest slightly against hers. . . .

He rolled his window down, to get air. "The moral," Murray was saying, "is not that the ladder was to blame, but that the brief break in his studies was. That's what we Jews believe man is made for, that's why our Sabbath is a day of rest and of study, so that—"

"Enough already," Charlie said. "Christ! What do we need stories about death for? Can't you see how upset the kid is?"

Danny was sitting forward on the seat, stiffly, his eyes fixed on the back of Murray's head, and Charlie reached back and touched his forehead. "You're Jewish, Danny," he said. "Believe me, okay? How could you be so smart if you weren't?"

"There are stupid Jews," Danny said.

Murray laughed. "But not so many," he said. "Ask Sol when he gets here."

"The Home is full of them now," Danny said, flatly. "And I've seen others sent away to mental hospitals and prisons and homes for retards who were all Jews."

"What made us smarter, historically speaking," Murray said, "were several things. First, the fact that every Jewish boy, in order to become Bar Mitzvah, had to know how to read so he could be called to the Torah. That's why—"

"I said to leave us be," Charlie said, but his voice was not insistent. "Okay?"

"I'm sorry," Murray said. "I just thought you'd be interested in the way things work out sometimes—how I read that story before sleep and then woke up in the middle of the night with a nightmare. That's the part I thought you'd be interested in—since you were the one who predicted it." The car held a curve that took it down a ramp and onto the West Side Highway, heading south. "In the dream I was mowing my lawn and trying to wave to somebody when I realized I was going over the edge of the swimming pool," Murray continued. "Then—you know the way it happens sometimes that things are happening to you and you're watching them happen at the same time—? I was watching the mower go to the bottom and there was only a black *yamulka* floating on top."

"I never dream that way," Charlie said.

"What I woke up thinking about this morning, though," Murray went on, "was about *Anita's* death. It was crazy—I told her while we were still in bed that what I worried about most if she died was not knowing the names of her flowers and what to do for them at what times of year."

"You could hire a gardener," Charlie said. "Money takes care of things."

Danny laughed and Murray looked at him coldly. "You're right," he said. "I suppose I could get Fred, from the school, if he had the time. . . ."

Charlie saw Lillian's finger trace a line along the contour of his hand, from the tip of his thumb and down along the webbing that stretched to his first finger, and then up and over and down—it went so slowly and her pressure was so light that he could never be sure of how long it had all lasted. It had been Sunday night, and they had won a football game that afternoon against the Colored Orphan Asylum and he had scored four touchdowns.

What he believed, even then, was that she had somehow wanted to drink the silence out of him. He had noticed that, of all the girls who hung out in the store, she had been the quietest, and, because she had also been the prettiest, the one the guys had left for him. When she moved her hand across the back of his she touched only the hairs, raising them the way the wind could, so that it had been almost unbearable and he'd wanted to smash the table with his other hand.

What, really, had they ever spoken about before their marriage? Was the quality that made him decide to marry related to the quality that made him decide to buy and sell?

And if there was a connection, would anyone who knew him then and now be able to sense what that connection was?

He wondered why Sol had encouraged the marriage, and he wondered if Murray suspected that he asked himself questions like these. But why then was he reluctant to show this part of himself to Murray? There was no one in the world he felt closer to. . . .

"Don't mind me today," he said aloud. "I was looking forward to seeing you, and the guys—but then this morning Max started in on Danny and it turned me."

"He gave me a test," Danny said, "and I answered all his questions."

"Sure you did," Charlie said.

"A syndicate is better than a corporation because there is no double taxation," Danny said. "You can avoid capital gains tax by trading land for a percentage of the proceeds of the structure built on the land. Distance is measured in minutes, not miles. Avoid lock-ins because without prepayment privileges you have no flexibility. Avoid net listings. Land values grow out of land use. . . ."

Charlie grabbed Danny's arm, above the wrist, and yanked. *"Hey!"* he said. *"Hey!* Stop it. It's my day off." But Charlie wasn't sure what was bothering him more—remembering what Max had done to Danny, or realizing that talking about it was taking his concentration away from what he had been seeing in his head. When he wiped his palms on his thighs he saw that he had an erection. He fluffed the hem of his sweatshirt, to disguise the swelling, and he longed to be lost again, in the memory of the ache he had once had. If he could lose himself in that feeling, and connect it to what he had *not* felt when he and Lillian had been touching, he thought he might still be able to discover what things he'd thought and felt when he was a boy. "Then when this test thing was over," he said, "Max went and pulled one of his crazy stunts. He said that what he decided was that Danny wasn't the age he says he is."

Danny spoke: "He said that maybe my name wasn't

Danny Ginsberg, and that maybe I was born to Christians who knew a good thing when they saw one and wanted me brought up with Jews so I could be smart."

"Max asked him how he could prove his age or if Danny had ever seen his birth certificate."

"It's not in my folder," Danny said. "I looked when I was there."

"Maybe it got misplaced," Charlie said. He saw signs for the Brooklyn-Battery Tunnel. "Come on, Murray, tell him —don't you think he's Jewish?"

They entered the tunnel. "Even if you're not the age you think," Murray said, "—let's say you're fourteen or fifteen —what's the difference? A boy as bright as you are . . ."

The car swerved and Charlie grabbed for the steering wheel. Murray whacked Charlie's hand with the back of his own. Charlie heard the tires squeal, the blasts of horns. "Don't ever do that again," Murray said. "You could have killed us."

"You were the one who swerved," Charlie said. "Pay attention."

"I *was* paying attention. There was a car passing that almost went into our side." He glared at Charlie. "The worst thing you can ever do is to interfere with the driver when—"

"Blow it out your ass," Charlie said.

"Apologize."

"What?"

"Say you're sorry."

Charlie laughed. "Listen, I'm not one of your kids—or one of your students either, so you—"

"Don't fight," Danny said. "Please. You're friends."

"A lot of good it does us," Charlie said. In his head he saw Anita's face, smiling.

"Maybe," Danny said. "Maybe it was the Angel of Death."

"He's learning from Max," Charlie said, but could say no more. He thought of Murray rocking him in his arms, and of Lillian's fingers brushing back and forth across his palm, under the table, tickling him so that he had to grit his teeth, and he thought that if he showed Murray this too—

101

how many hours his mind had devoted to replaying that moment with Lillian—he would not get Murray any closer. The truth, he knew, was that if he decided to try at all, he would try with the boy, since there was, literally, more future there. And there was this too—that no matter what Charlie said or did, he felt Murray would reduce it all to patterns and theories, the way he did with Sol, while the boy would see other things.

But what other things? Charlie looked at their eyes— Murray's angry, Danny's glazed—and he had his example. On the day of his fortieth birthday, when he stopped working, he knew that Murray's first reaction would be concern for him. But the boy—the boy's eyes, he knew, would be rejoicing.

He wondered: if he farmed Danny out to live with Dr. Fogel, would that help him get the land?

They were out of the tunnel, almost there, and Charlie felt better. He wanted to feel the thunk of the ball when Morty would rip a pass into his gut. He wanted—more— to feel himself blasting into the other guys. He wanted to stop thinking of Fogel and Sol and where they would live.

He looked left, across Murray, and saw the green fields of the Parade Grounds, where the others would be meeting them. They had played baseball and football here when they'd been boys at the Home, hitching rides on the backs of the McDonald Avenue trolleys. Murray had been afraid to ride the backs of trolleys. He had shown them all a comic book with the life story of Pete Gray, the one-armed Saint Louis Brown baseball player who had lost his arm from hitching on to the back of a truck and falling off.

Charlie remembered fighting bigger kids for fields. The fields had all been open then. Now there were fenced-in areas. "Something else happened yesterday," Murray said, "and I want to tell you about it. When we went to make *Havdalah* in the evening, we couldn't find the *tsumin* box."

Charlie saw that they were early. There were few players

on the fields. He should remember to put it on his list—*Tell Sol not to go to the racetracks, in Florida or anywhere else.* "The what?" Charlie asked.

"The *tsumin* box—we always keep it in the china closet in the kitchen, but it was gone. We used it last Saturday."

"I see Morty and Irving," Charlie said. "Christ, is Morty getting fat!"

They parked and got out. Murray locked the car doors. Danny stayed next to Charlie, and Charlie waved to Morty and Irving, rubbed the tips of his fingers against his palms, and then, without warning, punched Murray in the midsection. Murray coughed, gagged. "Soft," Charlie said. "You're soft even though you're thin."

"Don't do that," Murray said. "I don't like it."

Charlie punched him on his arm, below the shoulder. "Then I'll get you here." He punched him again and again, short rapid-fire jabs.

Murray drew his right hand back and tried to slam Charlie with the back of it, but Charlie had his wrist in his hand, and then he had his other hand next to it. "Indian rope burn!" he said, and he twisted his hands in opposite directions, tightly, rubbing Murray's skin so that Murray hissed.

"I mean it," Murray said. "Cut it out!"

Charlie dropped Murray's arm. "You're too serious," he said. "Have to hang loose before a game. Have to concentrate on relaxing—"

A car honked and some of the others waved from the window. "I can take it when I'm ready for you," Murray said. "I stay in shape." He lifted his sweatshirt and pressed a fold of skin on his pale stomach. Charlie saw the loaves of unbaked bread, rising, and he laughed. "No fat, I drink no whole milk, eat no eggs, no cheese, no pastries, no animal fats, no—"

"Who cares?" Charlie said, and he broke away, running toward the field and calling to Morty to throw him a ball. He ran hard, planted his left foot, cut right and took the ball—a soft spiral—above his right shoulder. He motioned to Irving to move, and when Irving waddled along, Charlie fired a strike into his stomach. Irving went down, in mock agony.

Hesh, Slats, and Louie appeared. They hugged each other, punched each other, teased one another about their pot-bellies, bopped one another on the heads, gave one another the old Manchurian torture, with knuckles on the tops of skulls. Others arrived—Stan, Jerry, Herman. They tossed the ball to one another, made phantom blocks, recalled the heroes of their childhood, imitated Dr. Fogel's admonitions, went over famous plays of games they'd been in, lined up in old school formations, asked about one another's families, talked business, stocks, and current sports, and chose up sides. Charlie felt, as always, elated. He ran without becoming tired, he drank in their memories of him, he relished the way they kidded him and Danny.

"I dub you our new mascot," Morty said, and he dropped a football on Danny's head. Danny's eyes looked into Charlie's, happy.

"The Maimonides Mascot!" Irving announced.

Danny was on Charlie's side, and on the first play Charlie handed him the ball and told him to follow him around right end. Charlie cracked into Murray, knocking him back flat, then rolled over Irving. Danny gained eight yards before being tagged.

Charlie heard Murray talking to Irving about Biafra. Irving taught at Queens College. "It's a racket," he always said. "College teaching is a bigger racket than the numbers game."

On the second play Morty suggested a reverse to Charlie —since he was so slow, nobody would suspect—but, going around the right side, Murray tagged him immediately, for a loss. Murray clapped his hands, then shouted, fist in air, "Way to go, Mendelsohn!"

"Let's make our parents proud on this one," Charlie said in the huddle, and the guys laughed, remembering the old joke.

He heard Murray and Irving, between plays, discussing

the probable number of Jews, of the fourteen million left in the world, who still observed ritual. Irving was president of the Men's Club at his synagogue. Murray said that if ritual ceased, then children would have no living memory of the past. He said that the absence of ritual in Jewish homes was like the destruction of Biafran villages. Both meant the end of cultures that had endured for centuries.

Charlie went out for a pass, a simple flare to the right side, and gained ten yards. They were past the midfield mark—Charlie saw the sweatshirts and jackets lined up for a goal line—and when the other side told them it was fourth down, Charlie replied that they weren't kicking.

"Is Dr. Fogel really still at the Home?" Herman asked Danny. "I still can't believe it."

"He was there when I left," Danny said.

"They're expecting a pass so we'll run straight up the middle," Charlie said. "I'll drop back, fake the pass, receivers go wide, and then Danny will take it from me and follow me up the middle. Keep your men blocked to the sidelines, right?"

"Hey—" Morty yelled to Murray and Irving. "I was wondering. From the way you guys are talking—are you Jewish by any chance?"

Charlie slapped his hands together. "Let's go!" he said, and, standing behind Stan and waiting for the hike, seeing the waiting smiles and imagining Danny breaking through for a touchdown and being lifted on his shoulders for a victory ride, he realized that what he really wanted from life was simple: for his friends to love his friends.

Money would give him the time to see them more often. He didn't want to stop the game, but he wished he could get Murray outside them all for a second, looking in, so that he would see that they looked like any group of men enjoying themselves on a Sunday morning. Why would anyone think there was, in Murray's words, something *wrong* with them? How would anyone guess where they had all been raised? . . .

The ball was in his hands and he raised it over his shoulder, with both hands, as Dr. Fogel had taught him, and yelled to his receivers to keep going. He saw one man coming at him, hands high, and he faked a pass and slipped under the flailing arms easily. "Let's go—!" he whispered, and handed the ball to Danny. The middle of the field was wide open and he had to force himself to keep from sprinting. Danny kept up with him, two steps behind. All the way, all the way, Charlie said to himself, and then he saw Murray angling toward them, running faster than he had ever seen the man move.

"Cut!" he called to Danny, meaning that Danny should move left as Charlie blocked Murray to the right. He had to give Murray credit—there was no one who played harder, and that had been true twenty years before. In games he had been a maniac, and, despite his lack of coordination, a starter on the Home's good teams, before Charlie had been old enough to play.

Charlie's elbows were set wide, his fists side by side, clenched against his breastbone. He ran low, then shot up fast just as Murray lunged; he popped him with a solid crack block, his forearms square into Murray's chest. Murray dropped and Charlie veered left, but too late. Irving had Danny and was swinging him around in a bear hug, yelling that he had stopped the touchdown and saved the day.

Charlie smiled, seeing the fury in Danny's eyes. The kid had almost made it. The feel of the block against Murray had been wonderful.

He saw Morty standing over Murray, offering his hand for Murray to get up, but Murray didn't move.

Charlie saw it all in an instant, and he felt gooseflesh spread wildly over his body. "No!" he cried silently. *"No!"*

"Give me a hand!" Morty cried. "Get some water—you cold-conked him."

Irving was down on his knees, listening to Murray's chest. "Something's wrong," he said. "It's not beating the right way."

Stan wandered over. "Stop being so melodramatic, Mendelsohn—" he called.

Charlie pushed Irving away, so that he fell over backward

on his rear end, feet into the air. Stan and the others, coming closer, laughed. Charlie pressed his ear to Murray's chest and heard a thump, a pause, a thump, a longer pause. He looked up and around, helplessly, opened his mouth, but heard only a gurgling sound, like air and water from a dentist's drill.

Danny was next to Murray and his head was bobbing up and down as if, Charlie thought, he was saying yes, again and again. His cheeks seemed especially pink.

"I'll get the car," Irving called. "I have a wagon—we can lay him flat."

"Where's the closest hospital?" Morty asked. "I don't know Brooklyn anymore—maybe they changed it."

Irving dictated commands: "Call the police—run into somebody's house and call. Get an escort. Give him artificial respiration. Somebody—"

Danny didn't move. Irving rolled jackets together and put them under Murray's shoulders, so that his head dropped back gently. Then Charlie reached down and wrenched Murray's mouth open, hooked his thumb in behind the lower teeth, inhaled, pressed his lips down against Murray's mouth and realized that he had, a moment before, blanked out and that Irving had taken over. Had anyone noticed? His mouth was sideways against Murray's and he did the breathing that he taught his own team at the start of each season. He tasted pipe tobacco. He blew long and slow, his head to the side, his four fingers keeping Murray's mouth open, the jaw jutted forward. With his other hand he pinched Murray's nostrils shut. He could hear the thumps, but they remained uneven. When he took his mouth away, he did not get a return rush of air.

Charlie was surprised at how quickly he could concentrate on the proper rhythm. Twelve to a minute, he told himself. Take your time, take your time. "I'll work his chest," Irving said, and Charlie moved aside so that Irving could go up and down on Murray's chest with the heel of his hand. Charlie saw the tears streaming down Danny's face and he saw that Danny was holding Murray's head in place between the palms of his hands. He heard the car approach them across the grass and he followed Irving's commands. He turned Murray over and hit him hard between the shoulder blades, and Murray's eyes flipped open and he took in a sudden enormous gulp of air. Charlie turned Murray onto his back. "Talk to me!" he yelled. "Come on. *Talk to me! Talk to me!*"

Gently, Irving getting in first, they lifted Murray into the car. Murray's chest moved up and down, in spasms, and Charlie crawled quickly into the back seat after him, grazing his head on metal. He turned back, looked out and around, grabbed Danny and pulled him in, then bent over Murray and began the artificial respiration again. The car roared off, swerved on the grass, and Charlie saw, where they had been, teenagers in a circle. He had the crazy notion to make them stop the car so he could see if Max were nearby somewhere, with his camera going. The car crossed the sidewalk and Charlie's teeth cracked against Murray's as they bumped over curbstone. He tasted blood.

Irving was on the other side, out of breath. "It's nothing," he said. "Keep working. You're doing fine. It means everything. Keep working."

Danny was hunched against the back door, knees to chest.

They slowed down and Slats yelled through the window that they'd gotten into somebody's house and telephoned and that a police car would try to meet them at the corner of Caton and Flatbush, picking them up for King's County Hospital. "The people were very nice," he said. "They said they'd call the hospital and . . ."

Herman was driving, with Morty next to him. Murray's skin seemed almost metallic to Charlie. He was too close to be able to see the entire face.

"Any signs?" Morty asked.

"Shut up," Irving said, and he bore down on Murray's chest with the heel of his palm.

When Charlie heard the siren he realized that some time

had passed—perhaps a minute and a half—and that he was relaxed: his breathing technique was perfect—if he had to, he could go on forever. It was really happening and he was in the middle of it and he could see himself, not as if he were on film, but as if he could actually reach out and touch his own face.

The experience, if Murray survived it, would serve to bind them even closer to one another, he knew, and Charlie wondered if that was, really, what he himself wanted. What Murray would feel about what happened, and about what Charlie had done, would all be, Charlie saw, after the fact. What then would they have to talk about? What would they have actually shared? He felt Murray's chest heave, catch, lie still. He heard Murray grunt, and he lifted his own head. He wondered about the second half of his own life—if Murray's family life were gone, would he be obliged to replace it?

"Don't stop," Irving said. "Don't stop unless he's choking."

"This is terrible," Morty was saying. "It's terrible."

Charlie enjoyed the sound of the siren rising and falling around them. He laughed silently at the silliness of it all—at the ordinary way his mind worked at such a moment, because one of the things he had been doing, he realized, in one section of his mind, was making a list—things to do if Murray didn't make it. And if, later, he revealed this to Murray, he knew that Murray would speak to him about one of his favorite topics—the way people confused their fears with their wishes. Charlie didn't, he felt, really need to go through a conversation like that.

But the question was there and it was real enough. Who else would handle all the arrangements? Murray had been a full orphan, without any living relatives Charlie had ever heard of. Ephraim was too young to take charge; Anita would be in a state. They would depend on him. He knew what others might make of it, but he didn't find it anything but ordinary that he composed a list: contact the funeral home, a rabbi, people at the school; go over insurance and finances with Anita; get money and securities out of bank accounts and safe deposit boxes; cancel appointments for next week to sit *shiva* with them. . . .

Danny would be a help. There would be groceries to be bought, the children to be kept busy, Anita to be consoled, medical bills—and, what he would find hardest, telephone calls to be made. At least, with most of the old crowd at the field, he would be spared part of the list.

If Anita had a doctor, he should call her doctor first.

But how would he get in touch with Sol?

What would Sol feel?

Should he call Dr. Fogel? And would Fogel think Charlie had some ulterior purpose in informing him?

There was no rabbi or synagogue or Jewish cemetery near them in New Jersey, as far as he knew. It was curious, he realized, how things were upside down: Sol—and not Fogel—was the one who was running out of money . . . Sol was the one who believed in Israel. . . . He was aware of Danny's eyes on him, and he had the feeling that Danny sensed his calmness, and that Danny approved. Even the thought of Dr. Fogel did not upset Charlie now.

But why wasn't he overwhelmed with grief?

And what was the difference between what he felt and what he showed? He had never been closer to anyone than he had been to Murray, and there wasn't anything Murray could say about him that would not be true, and yet, if you added up all of Murray's words, Charlie felt, you'd still wind up short.

Murray would know I thought this also, he thought.

The car slowed and there was suddenly less light coming in through the windows. They were at the hospital. "Remember to tell them about his attack four years ago," Herman said. "Maybe his doctor can phone in the history to help them. . . ."

Charlie knew nobody would blame him and he didn't blame himself. It had been a clean hard block. He gave Dr. Fogel credit for having taught him well, and he thought of

110

saying that to Murray. Murray would have said . . . what? He couldn't find Murray's voice in his head.

He crawled out backward, on his hands and knees, and watched them put the oxygen mask on Murray's face, transfer him to a rolling stretcher, and run him up a ramp and through a door. Was that the last time he would see him? Irving dabbed at Charlie's forehead with a handkerchief and showed him the blood, from when he'd grazed his head against the car roof. Irving patted him on the back, tried to say something, but bit his lip instead. Charlie nodded, knowing that Irving was thanking him for a job well done.

He wished he could know what was happening in Danny's head. The boy had so much going on there at the same time, all the time, that he made Charlie wonder even more about the things that had been passing through him when he had been that age. He thought of what Danny had said one day two weeks before, when they were driving home from practice.

Do you know what I really want to be when I grow up? Danny had asked.

What? Charlie had replied.

Normal.

There was a connection between that and what he had been feeling in the back of the station wagon. He liked the fact that his mind ran, sometimes, in ordinary grooves. It made him believe that the special part of his life was still to come.

They followed the policeman around and into a waiting room. Irving went to a desk and answered questions. Charlie sat. He heard a baby crying, saw that they were the only white people in the waiting room, and when he did he stood up, walked to Irving, and interrupted him.

"Make sure he gets a good Jewish doctor," Charlie said.

Irving squinted. Charlie's face was splotchy; he was sweating. "You'd better sit down," Irving said. "You don't look right."

Charlie felt that his words should have come forth with

strength and fury, yet he knew that they sounded soft and mellow. "I don't want him getting some half-assed intern or a foreign idiot, all right? Please tell them."

"Sit down."

Charlie turned. "Okay. Just remember that I told you what to do," he said, and he walked back and sat next to Danny.

"Will he live?" Danny asked.

Charlie shrugged, and saw Morty and Herman lean their heads toward him for the answer. "Who knows?" he said.

Morty was puffing, his stomach heaving in and out. Charlie was surprised at how polite all the black people were. None of them spoke, nobody spoke to them. They sat and waited. Though his business brought him into their neighborhoods, and though everybody thought he had a wonderful ability to get along with them, he decided that he really didn't know much about them, or understand them. "I always believed that each of us has a number," Morty was saying, "and that when your number is up, it's up. That's what I always believed."

"Maybe they dialed the wrong number," Herman said, and he chewed on his thumbnail. "Jesus, I don't know what I'll do if—"

"Shush," Morty said.

The others arrived and Charlie rose and stood with them, in a circle, wondering. They muttered and looked at each other and stared at the floor and watched the door that led out of the waiting room. Charlie imagined that each of them was trying to select a picture of Murray from the past.

He tried to imagine what was going on in Danny's head, and he found a feeling of repose there not unlike his own. He saw mists floating inside the boy's skull, like the morning fog rising from the playing fields at the school, and he thought that if the boy could have, he would have represented the mists with a saying. Charlie chose one the boy had taught him: *Paradise is Shabbos which never ends.* . . .

Charlie was surprised that nobody tried to tell a joke. They agreed that they shouldn't telephone Anita until they knew something definite. Charlie made a note to ask the boy, later, if that had been what he had, in fact, been thinking at that moment. He smiled. The boy would have answered yes, but that the thoughts had been part of what he had been imagining going on in Charlie's head. Morty talked about his blood tests, and the diet he never stuck to, and how Murray did stick to one, so what did it all prove? In the end, doctors didn't know so much.

Charlie saw himself with his arms draped limply over the shoulders of the men next to him as they swayed together, slowly, from right to left, and seeing this enabled him to see what he really wanted to see—a strong shot of himself with Murray.

He saw them as boys going to an old *shul* together where men were standing in front of the congregation with their *talises* pulled over their heads, and only their arms sticking out and stretching upward. Their fingers were outstretched and quivering, the thumbs and forefingers enclosing a circle of space, the tips not quite touching. He saw the men swaying and he heard them wailing like demons. The *talises* were white with black stripes and heavy knotted fringes. Murray had told him that the presence of God was supposed to lie in the air between the men's fingertips. If you looked at them while they had their heads covered, the Orthodox Jews said, you would go blind. Charlie recalled the foul, suffocating odor. That night he'd had chills and had crawled into Murray's bed and slept there. Neither of them had been able to sleep, apart, for several weeks after that.

Charlie realized that he was brushing Danny's hair, back and forth, back and forth, and it seemed softer and more golden than ever. He was pleased with himself—at how easily he was able to wait for the news. It told him that he did have, at his center, what Murray might not have suspected—a calm point, and that this spoke well for the life he would live after forty.

If Murray goes now, he thought, then I can fear less about my own chances of making it past forty.

A man appeared at the swinging doors that led away from

113

the waiting room. When Irving saw him he went forward, then behind the doors. Charlie sat down with the others, where they occupied parts of two rows, sitting silently like schoolboys.

When Irving emerged, five minutes later, he lifted his hands sideways, palms up, in a gesture of helplessness, and then Morty rose and the two men embraced, and cried.

"What happens now?" Herman asked.

"Come," Irving said.

They walked single file from the room. Charlie saw the black faces swiveling slowly to watch their departure. "Was the doctor Jewish?" Charlie asked, but nobody answered him, or seemed to hear his words.

They stood outside, near their cars. Irving said he would telephone his own home and then go with Charlie to New Jersey, to break the news to Anita and the children.

"My God!" Herman whispered.

They talked softly, as if they were afraid to disturb somebody, and they made arrangements to get together between five and six o'clock at Anita's house. Those without small children would come with their wives. Others would try to get baby-sitters. Irving and Charlie would see to the necessary arrangements. They took assignments for telephoning.

Irving said that they had opened Murray's chest but that the damage was at two ends—he didn't know the technical terms—and that it had been hopeless from the start. The doctor had said that there were few initial signs of arteriosclerosis or fatty deposits; it had been something congenital. There were weak walls. Irving said he really hadn't been able to concentrate on the explanations—it all seemed so stupid.

They embraced one another and said their good-byes. Charlie followed Irving to Irving's car. Irving had the keys to Murray's car, and they would pick it up at the Parade Grounds and leave Irving's car parked in its place. He would get it the next day.

Charlie thought, from the light pressure of his fingers, that Danny was feeling faint, and he suggested that they stop and get some food.

"I'll be all right," Danny said.

Danny sat in the back by himself and rested his head. Charlie tried to smile at him, to reassure him, but he saw something strange in the boy's eyes. "What is it?" he asked. "Come on. Talk to me—"

"It's nothing," Danny said.

"Talk," Irving said. "We should all talk a lot at a time like this. It doesn't matter what we say."

"Come on," Charlie said.

Danny nodded, and spoke: "I wanted to ask you if you were going to marry Anita now," he said, and his voice was suddenly strong.

"If *what*—?"

"Take it easy," Irving said, and put his hand on Charlie's arm. "The boy's upset."

"It's called a levirate marriage," Danny said, and his voice was flat again. "It's in the Torah. When a husband dies, his brother has to marry the widow."

II
Shiva

Five

The beautiful thing about what happens when a Jew dies is how quickly you're buried. A Jew is supposed to be buried on the same day he dies, but usually it's the day after.

Why this is good: It makes the suffering less and the pain more.

They had a Rabbi at the funeral yesterday who never met Murray and he said the Mourner's Kaddish is not a prayer for the dead but for the living! It's a public way to show you still have faith in God and intend to continue to be part of the Jewish community. It does not contain the word DEATH.

What I thought: He must have explained this 1000 times before at 1000 funerals of 1000 different Jews he never knew alive.

How much money does a Rabbi get for giving a funeral speech?

I'm glad to be home again with Charlie. Last night we slept at Anita's house in Ephraim's room and it wasn't good for Charlie to sleep there with Murray gone. I kept my eyes open until I was sure he was asleep but he woke up later when Eli was crying and he went to Eli's room and held him. Eli said his father would be scared in the

119

ground because it would be so dark and he wouldn't be able to see.

Rivka said Eli was stupid, that being dead was like sleeping and when she said that Hannah slapped her and told her she wasn't Eli's mother and then Anita was crying and Charlie was holding her. She looked terrible, with splotches on her cheeks and her hair raggedy looking. I saw Dov using his baseball glove for a pillow.

Charlie isn't so angry with me anymore. He told me if I wanted to write things down in my storybook the way he knows I do he would wait to go to sleep, but he fell asleep with the lights on anyway. I'll have to take his shoes off for him when I'm done. If I wasn't afraid to wake him up now I'd brush his hair back and forth the way he likes to brush mine.

MY SECRET: This afternoon I went for a walk with Hannah into the woods behind the shed where Murray keeps his mower and tools and we kissed again. She has soft lips which are bigger than mine and I don't think she knows that I never kissed a girl before. I think she thought I was a good kisser or she wouldn't have asked me to go with her again. She's less than 2 years older than me, which is a big difference now but won't be later, but I think she's too quiet. I don't know what she thinks about anything at all and she doesn't know what I think.

Today we kissed for over an hour and when we came back Charlie thanked me for spending time with her. I don't think anybody would guess because of her being older. I could feel her breasts against my arm muscles. While I kissed her I imagined her naked. When we stopped she didn't say anything so I asked her if she had a boyfriend and she said no. But I didn't ask her if I could be her boyfriend because if she said no I wouldn't have wanted to have her let me kiss with her again.

What I think: She wasn't even thinking about her father!

With things happening so fast it's hard to miss him yet, but even if she doesn't, I believe her life is changed now forever!

Today was the 2nd day of the week of SHIVA and their house was full of noise, and even laughing, espe-

120

cially when the guys from the Home were there with their wives and families. When only the people from near Mill River were there, then things were quieter and sad. All the non-Jews are too polite. They don't know what the Rabbi meant about life going on. They don't understand what the week of SHIVA means to a Jew!

For example: None of them talked about Murray the way Irving and Morty and their wives did. They probably thought it was forbidden to talk about the dead person, but when Murray was talked about was when his death was most real and at the same time when Anita was the least unhappy. She laughed when they told stories about him.

When he was a boy he once organized a hunger strike at the Home so that the boys would be allowed out by themselves, and he sent Herman out in secret to bring back candy bars. His strike worked.

Some religious Jews fast because they believe that being lighter brings one closer to God!

SHIVA comes from the word for Seven for the 7 Days of Mourning and from the word for Rest. Shabbos comes from the same word. During the week of SHIVA people come all the time to visit and talk and bring food. This is what the Rabbis teach: It Is Forbidden To Overstress Mourning For The Departed.

During the funeral I thought this was what Charlie was thinking: If I become a Rabbi will I use the same stories again and again or will I make up a new speech for every occasion?

The Rabbi said that the Talmud says that every Jew must say to himself, For my sake the world was created.

This is why: God created a single man in the beginning to teach us that if any man ever causes a single other man to die it is as if he caused a whole world to die because it is as if he had killed all those who would have been born to that human being until the end of the world.

His conclusion: The world exists so that each of us might be born into it!

Charlie's eyes flickered when the Rabbi talked about killing and even though he knows he didn't cause Murray's death I wonder how he'll ever feel truly free again.

He surprised me when they were talking about Murray yesterday and he said, Let's face it, he was never a likable guy.

Anita nodded her head in agreement and so did the others. Irving said that what Murray did for others came about because he wanted to succeed for himself.

I loved the guy, Charlie said, and he meant everything in my life. But he wasn't likable.

This morning Charlie told me he had a dream and in the dream he was coming home from the hospital and Anita came out of her house and he told her that he was in the delivery room and saw the child born. He said it was a girl. He said that later he would tell Anita about the dream and that they could laugh about how Murray would have analyzed it.

Before, when we were sitting in our room here and it was quiet, Charlie said that while the Rabbi was talking he was worrying about what would happen if a fire would break out in the funeral home. He said he saw himself running out of the home with the Torahs in his arms, saving them one at a time. I told him there were no Torahs in funeral homes. Charlie and I sat next to Anita during the funeral with the children on the other side. Before the service the Rabbi took a razor blade and slit the lapel of Ephraim's suit for a sign of mourning. Eli and Rivka howled.

Only members of the immediate family above the age of 13 are supposed to have their jackets cut, so I watched carefully to see what Charlie would do and he was watching me all the time he held his jacket lapel out for the Rabbi to cut.

What I said to him in the car right after Murray died is like a sword between us now and what I like about the sword is that I'm glad it's there and that I said what I did! It makes him respect me, that I could put him under my control with my knowledge.

He doesn't know what to do about the thing which surprised everybody: that Murray didn't have a will or any life insurance!

What Irving says: Murray thinks everybody has to live the way he did. He thinks everybody has to struggle.

Irving took Charlie aside last night and said that the truth was that Murray was a regular "shmuck" sometimes and that he would have beaten his brains in if he'd known about the will and insurance.

A good question: Years from now if I read this will I remember the things that happened to me and that I thought and that I did *not* write down?

I could make a 2nd diary with all the things I never list in this one!

They closed the school yesterday and a lot of the students were at the funeral, wearing their blazers. Their parents were there too, and what I noticed was how well-dressed their mothers were. If Charlie could buy and sell homes to them he could be rich fast, but he says families like theirs don't move so much.

He won't work now for the 7 days of mourning. Even though he's not supposed to say Kaddish he does, and he sits on a wooden bench the funeral home gave us. So do Anita and the children. All the mirrors in the house are covered with sheets or soaped up and Charlie won't shave until the SHIVA is over. None of the mourners wear shoes inside the house.

Other things you're not supposed to do during the week of SHIVA if you're mourning: leave your home, cut your hair, bathe, use make-up, greet another person 1st, work or talk business, study the Torah except for parts about mourning.

The only time I cried so far was at the cemetery when Charlie got in line and shoveled earth into Murray's grave. I liked the sound of the dirt falling on the wood. They buried Murray's Talis and Tephillin in the pine box with him.

What I thought even while I was crying and watching the others shovel dirt on top of the box: Now is a good time to show Charlie how well he can read.

I watched the gravediggers in back of the crowd and I hated them. They lowered the box with a machine and straps that did the work for them. I hated them because they don't know Charlie and what he feels and what he's like inside. They couldn't wait for us to leave.

This is what Charlie said after, just before we got into

our limousine: What's it all about, Danny? What's it all for?

I didn't say anything.

Irving put his arm around Charlie's shoulder but he didn't say anything either.

It's all so disconnected, Charlie said. To be buried in a place you never knew, to have a funeral where you didn't grow up, to have no relatives from your childhood who knew you when you were a boy. Don't you see? he asked.

It's shitty, Irving said. It's very shitty.

I wish Sol could have been here, Charlie said, and then instead of crying he made a fist and slammed it into a tree trunk so hard I thought he would break his hand. Irving grabbed him from around the back and held him with his own head resting against Charlie's back, but when I looked at Charlie's hand, his knuckles weren't even cut.

In the car, driving back across New Jersey, I sat next to Herman, with Charlie and Irving and Irving's wife in front of us. Anita and the children were alone in the car in front of ours with just Anita's sister. Anita's mother and father are dead. Her sister has been married and divorced 3 times and has no children.

Herman talked to me about his hobby. He enters contests and sends away for free things. It started when he was a traveling salesman going from city to city and selling leather goods. I liked to have mail waiting for me, he said, so I started clipping out coupons from magazines and entering contests. He put his cheek next to me and made me sniff his free after shave lotion.

His wife helps him now and he showed me her picture. She's 8 years older than him and lives in a wheelchair. They were married 10 years ago. They get 3 sacks of mail a week from the post office. 2 years ago they won a color TV set from a Reader's Digest Sweepstakes. Our names are sold from one mail order house to another, he said, and he invited me to visit him sometime to see his collection.

These are things he gets free samples of: stationery, stamps, soap, fabric, magazines, books, key rings, jewelry, silverware, photo albums, records, underwear, and spices.

The best part, he said, are coupons he gets worth over $15 a month. He and his wife belong to several Coupon Clubs. Charlie and Irving and Irving's wife were very quiet and it made Herman's voice get lower and lower until he stopped and said, It's just a hobby.

Hey, Charlie said to Herman, and he grabbed him above the knee and pressed hard. I'm not angry with you, all right? Herman nodded his head up and down, but he was sniffling and crying.

TUESDAY
(at Anita's House!)

I would have written more down about the funeral and what happened when we 1st got home from Brooklyn and how Charlie and Irving took care of everything, but Charlie woke up while I was writing last night and made me put the light out and get into bed. He said he was worried about Anita because her sister was too nervous for her, and that we would sleep here again tonight.

So I brought my notebook today without telling him. I told Hannah about keeping it but she didn't even ask me if she could look at what I wrote. I asked her if she wanted to know why I kept a diary and she said OK, but before I could speak she was tickling my right ear with her fingertip. I got angry and told her to stop and she pouted and said that the guys in school said it excited them to have her play with their ears.

She was worried that Dov was spying on us so we picked a different place today. First we went outside and then we circled back and went down into the cellar from the back of the house. There was an old couch in a storage room and we sat on that and I had a hard time concentrating on kissing because I was worried I'd forget my notebook somewhere.

We could hear people walking around on top of us. Once when we stopped to get air I asked her what she would think if her mother married Charlie and she said, I don't care what she does. I said I didn't believe her and she said she didn't care about that either. She made me put my hand on her breast, under her blouse and it was

125

soft like a baby's skin must be. I was afraid she would see my erection. She ruffled my hair and slid her finger down the back of my shirt.

I thought about how Larry and Steve and the other guys used to brag about what they would do to girls.

A question: How do grown-ups hide their erections all the time?

I wondered how old Charlie was the 1st time he kissed a girl.

I touched her ear the way she touched mine and she started wiggling against me. She stopped kissing me and she blew into my ear in a way that gave me shivers.

How old am I really?

IF MR. MITTLEMAN IS RIGHT AND I'M OLDER, THEN WHAT HAPPENED TO MY MISSING YEARS?

When I blew into her ear she moaned like an actress. She was laying almost on top of me and I know she could feel my erection against the inside of her legs but neither of us said anything about it.

What I thought while we were kissing: This will make good pictures for inside my head when I don't have her with me!

Charlie's wife and daughter came to the funeral when we were sitting in the waiting room before the service. Lillian kissed him on the cheek. I was surprised at how young and pretty she looked. "Oh Charlie," was all she said.

"Gee I'm glad you came," was what he said back, and they held each other for a while.

His daughter is very tall, almost as tall as he is, and she stands up like a ballet dancer. She has a beautiful long neck and her black hair was pinned on top of her head. Even though she's probably just a year or 2 older than Hannah she looked 5 years older, like a girl in college. She had Charlie's eyes. When Charlie told them my name and where I came from she looked at me in a way that made me want to tell her everything I feel about Charlie! She wore a tan suit made out of soft wool.

I wonder what she lets guys do to her. She didn't look as if anybody could ever mess her up in any way, she was so neat, and her clothes fit so right. She wore pale pink lipstick and she kissed her father on the lips.

This is the truth: I don't really like Hannah but I know I can't say no to her. Maybe she'll change. She said one thing which made me think she might have things inside her the way I do. She said, "Nobody knows what I'm like." I asked her what she meant and she said that her name and the way she looked weren't what she was like. I said I thought her name was beautiful and that in Hebrew it meant merciful but she said she didn't like it. My father treated us all like objects, she said, and that was the end of the conversation.

Did she get that sentence from her mother, or was it her own?

People seemed almost happy today. In the afternoon we had a Minyan and Irving was the leader and the guys kidded him about the way he chanted the prayers. He said he would be here in the morning early tomorrow so we could have a Minyan again and put on Tephillin. You can't say Kaddish without a Minyan. Ephraim didn't put on his Tephillin Sunday because it was the first day of mourning, but he does now. Dov took a stack of comics and sports magazines outside and sat in the treehouse all afternoon. He never says anything to anyone.

There were some students from the school there when we prayed in the living room and they looked in at us and I felt as if my heart were in flames. I was so proud because they could see Charlie singing in Hebrew with the others!!

This is what I thought: JEWS DON'T NEED PRIESTS OR CHURCHES BECAUSE WE CAN TAKE OUR RELIGION WITH US ANYWHERE. Wherever there are 10 Jewish men you can have a Minyan for a service, and you can have it in a home. That's why the men were laughing with Irving after, because doing it this way in a home shows that life goes on, for the individual and for the species too. Murray must have walked on the same spot we prayed on only 3 days ago and it didn't make us holy and silent.

What I think: With thoughts like these I could be a Rabbi too!

A good saying from PIRKAY AVOS: "Whole branches of Jewry may wither but the tree lives on."

What I know: The less I say to people the more I can write.

If I had to explain to Hannah why I write, I wouldn't have written all I'm writing today.

Then why did I ask her if she wanted to know why I write my thoughts and experiences down? The answer is that I wouldn't have asked her if I hadn't felt she would *not* be interested.

In the beginning I would have asked Charlie, but not anymore.

He was all excited after supper because a long-distance call came from Sol. He'll be here in 2 days. He saw Murray's obituary in THE NEW YORK TIMES.

Sol and Charlie

5 MINUTES LATER!

MR. MITTLEMAN JUST LEFT AND MY HEART IS STILL POUNDING! I can't even remember what I was going to write about Sol and Charlie, he got me so upset. I don't know how long he was standing next to me but when I looked up he was there. Well, well, he said, the historian of the event.

I'm still sitting in Murray's office at Murray's desk the way I was when he reached toward me with his hand and I flinched away. He said he only wanted to touch my hair the way Charlie always does. He said my hair invited touching.

I didn't say anything. I closed my notebook and he sat down on the other side of the desk and spoke very gently as if he was a different Mr. Mittleman. He asked me how Charlie was feeling and when I said OK he said to let him know if Charlie did anything funny.

He said I shouldn't be afraid of him, that he wouldn't take advantage at a time like this. I stared at his cigar and he said this: You're a very smart boy so you should understand about Charlie. Sometimes he's like a child and we have to watch over him, all right? Shirley and I agreed that I should speak with you since you're with him so much. We don't like him to think we're spying.

128

I said that I already said Charlie was OK but he just sighed and spoke very softly as if I wasn't there. I can still hear his voice! You're too young to understand, he said, but I'll tell you this: The hardest part of growing old is that your friends begin to die.

Charlie isn't old, I replied.

I wouldn't have thought it when I was his age, he went on. How much I would miss them. He leaned toward me then and said that sometimes he begins missing his friends before they're even gone! I wanted to keep him from speaking about Charlie anymore so I asked him what he thought of the Rabbi's sermon and he said he was very moved and that he liked the part about Murray's name. He laughed and said that when he worked with people more he used to call himself Mittleman the Middleman.

Then he stood and kissed me on the forehead just as if I was his own grandson and left!

This was what the Rabbi said in his sermon: that Murray's Hebrew name was Moshe, or Moses, and that it had been a fitting name for him for several reasons:

1. The original Moses was an orphan and a leader also.

2. Moses also stood for Moses Maimonides, for the name of the Home, and Maimonides was a great Jewish philosopher, Talmudist, and physician. He was called The Jewish Aristotle. "From Moses unto Moses," the Rabbis said, "there arose none like Moses."

3. Murray had the exact same full name as another great man in Jewish history, Moses Mendelssohn, who was a German Jew and a hunchback. Born into poverty, Moses Mendelssohn became a great philosopher and theologian and he fought for the emancipation of the Jews in Germany and Switzerland. He opened the 1st free Jewish school in Berlin in 1781.

When the Children of Israel were at the Red Sea and the Egyptians were pursuing them and they cried unto God, God said to Moses, "Wherefore criest thou unto me? Speak unto the Children of Israel, that they go forward."

God didn't make any promises. The Rabbi said Murray was like Moses. He went forth without promises. Born poor and an orphan, he never relied on God's miracles, but took responsibility for his own life into his own hands and went forth and created a beautiful Jewish family and home and became head of an innovative school which influenced educators from all over the country.

WEDNESDAY

This morning Hannah asked if she could visit one of her friends and Anita said she could go if she promised not to stay more than 2 hours. People aren't coming as much as they did the 1st day. I heard Hannah on the phone and one of her girl friends was supposed to call some guys to meet them there. They're from Murray's school so they have off this week.

Charlie and Irving talked about Sol today. Irving said that Sol's father was a typical German Jew, but I didn't know what he meant. Charlie said he felt that if he could know more about Sol's father he'd know more about Sol. He said Sol said his father used to hate poor Jews but not orphans. Sol's father believed that even the meanest Jew can rise by his own bootstraps. Sol said he was a very great man and had endured great humiliation from non-Jews even though he was wealthy and educated.

After lunch Mr. Alfred came from the Board of Directors and said they wanted to name the school after Murray. Anita surprised me and turned him down and Irving took her side against Charlie.

This is why Anita turned him down: She doesn't want charity or a widow's retirement money. SHE WANTS TO TAKE MURRAY'S PLACE AND RUN THE SCHOOL!

She got angry with Charlie and Irving for trying to help her. She wants to help herself. She said she has it all figured out. None of the other teachers can take over because she said Murray hired weak sisters so he could be in control. It's the middle of the school year and parents will want reassurance. These were her words: How can they say no? I have as many damned degrees as Murray. I was a teacher and a guidance counselor before we started repopulating the world with Jews, remember?

Irving said he thought it was a terrific idea but Char-

130

lie asked her what she would do about having the baby. He was looking at her stomach a lot.

She laughed at him and stood in the doorway with her arms around Ephraim and Rivka, pulling them close to her like a real mother. She said if the baby didn't come during spring recess she might have to take a week off but that Charlie could run the school if she did. She said she heals quickly after 5 children.

Charlie asked what she was going to do about money and said she could refinance her house and told me to explain what refinancing was to her but this got her even angrier. You really mean to see me helpless, don't you? she said. You're just like him in that way. She let her children go and stood over Charlie and I saw him smile at her anger. Irving tried to put his arm around her but she pushed him away.

When she asked if there were any more questions Charlie asked her what she was going to do with her spare time but she didn't laugh. I got brave and I said this: You can use one of Murray's favorite words when you go to the Board. You can tell them you represent Continuity!

That's wonderful, she said, but she turned away so quickly and left the room that I couldn't see how she meant it.

This is what I was thinking while the scene was going on: If Charlie didn't want her before, he'll want her now!

The most peaceful part of the afternoon was when Anita was talking about what Murray was like when she first knew him and his great desire was to be a martyr. She asked Charlie and Irving if they remembered the summer she and Murray went to a camp in Ohio to prepare for going to teach in Alabama. She talked about how Murray used to imagine the headlines there would be if he was killed helping blacks. She said everybody knew the government wasn't going to do anything until whites were killed also and she imitated Murray. I'm the most qualified, he used to say. A family man with small children. An orphan ...a Jew...

He changed, Irving said. He'd be angry if you brought it up now.

Morty and Herman came later in the afternoon and so did some of Anita's relatives and we had enough for a Minyan. We didn't have a Minyan in the morning. Then everybody reminisced some more about Murray and Herman told the story of how when they used to go to the movies away from the Home Murray would take a bag of warm oatmeal from the kitchen and he'd sit in the front of the balcony and yell suddenly that he was going to be sick. Then he'd open the bag and make believe he had to throw up and let the stuff plop down on guys under them.

When Murray was in college at Columbia, he took Charlie to visit him and Charlie was asked by the football coach to apply there. Charlie started to tell the story to show how good Murray was to him but when he got near the end he was depressed, as if he'd made a mistake.

Morty asked if Mr. Prentiss gave me to Charlie and I didn't know what he meant. He explained that at the Home, for summers and after school, they would be assigned to work for a Jewish businessman somewhere. Morty had worked for a children's dress manufacturer in the garment center and now he was a partner. He took out his wallet and showed me pictures of his family and his home on Long Island. In a separate envelope he had pictures of his swimming pool, his snowmobile, his snow blower, his electric barbecue, and his riding mower. What's money for if you don't use it? he asked.

Irving said he worked in a corner candy store for a husband and wife and that the brother of the wife had been a college teacher. He inspired me, Irving said. He was the only Jewish man I knew who wasn't rich but still had time to go to ball games and the beach!

Irving made more jokes again about what a racket college teaching is. He only teaches 6 hours a week and this gives him all the time he wants to read and do things with his family and friends. He talked about how angry he used to make Murray by telling him that if schools like Murray's multiplied and students came to college knowing how to read and write, it was going to make life impossible for professors. I used to love to tell him how popular the new film courses are, Irving said, and how we charge lab fees for them to pay for the pillows.

I didn't like to hear Irving make fun of education, so I left the room and went down to the cellar, where Hannah and I were. I didn't try to argue with Irving because I saw that he knew more than me, but I wanted to say to him that without our emphasis on education the Jews would never have survived and he would never have been born!

IF YOU'RE A JEW YOU SHOULD ALWAYS PRAISE LEARNING!

I started to masturbate, thinking of Hannah, but I stopped myself because of it still being the 7 days of mourning for Murray. I lay back on the couch with my hands folded on my chest and made believe I was dead and that Sandy was standing over me in my coffin and crying. Her heart was broken.

Going home tonight Charlie asked what I thought about Mr. Prentiss and I said, you meant apprentice didn't you?

He told me he wanted to invest in me. He believed in my brain, he said. Most people think money makes money, he said. They're wrong. Brains make money. He said he wanted to give me a stake of $25,000 and I would tell him what to do with it and after I was 21 I could start paying him back.

At how much interest? I asked.

He laughed and said he was serious. He would need incoming money in a few years because he would stop working by then. He said he told Anita that he was worth over a quarter of a million dollars in liquid cash and that he was telling me also.

What did she say when you told her? I asked.

Congratulations, he said.

The Jewish people who come to see Anita all kiss her. A lot of the non-Jews don't.

I think Irving admires me for my knowledge. When they talked about Sol's father founding the Home as the 3rd Jewish orphanage in America I said that the 1st orphanage in America was for children whose parents were massacred by Indians.

Before I came up here I went to see Mr. Mittleman in the office and I smiled at him but he acted like nothing ever happened yesterday. He was the old Mr. Mittleman. In a butcher shop in the 21st century, he said, they were selling human meat. The carcasses were hanging from hooks with prices on them. A Chinaman was $2.50 a pound. An Arab was 10¢ a pound. A Russian was $2 a pound, and a Chasidic Jew was $98 a pound. But why so much for a Chasidic Jew? a man asked. The butcher pointed to the frozen body of a Chasidic Jew which was still dressed in black coat and hat. Why? he asked. Tell me—have you ever tried to clean one of those?

From where I was I spat at him, but my saliva was too foamy and dry. It only went a foot or two. He didn't show me if he saw what I did. I prayed for God to put a curse on him. But if I had screamed at him about the sufferings that Jews have endured for centuries so that he could be born into the world he would only have found another joke.

I'm glad you never had a son, I said instead. He would have had to disown you.

Dogs copulate and have more dogs, he replied. Only man makes money.

I came up here and invented something to make Charlie smile. I asked him if he knew why the blue whale was probably a Jew.

Why is the blue whale probably a Jew? he asked, and he was smiling already.

Because he's the smartest animal next to man and he's the most endangered species.

Also: The mother can only give birth to 1 child every 2 years, which is the lowest rate of all animals.

This is what Murray believed: Prosperity is the enemy of the Jews because it leads to a declining birth rate.

I imagined Mr. Mittleman frozen and hanging from a hook with his eyes and mouth closed and his cigar stuck in where his penis used to be.

A question for Dr. Fogel: Even if you're a Rabbi, how can you ever *prove* to a Jew that he should care about being a Jew?

The answer is you can't.

But I would say this also: When they packed Jews into boxcars and ovens they didn't ask them how much they believed in being Jews!

This is what I imagine Dr. Fogel saying: The answer

134

to the question is HISTORY but if you don't know HIS-
TORY or feel HISTORY then it won't be the answer for
you!

SOL CAME TODAY!

I was sitting on the floor in Ephraim's room playing
poker with him when he appeared at the door and I knew
right away it was him, even before he spoke.

You must be Charlie's new boy, he said, and he
smiled at me in a way that made me feel good. He was
taller than I imagined him being and his face was shiny
as if it had all been polished, especially the top of his
head. He only had a little bit of gray hair left, over his
ears, and he wore small round glasses pushed forward on
his nose.

Hi Uncle Sol, Ephraim said, and as soon as he did
and Sol picked him up and hugged him, Ephraim was
crying. Sol told him not to be ashamed, to just let himself
go. This is what Sol said to him: Life has mountains and
life has valleys. He said it was something his father always said to him.

What I thought: He doesn't look like the kind of man
who had ever been a boy to a father! He looked as if he had
always been the age he was now.

He was dressed beautifully. I touched his suit and it
felt softer than Hannah's sweater. His shoes were gleaming black. He was shaved so close I couldn't even see the
little black spots of new hairs. His eyes were a pale gray
color that made you relax, and his forehead had 3 lines
running across it on top of each other.

You're the man of the family now, he said to Ephraim.
You take care of your mother. She'll need you now.

I thought of Charlie waiting for us downstairs and I
imagined him hugging Sol when Sol had walked through
the door into the kitchen. I wanted to run away so instead
I said, My name is Danny Ginsberg and I come from the
Home. Then he smiled very warmly at me and took my
hand in his and told me that Charlie was just telling him
all about me and why I was here. I couldn't stop staring
into his eyes, as if I was hypnotized.

135

Will you help save the Home? I asked, but he only laughed at that and said he could see why Charlie had picked me out. I like directness, he said. I like boys who look me in the eye.

I picked Charlie out, I said.

Did you? he said, and he winked at Ephraim the way Charlie does sometimes. Well, he said. More power to your elbow is what Uncle Sol says.

Ephraim showed him the postcards he'd tacked to his bulletin board and Sol said he meant to send him more. I thought of asking him where he was living but I was scared without Charlie there.

When we got to the kitchen Anita's eyes were all red from crying but Charlie's face was red from happiness. Irving and Morty and Herman were sitting around the table and this is what I thought: With Murray gone and a chicken roasting and plates and coffee cups and pots and paper bags everywhere the kitchen wasn't as neat as it used to be and that made it feel more Jewish to me.

I was surprised to see Sol put his arms around Anita and let her cry on his good clothing, but he didn't seem to mind. He said he wished he could have come earlier. All the men had tears in their eyes too, and I imagined each of them remembering Murray and themselves with Sol when they were boys my age. I saw Charlie in his football uniform with Sol standing next to him and smiling proudly but inside the football helmet I saw my own face.

Anita said she was sorry that Sol had to live to see this but he told her not to worry about him. He told her to worry about herself and her family. He took a handkerchief from his pocket and wiped Anita's tears. The handkerchief had the letter "S" in a corner, in lace. Anita said she knew what Sol must be feeling and he said we *never* know what other people really feel!

I thought he was going to say more but instead he said he thought the best thing was to leave Anita alone for a while. I'll take my boys out, all right? he said.

Anita kissed his cheek then and spoke in a soft voice and said this: Murray said you were the one person who always knew exactly the right thing to do.

Sol was as tall as Charlie. He picked up each of the children and lifted them to the ceiling and hugged them. He tossed Eli in the air and I saw all the children look at him the way they do at Charlie. He said stupid things to them like, Who's my favorite grandchild named Eli? when he was holding Eli, or when he made Rivka laugh he asked her, Are you Jewish—or just ticklish?

I could tell he'd said the same things to them before. They were the kinds of things Murray talked about and I agreed about never wanting to use them myself. It's easy to fool children.

Rivka was wearing her horseback riding clothes, with a black velvet hat and leather patches on her thighs. Murray promised to buy her a pony for her next birthday and to build a home for it in the back. I watched her eyes and I thought of Rivka in the Bible and how she deceived her husband Isaac in order to help her favorite son.

Rivka hugged Sol around the leg and said, My Daddy promised he was going to buy me a pony and now he's dead and I want my pony.

Anita got angry but Sol told her not to get upset. I thought he was going to say he would get the pony for her, but instead he took her out of the room by herself and when they came back inside a few minutes later Rivka asked if she could change her mind if she didn't want a pony anymore.

Eli started grabbing Sol's jacket at the door and asking him: Is today tomorrow? Is today tomorrow?

Charlie pulled him away and Eli cried. I remembered Murray saying how Sol would be proud of them bringing another Jew into the world, but I thought to myself: IF SOL'S A JEW, HE'S A PAGAN JEW.

In my head I was thinking of Dr. Fogel and listing the meanings of everybody's name.

Ephraim means fruitful.

Rivka means tie or bind, as when an animal is bound for slaughter.

Dov means bear, the animal.

Charlie's Hebrew name is Chaim, for life.

I was still afraid to ask Sol where he lives and where

his money comes from, so I said this: Dr. Fogel never calls us by our English names. But nobody paid attention to me. Eli was crying and yelling out loud.

I looked at Charlie's black curls and his dark face from not shaving, and I didn't even think of him as being very special anymore. Maybe he's only special when he's the way I saw him on those 1st times—making money or with football. I don't see what meaning his life has if he only does what he does and doesn't go beyond. Murray made more out of his life even though nobody looked up to him the way they do to Charlie!

I wanted to start reciting every saying I know and telling some of Mr. Mittleman's jokes but instead I got angry at myself inside for saying anything at all out loud and I told myself to start making new plans!

Whenever Sol looked at me I kept thinking he knew just what was going on inside my head!

Anita kissed Charlie on the cheek and told him to have a good time. Dr. Fogel is still at the Home, I said.

Who? Sol asked.

Dr. Fogel, I said, and I saw that I was almost shouting.

Lay off, Charlie said to me.

It's all right, Sol said, but in a kind way. He asked Anita if Dr. Fogel had visited her yet and she said no and Sol said that was just like Dr. Fogel.

Nobody ever called him, I said, and everybody's eyes went to Charlie because Dr. Fogel was on his list.

I called, Charlie said, and he wasn't even angry with me. He just wanted to leave.

Well then, Sol said, and he walked out the door.

Anita started laughing after they were gone and when she tried to hug me and kiss me I stiffened myself. You shouldn't have mentioned him to Sol, she said. But you didn't know, did you? Then she let me go and looked right at me and I could see she knew that I did know and she laughed again and told me she loved me.

FRIDAY AFTERNOON
(in Ephraim's room)

Everybody's downstairs now, getting ready for Shabbos!

Charlie said he'd call me when he was ready to go back home, so we could change into good clothes.

What I think: HE'S STILL UNDER SOL'S POWER! He still brushes my hair sometimes or says things like What's it all about, Danny? or What's it all for? but everytime I want to have a real conversation with him I don't know what to say and it's hard to remember how it was when we used to talk.

When I took my Tephillin bag with me this morning he didn't say anything about it. I put it on the car seat between us and this is what I said out loud to him: Talk to me. Come on. Talk to me.

He laughed at that. My name is Charlie Sapistein, he said, and I come from the Home, but he wouldn't say anything else. After breakfast he went into the city to see Sol at his hotel and bring him back here and as soon as he was gone Anita started worrying about not being able to work outside. She was worried about raking leaves if an early snow should fall on them and she said she still had bulbs to plant in the ground for the spring. She walked from room to room in the house talking out loud about all the things she had to do, until some of the neighbors came by with food they had cooked.

I remembered Murray saying Anita wasn't like Charlie and himself because she knew how to enjoy doing nothing.

A question: If Charlie stays calm and quiet will I have to start talking more? If he changes and I don't change too, how will we live together with neither of us ever saying what we're thinking and feeling?

Other things that happened so far today: I went into Ephraim's room in the morning when he was still sleeping. What do you think this is, I said, your birthday? and I tickled him under his pajamas with my cold hands. He got angry and called me a goddamned orphan and I said, It takes one to know one.

I still have a mother, he said.

So do I, I replied.

He got out of bed and got dressed while I made his bed for him. Then he put on his Tephillin the way he does every morning and I asked him to watch me while I put

139

mine on. I did it right. We prayed together in his bedroom like 2 old men, walked back and forth with Sidurim in our hands and Talises across our shoulders and the black straps wound around our arms and hands and heads. When we recited the שמונא עשרה we both stood together, facing east, and shuckled back and forth. I finished praying before he did and I told him that was the 1st time in my life I ever prayed with Tephillin on with somebody else.

He took his Tephillin off and so did I and we kissed the boxes before we put them in our Tephillin bags. He went into the bathroom and he put his face in front of the mirror and wiped away a patch of soap to see how dark his beard was getting. He pressed his pimples so they bled. His hair comes down to his shoulders like his mother's. He asked me if I'd ever kissed a girl and I said, Sure. He asked if we ever smuggled them into the Home and I said no. He said his father and Charlie once laughed about the time they dressed a girl up like a boy and brought her into the dormitory at the Home. All the guys chipped in for her. I thought about Larry Silverberg and the other guys in their hideout and for a few seconds I felt that I really missed them.

I asked him if he ever kissed a girl and he said only at kissing parties. He doesn't go to his father's school. None of their children do. He goes to a regular public school and he said his father didn't know about the sex parties the students in the Mill River school had every weekend. They take off their clothes and the girls let any of the guys pet them wherever they want. He said he even saw photos.

Hannah came into the bathroom in just her skirt and brassiere and Ephraim pushed her out. I turned my face away. What's the big deal? she said.

We sat in his room and he said he was worried about Hannah and about the effect Murray's death was having on her. They still kissed hello and good-bye on the lips, he said, even after she got breasts.

She'll get over it, I said.

Then I asked him to show me about his musical instruments and if he thought it was too late for me to start to learn. I blew some notes on his clarinet and his flute but I thought about how, to *really* learn, you'd have to be living in 1 place for a long time and have your own instrument and the time for practice.

We have some of the same favorite books: THE CHOSEN by Chaim Potok, THE CAINE MUTINY by Herman Wouk, PARIS UNDERGROUND by Etta Shiber, THE PEARL by John Steinbeck, and EXODUS by Leon Uris, and these are some of the other authors we both like: Ray Bradbury, Theodore Sturgeon, James Ramsey Ullman, Jack London, Franz Kafka, Isaac Asimov, and James Thurber. We agreed that our favorite book was THE CHOSEN. It was the 1st conversation we had that made us friends.

WHILE WE WERE TALKING I DECIDED THAT WHAT I'D LIKE TO DO SOMEDAY WOULD BE TO WRITE BOOKS TOGETHER WITH EPHRAIM! We could write books about the Jewish underground in Poland during the war smuggling Jews to Freedom, the way the French did in PARIS UNDERGROUND.

There were over 3,000,000 Jews in Poland before the war. After the war there were less than 300,000 left!

We could write a history of 2 great underground Jewish heroes who were boys like us, so that young Jewish boys would want to read our books and that way we could make them feel for the rest of their lives what it means to be a Jew! We could write about the Warsaw Ghetto and the frozen children in the snow and the soap the Nazis made from Jewish flesh and we could spend our lives learning the True History of what really happened even while we made up some adventures for the 2 boys to make the books more exciting!

We could make young people think about questions like this: If you were a Jewish leader and you could have saved 100 Jews by cooperating with the Nazis, what would you have done?

We could make one of the boys into somebody who escaped from the death pits of Babi Yar, climbing through the blood-soaked bodies and living out in the woods, until he meets the other boy, near the Russia-Poland border. We could take turns on different books on which of us would be the historian, getting the facts, and which of us could be the writer, making up the stories!

Today was too soon to tell him about my idea, but someday I will!

We played chess together but I couldn't think more than 2 moves ahead and I kept apologizing for losing so quickly.

You're just like Charlie, he said.

What Ephraim told me: He wants his mother to move to a different place now where there are more Jews so they can go to a regular synagogue instead of making all the services and holidays in their own house. He put on Tephillin every morning with Murray, and on Friday nights and Saturday mornings the family made Shabbos services in the living room, with Murray explaining the portion of the Torah for each week.

Charlie's calling me.

FRIDAY NIGHT AT HOME!

It's very late but Charlie is feeling good again, from the peaceful Shabbos meal we just had.

What I realize: The more I write, the more peaceful he looks. If I stayed up all night writing, he would stay up all night staring at me. If I left my notebook on his desk right now I don't think he'd even want to look inside, that's how peaceful he looks.

The question is, Do I want him to change?

Will just the act of writing down the beginning of my plan to change things make him start to change in a different way and if he does will his changing start to change me so that I won't need my plan as much?

What I think: There's a lot more. It's like a question with mirrors inside it, facing each other, with Daniel Ginsberg in between!

At supper Anita said the last fight she and Murray had was because he asked her what she wanted for her birthday and she said a stopwatch, and he said that was nonsense. I like to time things just to see how long they take, Anita said, but Murray couldn't accept something like that.

The table was beautiful, with a white cloth and candles. Nobody was sure what you did about Shabbos during the week of SHIVA so we called Irving, but he wasn't home.

We always did things Murray's way, Anita said, and Charlie told her to lay off him, that he couldn't answer back.

I said that Shabbos was the most important holiday of the year and that it took precedence over everything. If you couldn't have a funeral on Shabbos then you could probably stop the mourning period for Shabbos.

I used something I'd stored up and I said: THE SAB-BATH IS MADE FOR MAN, NOT MAN FOR THE SABBATH.

Hannah smiled at me for that as if I were older.

Before we made Shabbos, on the way back here, something happened that made me start testing Sol. Going around a curve a flock of birds flew right in front of us, swooping up as if they came from under the car. They were coming from old railroad tracks near the road and one of the birds was too slow and got hit by the front of the car so that specks of blood spattered across the hood and hit the windshield.

Charlie pulled to the side of the road. He got out and wiped the windshield and it made me feel weak to see him pick a piece of the bird out of the car's grill the way I feel weak when I think of how foolish it is to dream about us just continuing to live together, even if Charlie doesn't want to give me up!

I made myself think of what I would have to do if I were Charlie and I didn't like the answer!

When he got back in I said that Dr. Fogel once told us that in Yiddish his name means bird.

Charlie glared at me. Snap out of it, he said.

But Sol smiled at me and asked me if I knew what Faigele means.

He's just a kid, Charlie said to Sol. Lay off.

I couldn't stop what I was thinking from coming out and I DIDN'T WANT TO! The reason the Home is going to close is because of the new abortion laws, I said. There are hardly any Jewish orphans left. We're an endangered species.

Sol patted Charlie on the shoulder and asked him if he remembered how Murray used to have little sayings like that when he was a boy. I kept going and said: They don't make orphans like they used to, but Charlie didn't react even though Sol was praising me.

I've never believed Jews should have abortions, Sol said then and I saw Charlie's eyes look the way they did when he knew what Murray was going to say next. There were too many of us lost, Sol said. We need more Jews in the world, don't you see? We Jews have an obligation to re-populate is what Uncle Sol believes.

Then he began talking about Jewish history and his eyes got bright and I could see why Charlie and the others looked up to him when they were boys, even though he's like just an old man now.

He spoke right to me. Let's face it, young man, he said. We Jews are different for many reasons and the most obvious one is that we're more intelligent. The world needs our talents. It's as simple as that, though one doesn't say so too loudly these days.

I looked at the back of Charlie's thick neck and remembered him telling me how when he was a boy he used to imagine Sol inside a tent in a general's uniform, planning an attack and surveying battle maps and how he and Murray had once decided that if Sol were leading the Jews into battle, they would have done whatever he told them to. He said that Sol and Dr. Fogel were the same in one thing, that they got their biggest thrill when the Home's football team beat teams of non-Jews.

I can tell Charlie wants to speak to Sol about their living together but he doesn't know how.

Also: He's afraid he'll hurt me if he does.

Also: He'd like to ask me for the best words to use with Sol and that's what gets him so angry, BECAUSE HE DOESN'T REALLY WANT TO NEED ANYBODY!

"I have separated you from the nations that you be mine," I recited for Sol and this kept him going. He talked about the laws of Evolution and the Survival of the Fittest and said he'd even discussed his theory with 2 different Nobel prize winners and that they agreed with him in

144

private that Jews are genetically superior beings. He said that what happened was that during centuries of persecution all the unfit Jews had either died or been made into Christians. Without a Homeland Jews had only an idea to join them and make them remain Jews—the idea of the Torah and of being the people chosen to bring the Torah to mankind.

I agreed!

He spoke about the horrors of the Inquisition and of how Jews were expelled from one country to another, having to depend only on their wits and religion. Did I know, he asked, that until recently Jewish medical students right here in the United States of America were allowed to learn dissection only on Jewish corpses?

Charlie told him to stop scaring me, that the week had been hard enough, but he already had his wallet out and he took a picture from it of Jews hanging on meat hooks in Romania from 1940 with the words CARNE KOSER painted on their bodies. He said he kept it to remind himself and his Gentile friends that we're survivors of survivors!

Mr. Gitelman calls us an army of defectives, I said.

A what? he asked.

You shut up, Charlie said to me, but I didn't and I could feel my eyes starting to shine. Mr. Levine calls those of us still left in the Home retards and retreads, I said, and my voice was even stronger. And if you believe what you say about Jews and abortions and if you're so proud of the Home, then *why don't you help save it? Aren't we good enough for you anymore? We're Jews too!*

Enough! Charlie yelled at me.

Sol looked at Charlie and his eyes were soft again. I don't understand, he said. What does the boy want? Haven't I done my share?

More than your share, Charlie said. So let's close the subject, OK?

But I could tell from his voice that he knew his anger was only encouraging me. I'm not finished, I said. I want to know why if you care so much about repopulating the world with Jews, you were never married yourself!

But I said the wrong thing and the argument was over. Sol laughed and Charlie relaxed with him. Of course, Sol said. Of course. I always told my boys to follow my example and never marry, didn't I? He winked at Charlie and then at me and he gave me his punch line: And I told them they should give the same advice to their children.

Then I knew how right I was to have a new plan!

When we got home I left Charlie and Sol with Mr. Mittleman in his office and came up here to take my shower. Mr. Mittleman shook Sol's hand and asked, How's business? and Charlie tried to laugh but his laugh was forced. Sol patted Mr. Mittleman on the back and called him a great kidder.

It's not right, Mr. Mittleman said. A man should have a vocation.

His vocation is living, Charlie said, but I could see he was sorry he said anything.

Everybody lives, Mr. Mittleman said, and he sat down at his desk to work.

Charlie gave his saying about stomping the grapes, but it didn't make him or Sol feel better. Mr. Mittleman just shrugged. It's unnatural, he said.

I came upstairs and took off my clothes and got into the shower. I was thinking about the sound the bird made when it thunked against the car when suddenly the glass door to the shower opened and Mrs. Mittleman was standing there looking at me. I covered myself with my hand but she didn't move away.

I heard the water running, she said. And I thought all the men were downstairs with Max.

I'm sorry, I said, but I don't know why I said it.

That's all right, she said, and she smiled at me. I'm glad I caught you alone. It's nice, she said. I wanted to tell you that—it's been very nice since you came to live with Charlie. It's nice to hear your voices at night through the ceiling when you talk with each other. It's nice for him not to be alone so much and to share things. And I'm glad you were with him when it happened to Murray, don't you think?

146

I saw specks of water on her eyeglasses. She had one hand on the shower door and one hand on her hip. You wouldn't see it, darling, she said, but he's much less hostile to me since you came, so you shouldn't be sorry.

I'll get a chill, I said.

She started to close the door and then she smiled in a new way and raised her eyebrows. But I'll tell you this, she said. You're going to make the girls very happy someday, believe me.

Anita asked Sol to make the Kiddush tonight but he said Ephraim was the man of the family. We all wore Yamulkas and put shoes back on and when Anita covered her eyes to chant the blessing over the Shabbos candles I thought she would cry, thinking of Murray's absence. Instead she smiled. After she lit the candles we all kissed each other GOOD SHABBOS. When the phone rang nobody answered it. Anita wore a beautiful white dress with lace across her bosom. She said it was getting tight and this would probably be the last time she would have a chance to wear it.

Ephraim washed his hands at the sink, using a glass of water, and I did also. Dov and Eli were in line behind me. Then Ephraim made the blessing over the Challahs, which were covered with a napkin and we each made a מציא and ate a piece. Hannah served us chicken soup. When she came near me I could smell perfume on her like roses. She was so sweet and quiet that it reminded me she's not even 15 years old and she doesn't know very much about life!

It was very peaceful, after the company there was all week long, and when Anita spoke about Murray's love of Shabbos it grew even quieter. I looked into Hannah's eyes across the flames from the 2 candles and she looked right back into mine. Her dress was the color of violets and her skin was brown next to it, like toast. Ephraim's Adam's apple slid up and down and I saw tears in his eyes. Dov wouldn't eat anything. Anita said Murray always looked forward all week long to Shabbos and he used to say it forced him to say STOP to his life, and to linger over it and appreciate it. He never did any work at all on Shabbos and when Shabbos was over he would say what a feat this was for a Jewish Calvinist like himself.

After we passed a bowl and cup around to wash our hands and said the prayers after the meal, I helped Hannah and Ephraim clear the table. Dov brought in his baseball glove so Sol could help him oil it. Anita put Eli and Rivka to sleep. I wanted to kiss with Hannah but she seemed shy like a new girl and I was afraid she wouldn't want to in her good dress.

What I noticed: Sol never recited any of the Hebrew words.

He went for a walk by himself after supper. He goes for 2 walks every day. In New York City he takes a walk on the streets before he has breakfast when the streets are empty. He was still gone when Charlie and Anita went outside for a walk together. They were gone for more than an hour. She looked happy when she came back inside later.

A good place to stop.

SATURDAY

Today was a beautiful day. When I woke up Charlie was still feeling peaceful and I didn't ask him why. His face showed me he thought he had no worries at all.

Teach me to read, he said.

I didn't even wait to get dressed. I picked up the real estate book and when he made a face I told him it was a good book to start with because it was something he cared about. We sat up in bed together with our backs against the headboard and the covers across our knees and he started reading from a section called THE RISKS OF USING BORROWED MONEY. He read 3 sentences before he got stuck, but I said the next word for him and he was able to go on.

Mrs. Mittleman knocked on the door and came in with a tray full of good things to eat: Danishes and toast and jam and scrambled eggs and juice and coffee for Charlie. Charlie wasn't even embarrassed. He just smiled at her and said, Who's my favorite woman in this house? and she bent over and he kissed her under the ear.

We read 2 pages before we stopped and I saw how he

148

mixed up letters in certain words so that DEBT would be BED and DEAR would be READ and WAS would be SAW. I wrote out the following sentence for him: NAME NO ONE MAN, and told him to read it both ways.

We laughed and ate and worked some more. The more we read the worse he got and I tried to be very patient with him so he wouldn't get angry with himself. I watched his eyes and saw how they jumped, even though his body looked relaxed. When he finished a paragraph sometimes I asked him to tell me in his own words what he just read but he couldn't. They're just words, he said to me. He wanted to stop a few times but I told him how well he was doing and that from the things I'd read what he was able to do showed he could probably be cured very quickly.

I see words faster than I can read them, is what he said then.

He told me he wasn't going to bring Sol from the city today because Sol had people to see there and I thought that was the real reason he was relaxed with me. He said he always worried that he had brain damage and I said I didn't think so because the only thing he had trouble with was reading. If he had brain damage it would have slowed him up in other ways. Brain injuries are called ALEXIA, I said, and he had DYSLEXIA.

I told him that Leonardo da Vinci wrote from right to left and he said it didn't make him Jewish.

I covered words with a card and made him read slowly, so he could only see one line at a time. I made him read sentences over and over with his finger on each word. We took long pauses between sentences and paragraphs, to eat and to talk. He said Hebrew was always easier for him because it went the wrong way.

I told him I read that sometimes you didn't even need a lot of training, you could improve just from taking hormones or vitamins, but he said he didn't want anybody messing around with his glands. I told him to close his eyes and then I touched his fingers one at a time and he could tell me which finger I was touching each time, to show him his brain was OK.

I told him to imagine he'd lost all his money and Mr.

Mittleman was standing over him and laughing at him and blowing smoke in his face, and he laughed at me, but I said I meant it. He said he'd put it on film in his head and he did and it got him so upset that he began to read more quickly, until his anger wore off.

He could read titles easily, and sections with numbers and tables and amounts of money. We found a section about the FHA and "608s" and Charlie said that had been how Mr. Mittleman became rich originally. Just after the war the FHA insured mortgages for 90% of the real estate value in order to stimulate construction of garden type apartments. Charlie explained to me how Mr. Mittleman bought low cost land and valued it higher than the price he paid so that he got mortgages for more than 100% of the cost of the projects and long term loans at low interest rates to pay them back! The result: He actually got cash above his cost even before he sold or rented the land and apartments.

When Charlie read the words in the book and saw that they said the same thing he said, his eyes lit up and he slapped me on the back and said, Hey—what do you think of that?

I had him stop before he got tired. We got dressed and came downstairs and Mr. Mittleman asked Charlie what he was going to do and Charlie said: Nothing. It's Shabbos.

I said, He's practicing for his retirement.

Mr. Mittleman said, You're both Mishugah.

The Sabbath is a day of study, so we studied, right? Charlie said to me.

This was my reply: When you're in love, Charlie, the whole world is Jewish.

Then I asked Mr. Mittleman if he knew why we would benefit most if the whole world were really Jewish and when he didn't know I told him it was because the Talmud says that orphans don't ever have to pay taxes and that their land is considered sacred whether they're rich or poor! Charlie was proud of me for knowing that, even though I think it made him think of Dr. Fogel's land.

We took a walk to do some shopping for Mrs. Mittleman and Charlie talked about Murray as if Murray lived

a long long time ago. He said I shouldn't be fooled by
Anita, that she had loved Murray very much. He told me
about the time Murray found out about Jewish orphanages
in California which had something called The Cottage
Plan where the orphans lived in regular houses and went
to regular schools and where boy and girl orphans lived
next to each other.

Murray wrote out a petition and plan to transform
the Home into The Cottage Plan and proved it would
save money, but nothing ever came of it. Murray said
they were worried about controlling us if we got outside
too much, Charlie said.

We walked through a park near our house and sat on
a bench watching kids younger than me play football.
Charlie told me that Sol used to tell them statistics on
how bad it was for Negro orphans and how lucky they all
were to be in the Home. They posted newspaper pictures
on the walls whenever there were fires in Negro orphanages, and he always remembered what Sol said about half
the Negro orphans dying before they reached the age of 5.

He exaggerated, I said.

Did he? Charlie said, and he shrugged as if to say
that it didn't matter. What was important was that he
remembered it.

What happened between Sol and Dr. Fogel? I asked,
and Charlie didn't get angry with me for asking. He said
he never really understood all of it. He said it happened
before any of his group had come to the Home but that
Murray found out the whole story and that it was mostly
about religion. He said Dr. Fogel wanted to be Director of
the Home before the war but that Sol made the Board of
Trustees vote against him because he didn't want the
Home to be Orthodox. In those days Sol believed the
Home should be American 1st and Jewish 2nd.

Then Charlie laughed about how upside down things
can get sometimes, and how Dr. Fogel wound up being the
one with the land and the money and Sol wound up being
the one who believed in Israel. I asked him if he was going
to tell Sol about Dr. Fogel's land but he didn't answer
that question.

I remembered a joke he made about imagining the 2

151

of them living with him and taking care of each other in the house he was going to buy for us and I asked him this: Do you ever imagine them coming to your funeral together?

This is what he said back: You know me, don't you?

After lunch we took a nap together and then went to Anita's house. Charlie made a fire in the living room fireplace and we all sat there in front of it. Slats and Louie and Jerry and their families came and after the 1st hugs and words about Murray, people were cheerful. Slats and Louie and Jerry live together in the same apartment house in Brooklyn, on Ocean Parkway. Slats and Louie own a hardware store together and Jerry is a bookkeeper for a pocketbook manufacturer in Queens.

When the women were out of the room Slats and Louie talked about the fart wars they had in the dormitory when they were boys and they teased Slats and asked if he could still play the 1st line of MY COUNTRY TIS OF THEE in farts. Jerry asked Charlie what ever happened to the jar of beans the guys gave him when he married Lillian. He was supposed to put 1 bean in the jar for every time they made love the 1st year and take 1 bean out for every time they did it the 2nd year, and Jerry gave 10 to 1 odds there'd still be beans left at the end of the 2nd year.

Then Louie danced around the room like a fool and sang:

> Beans, beans good for your heart,
> The more you eat, the more you fart!

Slats whispered to Charlie that he spoke to his brother-in-law who's a lawyer and that nothing could happen to Charlie for how Murray died. Slats, Louie, and Jerry sat on the couch side by side, facing us, and talked about how much private schools cost for their children in Brooklyn. Jerry asked, if an Arab and a Negro both fell from the top of the Empire State Building at the same time, which one would hit the ground 1st, and when nobody knew Jerry answered, Who gives a shit?

He talked about the workers in his factory who come

152

up from Colombia in South America. They're happy as long as you give them overtime, he said. They stay 5 years and save money and go back and new members of their families come to take their places. Louie said he kept a gun in his dresser under his underwear. They talked about a guy named Pikeface who was at the Home when they were boys and who made a zipgun in workshop and was sent to reform school and was eventually killed by gangsters.

Charlie sat without talking and cracked walnuts in his fingers for Dov. Slats remembered when Sol used to say that Charlie was so fast and strong he could throw a strawberry through a battleship!

When they were gone we gathered in the kitchen for Havdalah to end Shabbos. Ephraim chanted the blessing over the wine and Anita opened a jar of cloves because the Tsumin box was gone and we sniffed them. Then Hannah and Rivka held a braided candle up and Anita lit it and whispered to them: Hold it as high as you want your husband to be!

After supper Charlie and Anita went outside together again for a walk until more people came to visit. They were parents of students from Murray's school and they brought baskets of candy and fruit. I stayed away from Hannah even though I could tell she wanted to be with me. Guys from the school football team came but Charlie hardly noticed them.

Anita was tired so we came home early and sat downstairs having milk and cake with Mrs. Mittleman. Mr. Mittleman was in his office typing. His movie projector is put away for the whole week. Mrs. Mittleman talked about how young Sol always looked for his age. She told us a secret: that she's trying to talk Mr. Mittleman into retiring with her to Florida. Her bones hurt her when the snow comes.

This is what she said: I'd like to spend my reclining years in the warm sun.

When we came up here Charlie and I laughed about what she said. It's been a beautiful day but that doesn't mean that his change is permanent. *I have to be ready!*

153

I don't care if he did it just to throw me off guard or if he doesn't know what makes him different, so I went ahead and telephoned Dr. Fogel!

When I woke up this morning Charlie had already gone into the city to get Sol to bring him back. The 7 days of SHIVA were over in the morning but we stayed at Anita's all day until the sun went down. As soon as we came home Mr. Mittleman gave Charlie a stack of phone messages from all week long and Charlie started telephoning and talking to Mr. Mittleman about houses and money.

I sat in the office watching him and I couldn't hide the feelings that showed in my face. This is what Charlie said to me between calls: Life goes on, Danny. Didn't you hear what the Rabbi said? Life goes on.

I told him that close relatives are supposed to mourn for 30 days and he didn't answer me.

I can hear him shouting at Mr. Mittleman now. If he comes up I know he'll make me stop writing. I'm glad I started the 1st part of my plan yesterday even though it was peaceful between us then.

After supper Mr. Mittleman took out his movie projector and sat in the living room watching. In the movie Mrs. Mittleman and 2 friends were in a canoe. Mr. Mittleman told us the man and woman both died years ago. We spent our honeymoon with them, Mr. Mittleman said. They had 2 children, a boy and a girl. When the boy was 15 and the girl was 14 they were both killed in an auto crash. The parents died shortly thereafter.

This is what Mrs. Mittleman said: A wife who loses a husband is called a widow. A husband who loses a wife is called a widower. A child who loses his parents is called an orphan. But in Yiddish they say there is no word for a parent who loses a child, that's how awful the loss is!

What I wondered: Is there a word for a friend who loses a friend?

THE MOST IMPORTANT THING THAT HAPPENED TODAY IS THAT MY PLAN STARTED TO

154

WORK! DR. FOGEL CAME AND CHASED SOL
AWAY!

When Dr. Fogel drove up to Anita's house in the
morning Sol was in the middle of telling us about all the
boys he visits on his cross country trip. He told us something about each family. There were a lot of people in the
living room listening to him. Morty and Irving and Herman and their wives and children were there, along with
neighbors and people from the school. They all came early,
bringing things for breakfast. Sol talked about one of his
boys who was a ventriloquist and some of the visitors
had seen him on TV. Sol said he may get his own show
soon. Some of the boys he talked about seeing were
younger than Charlie and his group, and some were older.

When Dr. Fogel entered the living room with Anita
holding his good hand everybody's eyes turned to them.
Dr. Fogel was dressed in the old brown suit he wears to
school and his face was the color of ashes. He wore a
Yamulka.

Charlie stood before anybody else and his hand was
on his chest and I could tell he was listening to his heart
through his fingertips. Dr. Fogel told him about me telephoning and he stared at the cut in the lapel of Charlie's
jacket and at Charlie's beard but he didn't say anything
about them. Instead he told us all we should be wearing
Yamulkas. Doesn't it matter to you even now? he asked.

Herman kept whispering to Morty: He looks just the
same. He looks just the same.

Then Sol got up and walked to the door and put his
hand out to Dr. Fogel. Well, Mister Fogel, he said. It's
been a long time, hasn't it? I'm sorry we have to meet
on such an occasion.

Dr. Fogel's limp arm was swinging lightly at his side
and he cocked his head to one side but his Yamulka didn't
fall off. He looked at his right hand and he laughed at
Sol very quickly and then looked away and motioned to
me to come to him. He called me by my Hebrew name
and asked me where he could wash.

I knew who he was when he walked in, Anita said,
and her face was glowing. I recognized him from Murray's descriptions.

155

Dr. Fogel said he was very hungry from his long ride and when I told him Anita was Kosher, he said, It's why I could come, yes? Then he spoke to the room and said that it showed how such a law kept us together as Jews. He said that the day of burial counted as a day of SHIVA and that the week of SHIVA was 6 days plus 1 hour to show that we Jews don't believe in making grief worse. He took Anita's hand and told her he was glad he got here in time.

By then Sol was stalking out of the room and it made me laugh to see how quiet and stunned the non-Jews were at the scene. Charlie started to go after Sol but Dr. Fogel said to let him go because even if he stayed there wouldn't be enough Jews for a Minyan. I said that the closest Shul was over 30 miles away and that it was Reformed. Dr. Fogel held Charlie's wrist and whispered to him that they should talk about the land when the SHIVA was over.

I've never seen Charlie angrier with me than he was then! He glared at me and yanked his hand away from Dr. Fogel and left us and Anita excused herself also, saying she would see Sol to the door if he was leaving.

Dr. Fogel was happy. Please continue your conversation, he said to the room and he let me lead him to the bathroom where he washed his hands and made a blessing over them. He was happy to see the mirror over the sink soaped up. While we were in the bathroom, Dov and Rivka came to the door and stared at us.

Is somebody sick? Dov asked.

He's not that kind of doctor, I said.

When we went back into the living room everybody was gone except Herman, Morty, and Irving.

He looks just the same, Herman kept whispering. He looks just the same.

Ephraim came in and I introduced him to Dr. Fogel and Dr. Fogel kissed Ephraim on his forehead and said something quickly in Hebrew, with his hand on Ephraim's forehead.

Tell me about yourselves, Dr. Fogel said to his former students, and he called each of them by their Hebrew names to show he remembered. He smiled warmly at them and apologized for not having come sooner in the week. He said he was truly interested in what had become of their lives.

They talked very easily after that, with Irving starting, about themselves and their jobs and their homes. They brought their wives and children in to introduce to him, and the children sat on the rug with Anita's children and listened to Dr. Fogel ask questions. He wanted to know if they kept Kosher homes and Morty and Irving's families said they did but when Herman said he didn't Dr. Fogel didn't cluck inside his mouth. He praised the children for being able to give their Hebrew names and he gave each child a nickel, a penny, and a piece of sucking candy. They all stared at his arm and whenever he caught one of them doing it I saw him smile. This is a riddle he asked: If you want to get something precious from the other side of a Shul, do you go through the Shul to get it, or around? Ephraim knew the answer from Murray, and why. You go around, he said, because a Shul is not a means to an end.

Just before 10 o'clock Dr. Fogel went to Murray's study and found a prayer book he wanted. He prayed by himself from Tihilim. Then he went around from room to room and took sheets off mirrors. The SHIVA was over. He told Ephraim and the others they could put their shoes on. He went into the kitchen and ate some food and made Anita and Ephraim eat with him and then he asked Charlie to telephone for a taxi. Charlie will take you back, Anita said, and Dr. Fogel didn't wait for Charlie to answer. Good, he said.

Charlie didn't tell me to come along. Before he left he went into the bathroom and shaved off his beard with Murray's razor.

Also: I asked Dr. Fogel about the Home's motto and he smiled at me for knowing! He said he never told anybody to change it because it always reminded him of Jews like Sol's father who built the Home!

These are other things that happened today after Dr. Fogel left: I practiced my Haftorah. Mr. Alfred and a new man came and spoke with Anita in Murray's study. Dov fell out of an apple tree but he wasn't hurt. During

157

lunch Eli fell asleep on the floor and wet his pants. Hannah handed me a note and I went into the bathroom and read it and this is what it said:

Don't you like me anymore? I still like you. Please don't be angry with me for going to my girl friend's house. I hope I'll see you a lot even after this week is over. I think you're very special and different. Why don't you want to be alone with me?

In the car going home I got Charlie angry by saying that someday he would meet all of Sol's other boys at Sol's funeral. He slapped me across the face and didn't say he was sorry.

What I think: Charlie got angry because he knows that I know that he thinks that Sol thinks the exact same thought in his head every time he goes around the country and wonders if it's his last trip. That's what I decided Sol's life is for!

Ephraim and I went for a walk together in the woods. He knows the names of birds and trees and wildflowers. He told me he once told Murray that Murray wouldn't have cared so much about being Jewish if he hadn't been the only Jew where he lived. I called him a would-be Jew, Ephraim said, and I never took it back.

When we said good-bye tonight Anita hugged me and kissed me and whispered into my ear, "I love you." Ephraim said he's not going to shave or cut his hair or put on new clothes for 30 days. The 7 days of Mourning come from the 7 days Joseph mourned for his father Jacob and the 30 days come from the 30 days Israel mourned for Moses. Nobody knows where Moses is buried because he didn't want people to come to his grave and worship him.

What I decided: When I die, even though I believe that burying bodies in the ground is a waste and doesn't do anybody any good, I won't give my body to science or for anything else. I'll leave instructions to be buried like a Jew because I want to be buried the same way Jews have always been buried for thousands of years.

Rivka and Dov wanted to watch TV right away after

SHIVA was over but Ephraim wouldn't let them. Anita said they'd discuss it later. Charlie didn't say what he and Dr. Fogel talked about when he drove Dr. Fogel into Brooklyn. He telephoned Sol and they have a meeting for tomorrow when Charlie will offer him his plan!

Here he comes now. This is the truth: If Murray hadn't died when he did I would have to do what I'm going to do anyway!

III
New Zion

Six

Charlie watched in disbelief as the runner stumbled across the goal line. *Danny's gone,* he thought. *Danny's gone.*

He sent in substitutes and called two players who'd missed tackles to him. Charlie thought one of them was smiling at him. He grabbed the boy by the face guard and yanked. "Does that hurt?" he asked. The boy tried to twist away. "Does it?"

"Cut it out," the other boy said. "We don't get paid for football."

"It doesn't matter," Anita said, standing next to him, her head enclosed within a dark piece of fur. "You should relax."

Charlie shooed the boys away, but he still could not find words quickly enough. Sol was gone also, to California. "You get lost too," he said to Anita, and he stalked away, down the sideline.

For the third week in a row his team lost. In the locker room, while his players were changing, there was a knock on the door. "Is everybody decent?" Anita called. When there was no reply, she entered.

"This is the men's locker room," Charlie said, but Anita did not acknowledge his words. The boys giggled. Her fur hat was off and Charlie could smell perfume in her hair. Anita spoke: "I just wanted to tell all of you that even though you lost, I know you did your best. . . ."

163

"Bullshit," Charlie said.

Anita smiled at him. "I'm glad nobody was hurt today," she continued. "That's important."

Charlie rolled his eyes, but said nothing. It was useless. Everything was upside down. He saw Sol laughing at him. "I want to speak with you afterwards," she said to him. "Can you come by the house?" Charlie nodded. She drew him to the door. "They're only boys," she whispered. "Why take it so hard? Honestly, Charlie—they're still wet behind the ears—"

"Sure," he said. "And I'm the king of France."

"I'll see you later," she said, and touched his hand with her own.

He wished Danny could have seen the difference. Weekday afternoons during practice the girls from the school would now stand along the sidelines, flirting, and Anita forbade him from making them leave. Losing interest himself, he would look past them, to the hill where he had first seen Danny. He didn't argue with Anita. She had the support of the Board and of the teachers and of the students. There was no more marching silently from class to class, no more required uniforms, no more standing when adults entered classrooms, no more sitting quietly in rows. Students were encouraged to call teachers by their first names. "The Reign of Terror is over," she told a meeting of faculty and staff on her first day as headmistress.

He remembered a story Dr. Fogel had told them, of how, when Noah's sons found their father lying drunk and naked in his tent, they had entered the tent with a garment over their heads and walked backward, so as not to set eyes upon their father. They had covered him with the garment. The story showed, Dr. Fogel had taught, that Judaism assumed that as a man grew older he grew wiser, and so it demanded that the young give respect and honor to their elders at all times. But Charlie didn't dare try to tell the story to Anita or his players.

He wasn't even certain that he remembered it correctly. Danny could have helped him on that, but he wasn't ready

164

to give in to the boy's demands either, especially when he was, as now, feeling slightly unsure of himself. If he went after the boy because of the boy's threat, how would the boy respect him? Yet he sensed that if he waited for the boy to come back to him, he might wait forever.

He came to Anita's front door smiling, realizing that he did not, for this very reason, *need* to go to Danny. A boy with a will like his—with such desire—would survive, with or without Charlie Sapistein, in the Home or out.

Anita opened the door, drink in hand. "I'm sorry I bit at you before," he said.

She kissed him on the cheek. "I love to see you angry," she said. "It's what makes the boys admire you. You have a marvelous temper."

Charlie stepped inside and took his parka off. Eli and Rivka ran to him and he picked one child up in each arm and swung them around. Anita told them that she and Charlie wanted to be alone. The children were to play in their room. "I built a fire," she said, and led Charlie to Murray's study.

In Murray's study, she closed the door behind them and handed him a drink. "No thanks," Charlie said. "I'm still trying to get back in shape from the week's layoff."

"As you wish," she said. She patted the couch next to her, and he sat. She touched his right ear with her fingertip. "Don't worry so much, Charlie—we'll support you, win or lose. We might even give you a raise for next year. The new headmistress is most impressed with your qualities."

"I'm a worthy cause," Charlie said.

"What?" Anita said, and before he could repeat himself, she was leaning on his shoulder, her mouth near his neck, laughing. "The way you put things—it breaks my mood, don't you see? I had things arranged so that we could relax together in an intimate setting, and then you come up with one of your sayings—"

"It's not mine," Charlie said. "It's Danny's. It's what he wrote in his note to me."

She drew away. "Oh."

165

"I miss him."

"I could tell." She rested her cheek against his shoulder. "But can't you forget about him for a little while?"

Charlie stared ahead, at the picture on Murray's desk—a gold-framed wedding photo of Murray and Anita. Murray had been heavier then. "Don't you think we're rushing things," he said. "I mean, it hasn't even been a month. Think a little."

"Life goes on, Charlie," Anita said. "Isn't that what the rabbi said? Isn't that what I heard you and Sol and Irving and the others tell me the whole week long?"

"Sure," Charlie said, but as her fingers stroked his cheek he realized that what bothered him about her touch was not anything that had to do with Murray, but the fact that he did not feel any real desire for her. "But listen—we need to talk. I mean, do you know what you're getting in for, playing around with a guy like me? Remember, I was married and divorced."

"I loved Murray," she said. "But he has no hold on me."

"I know that."

"We've known one another as long as I knew Murray. We've waited long enough, haven't we?"

"I keep seeing him on the ground, after I put the block on him."

"Was it a good block?"

"It was a terrific block," Charlie said, and he smiled at her, then laughed. "Murray would have admired it, I guess. It's not such a bad way to go, when you think about it—given his life and our friendship."

"No."

"But you should give me some time."

"The children love you and quickness is everything now, don't you see? It's why I'm succeeding as much as I am. At the school, at home—" She licked her lips. "By startling everybody with my speed I'm getting what I want."

Charlie knew that he was hearing her words, yet in his body he felt as if he were not with her. He saw Sol sitting in the front row at St. Nick's Arena, watching a boxing match

166

and explaining the fine points to him. Sol had said he believed that Jews were superior because of their history—because only the fittest had survived suffering. Did this mean, then, Charlie wondered, that without suffering the quality of the race would decline? Charlie smiled. It was, he knew, the kind of question Danny would have asked. The boy had infected him.

"You know about my plans to become a rabbi, don't you?" he said.

Anita sat back, her hand still on his shoulder, and laughed. "You're wonderful, Charlie Sapistein, do you know that?"

"But I need to learn to read first," he said. "Danny was helping me. I'll have to go to a doctor and get checked out. I read Hebrew pretty well because it goes from right to left." He saw lights outside the window, and thought of Murray, on his mower. "There's hope for me, I guess."

"I know all about Rabbi Akiba," Anita said. "And I'll bet I know something you don't know—that whenever his disciples praised him, he told them he owed all to his wife. Did you know that? She was the one who made him return to his studies after he couldn't learn to read. His wife was the one who believed in him and gave up everything so that he could become a great scholar. . . ."

"Sounds more like his mother," Charlie said.

Then she was across his lap, her arms around his neck. "Do I look like your mother?"

"Not really," Charlie said. "You're both beautiful. My mother was the most beautiful woman I ever saw. I think I said that before. You're beautiful too. I've always thought that. But no—you don't look the same." His head felt light, from not having eaten. If he ate before a game he became nauseated. "As a matter of fact, you remind me of Murray."

"Stop it," she said. "Stop teasing."

"Murray was beautiful when he was a boy, and do you know what?"

"What?" Her head was against his chest, her hair against his mouth, and he told himself that he would have to ask Dr. Fogel the question: if God had singled out the Jews as

167

His people, for suffering, and if the Jews did well and prospered, would this mean that God had abandoned His people?

He spoke: "You and Murray look alike. Married people always do. It's one reason Lillian and I divorced—we wanted to do it before we got to look too much like each other—while there was still time. . . ."

"I always liked to listen to you—I must be like one of the children."

"What about Danny?" Charlie asked.

"What about him?"

"The Home isn't the right place for him now—not the way it is."

"You'll forget about him." She was staring directly into his eyes. Her eyes seemed kind enough, he thought. There was no reason, really, not to go along with her. The truth, which he didn't need to share with her, was that in general he found his need for women had diminished. He remembered stories from the Home about older women paying eighteen-year-olds. A woman isn't really interesting until she's past thirty, Sol had always told them, but he'd never said why, if this were true, God had created man so that his own desire for sex was declining by then. Charlie imagined that Murray and Irving and the others had talked about this when they'd been in their early twenties. But he'd been married then, and without sharing the discussions he didn't know what to make of it, other than to see the joke.

He looked into her face and he imagined Murray kissing her. He wondered how often they had made love—how many times a week, and if they had, in recent years, ever made love more than once a day. Was it normal, he wondered, to have little desire to regain the desire he'd once had? There had been days, half his lifetime ago, when he'd thought of nothing from the time he awoke but the touch of Lillian's body against his. Would he be obliged to tell Anita that he and Lillian still went to bed together several times a year, even though, away from her, his craving for her disappeared?

"All right," he said. "Life has mountains and life has valleys, right?"

"Yes," she said, and he kissed her. He tried not to think of anything else, in order to enjoy himself, but he wondered what thoughts had gone through Murray's head the last time he and Anita had made love together. . . .

He opened his eyes very slightly and peeked through the lashes, so that Anita would not be able to tell that he was looking at her if she opened her eyes at the same time. Her eyes were closed. She took his hand in hers, and, gently, placed it upon her belly and made him move it slowly, in circles. Her other hand held him behind the neck, tightly. He wondered how different she was—if she kissed differently —from the girl she had been before she'd had her first child. How long had she dreamt of this moment? Was it easier for her to forget Murray than for him? If Murray were looking at them now, would he be jealous, or amused?

He pulled back and she smiled up at him. "Jealousy is the illusion of possession," he said.

"Did you make that up yourself?"

"I think so."

They kissed again. Her lips were full and warm and he didn't think she could tell that she was not arousing him. He'd never had trouble satisfying a woman before and he saw no reason to start having troubles now, so he touched her eyebrow with his finger, let his finger move down to the corner of her mouth, where their lips met. She licked his finger.

In his head he began making a list of the women he'd had during the past few years. Then he thought of each of Anita's children and he stood them in a row, at attention, in the courtyard of the Home. He imagined Danny looking down on them from the window of the dormitory, a movie camera in his hand, the viewing lens pressed against his left eye. Touching her stomach—the circular motion—relaxed Charlie, forced him to go more slowly. Her mouth opened for him and he felt mildly repelled by her warm breath. He thought of toothpaste. Eli had a toothbrush that trained him by making music when he moved it up and down. Charlie moved his tongue forward, past her teeth, felt her body press closer to him, and then, as she bit down, he winced and pulled back.

"Hey—!" he cried. "What's the matter with you—?"

She was lying back in the corner of the couch, laughing, looking suddenly younger than he had ever remembered her looking. She might have been his daughter's age. He pulled a handkerchief from his back pocket and held it against his tongue, then looked at the points of blood on the white cloth. "Christ!" He stood. "That hurt."

"Oh Charlie," she said, and her voice was soft. "I'm sorry. You forgive me, don't you? It's just something I've always wanted to do, don't you see? For years."

"You must be in shock," he said. "You should see a doctor, doing a stupid thing like that."

"Don't be silly," she said. "I knew just what I was doing. Don't you like to be—well, playful sometimes? Or are you—?" She broke off and sat up straight. "Please laugh with me," she said, and reached toward him with both her hands. "Don't you see that it's just something I always wanted to do and never could. Not with Murray." She laughed to herself, then brushed her hair back. Charlie couldn't move. He wanted to hit her, and he was shocked to find that he enjoyed the feeling. "I've done it before—years ago—when I first went away to college. It was something my mother taught me to keep away the wolves. 'Do that the first time and they'll know the kind of girl you are,' was what she said to me."

Charlie dabbed at his tongue with the handkerchief. "I don't care about the reasons," he said. "You should be locked up."

She waved his words away and walked to the window. He heard steps on the ceiling, then scuffling. "It's nothing to get so excited about." She spoke with her back to him. "I said I'm sorry, all right? I didn't mean to hurt you." She faced him. "Will you forgive me?"

"You're crazy," he said. But his tongue didn't really hurt anymore.

"Well," she said, to herself. "I did it and now it's done and I feel better, all right?" She looked up at him and smiled, as if to a child. "Let me ask you something, Charlie Sapistein: if you're so rich, why aren't you smart?"

"Just lay off," he said. "You scared the shit out of me."

She was standing behind Murray's desk, leaning upon it with both hands. "Let me ask you something, Charlie Sapistein: how long do you think Murray's school would have lasted, with his rules? Isn't it clear to you what he was doing? The pattern he was repeating?"

"Have another drink," Charlie said. He put his handkerchief away. "I need to get home and sell some houses."

She shook her head sideways, as if pitying him. Her mouth seemed enormous to him as the words came from it—four or five times its normal size, like the mouth of a girl on a billboard. He couldn't stop staring into it. "You believe I was against him, don't you? Against the things he believed in—privacy, family life, inner discipline, ritual, respect for elders—do you want the whole list? You think I was against him."

"I didn't say that." He shook his head to clear it. She pulled at one of the drawers in the desk, and for a split second Charlie expected to see her hand rise with a revolver in it, pointed at him. Instead, she held up a stethoscope.

She winked at him. "Wanna play doctor with me?"

"You're bats," he said. "You really are—"

She was sitting in Murray's chair, laughing. "Oh Charlie," she said. "Please forgive me. It's not what you think." She held the stethoscope up and pressed the black rubber tubing to her cheek. "It's not what you think at all. I'm just trying to have a little fun, don't you see? I've wanted you for so many years. I've wanted to be able to do things with you that . . ." A tear slid down her cheek even as she laughed, but he made no movement toward her. Women's tears had never moved him. He preferred anger to weeping. In all the years I knew him, he thought, I never saw Murray cry. "This isn't what you think. Murray and I used to listen to the baby's heartbeat while the baby was inside me—for each of our children. I didn't mean to scare you. I thought you might like to listen to the baby, that was all. I'm sorry." Her eyes seemed

171

rounder to him, and he didn't trust himself. "The heartbeat is twice what ours is now, while the baby's inside—"

"I have to go. You take care of yourself, okay? Call me if you need anything. Promise?"

He opened the door. "Is poor Charlie's little tongue hurt?" she cooed. "Does Charlie want Mama to make it all better?"

"Promise," he said, but she only laughed.

On Monday morning, earlier than usual, Charlie left the house. "The early bird catches the worm," Mr. Mittleman said to him, without looking up from his desk.

"Like father, like son," Charlie replied.

Charlie drove into Brooklyn and saw the sun rise, from behind the city. He had made his decision. He would visit the Home, speak to Danny, and leave it at that.

This is the truth [the boy had written]. I want you to adopt me. I looked it up and you can do it legally. Whether you marry Anita or not, as a man who was once married and being of the same religion you are allowed to do it. I can't stay with you like this forever, not knowing where I stand. I'm returning to the Home to be with the others, where I belong. I'm an orphan just like you were and I asked you to do something special when I first met you. I asked you to save the Home. You said people should let dying things die and that you would let the Home die but that you would save me, so I'm saying OK to that and I'm telling you, to use your own words TO PUT UP OR SHUT UP. I believe that I'm a worthy cause. You can adopt me or you can let me die with the others. My fate is in your hands. I also want to say that if I never see you again I want to thank you now with all my heart for letting me stay with you during these past few months. I'm sorry about Murray for I know what he meant to you. ("Give me friendship or give me death!") Good-bye and good luck.

The boy had signed the note, "Your loving friend of indeterminate age, Danny Ginsberg."

The question appealed to Charlie—why did he, in fact, in one part of him, agree with the boy, that they were both members of an endangered species that demanded saving? He remembered what the boy had told him about Jews in Poland marrying two orphans during an epidemic, in order to find favor with God. Did that mean, Charlie wondered, that if there were no Jewish orphans left and God visited a plague upon mankind, there would be no way of saving the Jews?

In Brooklyn, as he came closer to the Home, he became conscious of how much he looked forward to seeing Danny. He wanted to tell him about Sol, not only because he felt it would make Danny stop worrying but because he knew Danny would enjoy hearing about what had happened. It was, Charlie told himself, something good the boy could put in his storybook.

Charlie smiled, remembering how uncomfortable he'd felt in the hotel room in New York when he'd presented his plan to Sol. Sol had said he would have a surprise for Charlie when he was done. He'd listened without smiling and had acknowledged that Charlie was right about many things—the money he'd inherited had run out, he wasn't visiting as many of his boys as he used to, he'd given up his apartment in Brooklyn. . . .

But guess what your Uncle Sol does now? he'd asked then, and when Charlie had shrugged, unable to say, Sol's face had broken into a broad grin. *He sells real estate too! That's the surprise he's been waiting to give you ever since he arrived!*

It was a surprise, Sol said, that he knew would please Charlie more than anyone else in the world, and Charlie wanted to share that news with Danny now. "Your Uncle Sol is a prudent man," Sol had said, "and that's what pulled him through." Then Sol had explained that many years before, when he realized that he might outlive his inheritance, he'd bought a large three-bedroom apartment in a senior citizen city in California. He'd bought it outright and had first entered into the real estate business, he joked, by trading the apartment down several times until he'd wound up with his present place—a one-room efficiency unit. He'd lived on the profits of the trading until a year before and then had begun working for the senior citizen city itself, selling homes and apartments in a new condominium they were building.

"I was worried at first, to tell the truth," Sol had told Charlie. "Imagine—a man my age, taking his first job! I was like a nervous rookie before his first major-league tryout, and believe me there were many nights I wanted to call you to get some good advice! But I didn't. I decided to see it through on my own. And the thing that enabled me to do it, and to succeed—I was their top man this winter in unit sales!—was my desire to see the look in your eyes today when I would tell you all about it. . . ."

Charlie had been so stunned that he'd been unable to say anything to Sol for a long time, and he saw now that this had pleased Sol most of all. He saw Sol smiling at him from the mirror in the hotel room, while Sol attached his collar to his shirt. He heard Sol telling him about his plans for the future, about how he was thinking of branching out and selling land in Arizona and Nevada. . . .

A breeze, coming through the car, brushed the hairs on the backs of Charlie's hands, and he remembered, in class, being ashamed of the hair there because Dr. Fogel had remarked on it and had likened him to Esau and Murray to Jacob. He had had no tongue for arguing then, though what he had believed then still seemed to him a true question—if God had wanted Jacob to have his father Isaac's blessing, why had he let Esau be born into the world first? Wasn't *He* all-powerful?

He saw Murray, a sheet draped across his shoulders, a staff in his hand—dressed up as Jacob for a play—with cotton glued to the backs of his hands.

The idea of adopting Danny was crazy—yet it had been, he realized, just as crazy to have let the boy stay with him. Danny had been right to call his hand; how long could it have gone on, on a temporary basis?

174

The wonder of it was that while it had been happening —while the boy had been with him—it had all seemed so normal. So normal, in fact, that nobody—neither Max nor Shirley nor Murray nor Irving nor Lillian—had ever said anything to him that indicated they thought it was strange. Or had they been making allowances? Had they been indulging him?

Charlie arrived at the Home a few minutes before seven o'clock and found the gate padlocked. A large wooden sign was wired to the iron bars, stating that the Home had been closed, that all inquiries should be made at the Federation of Jewish Philanthropies, and that trespassers would be prosecuted.

Charlie blinked, reread the notice without difficulty, and wondered if the place had been closed before or after Danny had returned to it. He tried to think the question through logically, but instead he found himself thinking of the photos on the walls. What had happened to them? And what had happened to the records in the main office? Where were the trophies and medals?

He walked around the block once but saw no lights on inside the buildings. Several windows were already broken, and the amount of dust on others suggested that the Home had, in fact, been shut up for some time before Danny had run away from him. If so, he wondered what had gone through the boy's mind when he had arrived and seen the sign on the gate.

Or had he known it was closed even while he was writing his farewell note?

Charlie stood in front of the gate again, his eyes on the Home's bronze plaque. The words mirrored backward, unintelligibly, despite the fact that he knew what they were without looking at them. If the boy were truly intent on having Charlie find him, Charlie reasoned that he would have found some way to let him know, so he could follow. If, that is, he'd had a choice. It was possible, Charlie realized, that the closing and the move had come too swiftly, even for Danny.

Or had the boy imagined the moment Charlie was now living in? Had Danny known Charlie would come, if only to talk, and had he wanted Charlie to go through what he was now going through?

The street was deserted—no people, no cars, no animals, no sounds. In his eagerness to start out and avoid any conversation with Max or Shirley, he'd had no breakfast, and now he felt mildly faint.

There was another possibility, and Charlie had been aware of it from the first moment, that Danny was being true to his word, that he was there, within the walls, somewhere inside the deserted building, waiting.

Charlie rubbed his hands together for warmth, then walked along the street, away from the gates. He stopped when he came to the spot he remembered. The wall was as it had been twenty years before when they had used it to sneak back in at night, after hours. Three feet above the ground a brass water-main attachment, for two firehoses, stuck out from the wall. Charlie put his right foot on it, reached up, and slid his hands into two openings, where bricks had been chipped away. His fingers went in, to the knuckles. He stood on the hose connection with both feet, then lifted his right foot again, placed it upon a rounded stone that protruded a half foot from the wall surface, put his hands on top of the wall, and hoisted himself so that his stomach lay across the top edge. He stretched his right hand across, grabbed metal piping, and pulled. He avoided the cut glass, which ran all along the four-foot-thick wall in a line several inches wide. Two of his fingers bled slightly. Charlie sucked the blood, and, standing, he looked down into the courtyard.

He saw no lights, no movement. His breathing was even. The line of glass, along the wall in both directions, did not glitter. Charlie squatted and touched the dull green and blue glass pieces; their edges were, mostly, rounded. Was Danny looking at him from one of the windows? Charlie smiled. He believed he could feel what the boy might be feeling at this moment, seeing himself—Charlie Sapistein—standing on the wall, and Charlie saw that he was somewhat frightened and, to his surprise, very happy. He jumped, landed on his toes, felt his body vibrate in the hard dust from the impact—but his balance was good and he did not fall.

He looked up, to the spot where he'd been standing. He remembered Murray, angry about some regulation, leading a parade of boys around the block, seven times, outside the walls, and blowing a bugle at the end. The walls had not fallen. It was a story he told himself to remember to share with Danny.

The stillness unsettled him; he imagined, for an instant, that he was seeing the place before any boys had ever lived in it. The courtyard seemed small, as it always did to him the few times he'd been back. Murray had claimed that this was so not only because it would always seem impossible that so much—so many ball games and conversations and years —had once filled it, and not only because a child's view inevitably made things larger than life, but because one generally regretted what one had become.

Charlie didn't agree. He believed it was better to be an adult than a child, and it pleased him to find the courtyard smaller than his memory made it.

He opened a door and called into the corridor: *"Danny!"* There was no answer. "Hey, Danny!" he called again, cupping his hands around his mouth. "It's me—Charlie. Talk to me—okay? Come on—"

The walls were bare, the corridor empty. Charlie walked a few feet, his heels clacking on the wood floor. He looked behind, but saw nobody. He opened the door to Mr. Gitelman's office but it was empty. Had the records been transferred—or destroyed? He had never thought about it before, but now that he was here, and had asked the question, he decided that he wanted information about himself, from the years before he'd come to the Home. He wanted to know about his real father. His mother had kept photos of Charlie's father in a cigar box, he recalled, but he couldn't remember anything about them. The photos were gone by the time—when he was married—he'd realized he was interested in them.

"Hey Danny!" he called again. There was no answer and,

177

despite the length of the corridor, no echo. Charlie saw rusty marks on the floor, where the trophy cases had once stood. The gray walls were broken into whitish rectangles and squares, as if spray-painted, from where the photos had been. He walked to the end of the corridor, went through a swinging door, and called to Danny again. He thought he could hear the sound of his own brain, whirring and clicking like a movie camera, but it was Danny he saw using the camera, filming him as he walked through the Home, and in his head he saw himself from behind, walking down the corridor he'd just come from.

He went back into the courtyard, drew fresh air. "Hey Danny!" he called, toward the second story, where the dormitories were. "Come on down!"

He felt better. Outside, his mind worked the way he wanted it to; he made a note in his head to call the Federation and ask if the buildings and grounds were for sale. He could sweet-talk somebody there into selling the place to a former orphan-made-good. He'd talk to the man from the city. Maybe he could sell it for the city to use as some kind of manpower training station. The facilities were perfect.

He crossed to the opposite side of the courtyard and opened one door after another, calling Danny's name. He saw himself laughing with Danny when he would point out how things were upside down again; how just when he was getting set to retire from the real estate business, Sol was starting out. . . .

He smiled. Maybe the boy was in the *shul,* he thought, practicing for his Bar Mitzvah. Charlie walked down the steps and opened the door. The wooden ark was in front of the room, as it had always been, but the velvet curtains that had covered it were gone. Charlie slid open the doors to the ark, to see if the Torahs were still there. They were not. He touched the combination lock on the door to the *Genizah,* then spun it around, listening to the clicks.

"Stay right where you are, put your hands over your head slowly, and press your body flat against the door."

Charlie turned, saw a policeman in blue winter coat

standing in the entranceway to the *shul,* a gun in his hand. "Hey—!" Charlie said.

He heard the gun click. "Do as I say and you won't be hurt. Stay where you are, put your hands over your head, and press your body flat against the door."

Charlie heard his heart pumping, glanced down and saw his jacket move above it. He swallowed. "I was looking for somebody," he said. "A boy."

Charlie felt the barrel of the gun in the small of his back. His palms were already moist, against the door. The policeman frisked him, along the legs and calves and thighs, around his torso, under his arms. "Now turn around."

Charlie turned and stared into the policeman's eyes. They were tired, rimmed in purple. The two men were the same height. A slender pink scar ran diagonally from the man's lip to his chin. He pressed his gun against Charlie's stomach and, automatically, Charlie flexed his muscles there. The policeman jabbed him, hard. "Don't move," he said. He reached inside Charlie's parka, patted Charlie along the chest, then checked each of Charlie's pockets. "Lie down," he said. "On your face."

"Hey, come on—" Charlie said. "What is this—?"

The policeman held Charlie's wallet in one hand, but he did not look inside. "Do as I say."

Charlie got down on his knees, then lay face down. "Cheek against the floor." Charlie saw the dust shift from under his head. He looked sideways, at the open ark.

"You Charlie Sapistein?" the policeman asked.

"That's right."

"You realize that I could do whatever I want to you, don't you? I could tell you that you're free to go and shoot you in the back. You do realize that, don't you?"

Charlie's nose itched, but he was afraid to touch it with his hand.

"Answer me," the policeman said.

"I realize it," Charlie said.

"Tell me what you're doing here."

"I told you—I was looking for somebody—one of the orphans. Christ!" Charlie could not see the man's face. Although it was not so, he imagined that the policeman was black, and that he had thick lips. He knew how black cops treated black kids, when they had the chance. "I used to live here is what the story is—you could look it up. Telephone New York, to the place that owns the buildings—they could look it up for you. My name is Charlie Sapistein and I grew up here, is all."

"But you said you were looking for somebody."

Charlie saw himself looking down at Murray's face in the grass and he remembered how Irving had had to tell him what to do. If he was no longer a hero—if he had lost the ability to always do the right things in times of crisis—did that mean that he would come to desire things more? He drew in breath, between his teeth, and tried to concentrate on getting free. "Okay, okay. It's the truth—a boy named Danny Ginsberg—you could tell them to look him up too. I knew him and I wanted to visit him."

"But you saw the sign. I saw you read the sign."

Charlie thought of telling the man he couldn't read, but he was afraid to say the words aloud. Where would they lead? "I thought he might have been hiding here. He ran away from the Home."

"How do you know?"

"Hey look," Charlie said. "This is crazy—I mean, you see I didn't take anything if you've been following me. You see who I am from my wallet. You can search my car. You can telephone people and they'll tell you my story is true. Come on—what gives?"

"Why were you looking for the boy?"

"Because I miss him."

The policeman laughed. "That's a very good answer."

Charlie saw his opening. "Look—could I ask you a question, Officer," he said. "I mean, are you Jewish?"

The policeman laughed again, heavily.

"There are black Jews," Charlie said, before he could stop himself. "When I was a kid here I once met an orphan who was a black Jew—we played against him in a football game. They wouldn't let him transfer to our Home, though." The policeman was still laughing. "Maybe he wasn't really Jewish," Charlie offered. "Maybe he just thought he was."

"You're a pretty funny man," the policeman said, "but you should be more careful. Why should I believe that a grown man such as yourself with over three hundred dollars in his wallet would climb a ten-foot wall in order to search for a boy when there's no sign that anybody has been in these buildings for weeks?"

"No reason," Charlie said.

"We have to be very careful," the policeman said. "Our trust is sacred, right?"

"Sure," Charlie said, and he knew what he had to say.

"What motive would a man such as myself have for doing something to a man such as yourself, except duty?"

"I'm sorry," Charlie said, and felt no shame. "I really am."

"I know you are," the man said. Then, more softly: "Were you really an orphan?"

"I was an orphan."

"That's in your favor. When I was a kid I always wanted to be an orphan. My grandmother lived across the street from a Catholic orphanage and when I visited her they'd fight with one another to invite me in and show me how they lived. They'd get very excited when a stranger like me would come by and they could show me things."

Charlie tried the standard gambit. "Look," he said, "if there's some kind of fine I have to pay—I don't know much about how these things work—but can't I just pay it now and we'll be done?"

The man laughed. "Are you kidding? With your looks you could be setting me up. Your money could be marked. I'm not interested in taking you in, for trespass *or* bribery."

Charlie sneezed, his mucus spraying dust. "Shit!" he said.

"Leave your hands where they are." The policeman was silent for several seconds, then spoke again: "Okay. I believe you, that you were an orphan. In my work, you see, I have to read people's faces. I meet a lot of interesting people. You'd be surprised. My hobby is having conversations with interesting people from different walks of life."

Charlie said nothing.

"I want you to count to sixty, and then you can get up and leave. I'll be watching you. But if I ever see you here again you won't be as lucky. Is that understood?"

"It's understood."

"A man your age shouldn't be doing things like this. With your looks and your build you should have learned to stay away from young boys."

"Hey—!" Charlie called, without thought.

The policeman's heel struck him hard, near the end of his spine. Charlie bit his tongue to keep from crying out. "I told you to be careful. I'm your size, Mr. Sapistein. The next time you consider doing something foolish, remember what I could have done to you and didn't. That's how easily it can all end, don't you see? You'll find your wallet outside the door. You don't know my name, do you?"

"No."

"But you'll remember our conversation for a long time, even if we never see each other again, won't you."

"I'll remember."

"You're a very lucky man, in my opinion. You can start counting to sixty, slowly."

Charlie did as he was told, then stood up. He reached under his shirt with his fingers to see if the policeman had, on his back, drawn blood. He had not. Charlie took his handkerchief out and wiped the sweat from his face. He saw blood on the handkerchief. He stepped outside, picked up his wallet, and counted his money. It was all there. He took off his wristwatch and, using the silvered back for a mirror, saw that the left side of his face was scratched, from where he had rubbed the skin against the floor. He remembered when he'd been assigned to flannel the floors of all the dormitories, meeting rooms, and game rooms.

He walked across the courtyard, then scaled the wall and jumped down, onto the street side. The sidewalk was hard and he stumbled forward, let himself roll slightly, football-style, on his shoulder. His back did not hurt, though he knew he was bruised there. He tried not to think of anything or anyone, and he tried not to allow himself to recognize the measure of his anger. He opened the door to his car, got in and drove away, his heart beating as rapidly as it did when he finished wind sprints, and he didn't stop the car until he had driven twenty-five blocks. Then he pulled to the curb, in front of a diner, looked all around, and reached across.

When he saw the crumpled newspaper inside the glove compartment, he exhaled with relief and told himself that he was even luckier than the policeman had imagined. Charlie unwrapped the newspaper. His fingers were trembling. He glanced up, into the rear-view mirror, but saw no cars approaching.

He held the silver *tsumin* box on his lap, just below the steering wheel. The bells tinkled gently. The metal felt ice-cold. Charlie looked into the side-view mirror, then lowered his head, opened the door, and inhaled. The fragrance of spices made him salivate. If what had just happened was crazy, he told himself, then having taken the *tsumin* box was even crazier. Could he even remember the reasons he'd given himself? How honest had he been with himself when he'd promised that he was only taking it for a few days, to show to a dealer in the city so he could get one like it for Danny? He'd had only a week—but why hadn't he taken care of it during that week?

He felt moisture along the insides of his thighs. It wouldn't be safe to drive, he knew. He needed food, warmth, time. He sniffed the spices again, crumpled the newspaper around the box and placed it back in the glove compartment. He told himself to lock the glove compartment. When he stepped out of the car he locked all the doors and went around the car a second time, double-checking.

Charlie entered the apartment building and walked to the second floor. Lillian opened the door. She was in a sheer pale blue nightgown, a coffee mug in her hand.

"Sandy's still here," she said.

She gave him her cheek to kiss, but he put both arms around her and pressed his mouth against her neck.

"Hey—" she said. "What gives?"

Sandy stood behind her mother, schoolbooks in her arms. "Oh," she said. "It's just you."

"Hi sweetie," he said, and he went to her. She let him kiss her on the lips.

"I have to meet my friend Jennifer before school, to get the history assignment," she said, and left the apartment.

Lillian sipped her coffee and smiled at him. "Okay," she said. "Come on—" She walked down the hallway to her bedroom. "Once she goes she won't come back."

"I didn't come for that," Charlie said. "I was in the neighborhood, is all. I needed to be with somebody, to get warm."

Lillian didn't seem to hear what he was saying. She laughed at his words. He followed her. "I don't have much time," Lillian said. "I have to be at work by nine—don't let me fall asleep after, all right?"

When he entered the bedroom she was already under the covers. The venetian blinds were drawn. "Something crazy happened just before," he said. "Remember the boy who was at Murray's funeral—the one from the Home who was staying with me?"

She turned her back to him. He took his shoes off. "My name is Danny Ginsberg and I come from the Home," she recited, and shuddered. "He gave me the willies, being there. He reminded me of your mother—"

Charlie got under the covers, but he was afraid to touch her. "You never met my mother."

"You used to tell me how beautiful she was. You once showed me a picture of her when she was young—from before she was married."

"Do you want to know what happened this morning?"

He saw her hand reach out and turn the alarm clock, on the night table, toward her. "If you make it quick, sweetie. I really—"

184

"We don't have to do this," he said. "We could have coffee and just talk."

"Make up your mind." She turned to him, her eyes mildly angry. "You told me you needed to get warm, didn't you? What is it you're trying to do to me?"

She ran her forefinger down the middle of his face, between his eyes, down his nose, across his lips, to his chin. "You look tired," she said. "You work too hard, don't you think? You should relax a little bit more. We'd be glad to go places with you if you'd give us notice. Now that you're a rich man . . ."

She laughed and slid toward him. She was still wearing her nightgown. She put one arm over his shoulder and he shivered. "Hey," she said. "You're really in a state, aren't you?" She reached down. "You're not even—"

He turned over, on his side, away from her, and she pressed against him from behind, her arms around his chest, "I'm sorry," he said. "I went back to the Home and found it was closed and I climbed over the wall—then this crazy cop found me there and threatened to kill me. I told him I was looking for Danny. I forgot to mention that—that the boy ran away and I was worried about him. So I came here. I had breakfast over on 18th Avenue and realized I wasn't in such hot shape."

"Poor baby," she said, her fingers playing with the curls on his chest. "You like it best this way, don't you—when I hold you from behind? Tell me the truth."

He nodded.

"I know," she said. "You like me to talk to you like this too, don't you?"

He nodded again.

"We never talked much before we were married, but now that I'm heading for middle age and grandchildren—now you like me to tell you everything that's happening, don't you?"

"Please . . ." he said.

"I wish I had the time," she said. "I'll probably be the

185

youngest grandmother in the neighborhood." She pulled away. "It's getting toward eight already and I have to put makeup on and get dressed and get to work. Can you come back tonight? We could talk then." She stroked him with her fingertip, just below the navel. "I like you down here. You're nice and flat." She licked his shoulders. "It sounds like you were the crazy one, if you ask me—what's a cop supposed to think, finding a big guy like you in a closed-up building?"

"Okay," Charlie said. "Just hold me then."

"You always get big more quickly this way, don't you, but listen, hey—" she whispered in his ear. "I don't mind even a little bit. I like it too. I like you and I like being able to say what I want to you and I like that you need me and just come barging in, like this morning."

She had both hands between his thighs, spreading them. He felt his muscles contract, involuntarily. She ran her tongue down his spine and he didn't know how to tell her that this wasn't really what he had come for. "I took something from Murray's house," he said. "It's in the car, locked up."

"Mmmm," she said, then stopped, briefly. "I'm so sorry about that, Charlie. I really am. I know how you loved him."

When she was dressed, he offered to drive her into the city, but she said she preferred the subway. It would give her time to rest, without talking.

Charlie drove through Brooklyn, down Flatbush Avenue and across the Manhattan Bridge. He'd wanted to tell Lillian about Sol, but there hadn't been time. Lillian had always liked Sol. He drove to the office of the Federation of Jewish Philanthropies and spoke to several people before he found somebody who had information about the Home.

Charlie sat in the man's small office and explained that he had grown up in the Home and had taken an interest in one of the boys now there. The man found a folder and told Charlie that all of the remaining nine boys had been transferred to other facilities, but that there was no listing for any boy named Daniel Ginsberg. He showed Charlie a small photo of each boy, in case Charlie had the wrong name, but Danny's face did not appear among them. Perhaps, Charlie suggested, Danny had been transferred somewhere else just before the Home had closed.

The man looked through more folders. "Here's a complete roster of all the boys who were there during its final eighteen months, with the disposition of each case. There's a small snapshot of each boy, and fingerprints." He passed one sheet to Charlie. "There's a Greenburg here—Martin Greenburg—but I find no Ginsberg."

Charlie looked at all the pictures. "I don't understand," he said.

"When was the last time you saw him there, Mr. Sapistein?"

Charlie scratched his head and acknowledged that he might have been mistaken. It had been a while. Things got away from him sometimes. The man did not show that he was in any way suspicious of Charlie's inquiry, but Charlie warned himself to be careful, to keep from saying anything about Danny having stayed with him. "It's funny, though," Charlie said, standing to leave. "I mean, that the place is closed—that there won't be any more Jewish orphans."

"It must be," the man said, and he stood also. "And there's one bad effect in all this too—I mean the black market in Jewish babies."

Charlie felt nothing.

"It's soared out of sight. This is off the record, of course, but I've been told that Jewish parents without children are willing to pay up to fifty thousand dollars to obtain a certified Jewish baby these days. And even then they can never really be one hundred percent sure." He walked around his desk and opened the door for Charlie. "I feel sorry for them." Charlie saw the gold-framed photographs on the man's desk, of wife and three children—two sons, one daughter.

"I have a daughter," Charlie said. "I was divorced, but I still see her. She's a big girl now."

The man smiled. "If we can be of any further help, just call on us. I have your address and phone number should anything come across my desk."

Charlie left the building and was a block away before he realized that he had forgotten to ask about what had been done with all the records and photographs and trophies and medals. He wished he could have seen his own file—to see information on what he'd been like, according to others, when he'd been a boy.

He walked toward Grand Central Station, along 42nd Street. He imagined that most other people had a similar curiosity about the past—not about themselves, perhaps, but about the childhoods of their parents and grandparents. You could never ask older people—Sol or Mittleman or Dr. Fogel —to talk about their own boyhoods, though. You had to wait on older people. They told you stories about themselves when they were ready to tell them.

Charlie wondered if Danny had been in touch with Dr. Fogel. He wondered how Dr. Fogel was filling his days, without the Home. He imagined himself in Dr. Fogel's living room, telling Dr. Fogel and Danny about Sol's new life. He saw himself saying that when he thought of Sol now he thought of a story Max had read to him, from the newspaper, about a man who went around the country, from town to town, placing an ad in each local paper. The ad gave a post office box number and said, simply, *Last Chance to Send in Your Dollar!* The man had averaged between three and four hundred dollars a town before he'd been stopped. Max had tacked the item to the corkboard beside his desk. Charlie wanted to remember to give the story to Sol, the next time Sol telephoned.

When he entered his car, Charlie checked the glove compartment. The *tsumin* box was there. In truth, he reasoned, the absence of any records concerning Danny helped to explain things. He figured that the boy had reached the Home a day or two after it had been closed. There was no mystery to it, really. Gitelman and the others had decided, simply, that the easiest way to close the Home's books at the end— to balance things—was to eliminate the boy's records. If they had admitted he was missing there would have been too many problems—with the police, the FBI, the Federation. . . .

But how, he wondered, had Danny reacted when he'd arrived, with his sack and books, and had seen the gates closed? Had he realized that no records of his life existed? And if Gitelman and the others had actually destroyed information, how, in his future life, would Danny ever be able to prove he really existed?

Charlie smiled: it was a problem that would have delighted the boy! Endangered species was right, and Charlie imagined himself meeting Danny and surprising him with the information that he had, alas, become extinct.

Back in Brooklyn, Charlie collected rents. He mentioned Danny to each person he visited, asking if they'd seen him during the previous few weeks. Nobody had. If they did meet him, he asked them to tell the boy to telephone New Jersey collect, that there was an important message for him.

After lunch he drove to the Grand Army Plaza library. Danny had once told him how much he'd liked the place. Charlie had not been there since he had visited it with a class from the Home, over twenty years before. He walked inside and felt, in the immense hollow of the lobby, comforted. The large squares of wood paneling, which rose on top of one another to the full height of the building—perhaps one hundred and twenty feet—seemed warm and inviting. Maybe, he thought, after my fortieth birthday I'll move back to Brooklyn, to this neighborhood.

He walked from room to room but did not find Danny. He sat in the reference room for a while and enjoyed the quiet. Three old men were reading newspapers and passing them around to one another. He dozed briefly, and when he awoke the men were still there and he realized suddenly that he could, in fact, find pictures of himself as a boy without having to return to the Federation office.

He took his coat off and sat at a desk for over an hour, looking through 20- and 25-year-old copies of *The Brooklyn Eagle*. A woman brought the large yearly volumes to him, one at a time. He saw photos of himself in uniform, playing football and baseball and basketball. He saw his name in articles and in scoring columns and in lineups of All-Star and All-City teams. He was amazed, from the pictures, at how little he had changed. He had lost no hair, he had put on almost no weight, and only his mouth and chin looked a trifle older. But even there, the yellowish quality of the paper and the darkness of the photos made him seem slightly more tired than he had actually been at the time.

He looked up often, hoping to see Danny, so that he could show him the articles about himself—about how good he had once been, how important to the life of the Home. The others had all changed so much in comparison to himself. They had all aged so quickly! He wished he could bring them down sometime, in a group, to look through the papers together.

When he decided to stop he realized for the first time that he had had no trouble reading any of the newspaper columns. He put his fingertips against his wrist, looked at a wall clock, and counted twenty-seven beats in fifteen seconds.

He left the library but did not go to his car. Instead he walked along Eastern Parkway and went down into the subway. He wanted to go downtown, to one of his banks, and he knew how bad the parking situation there would be. He only had to ride three stops.

In the subway, he wondered why, really, he wanted to look at the newspapers with the other guys. They would only try to relive their youth as if those days and games had been the high points of their lives. What Charlie thought he wanted to do was something different—to show them how far they'd come—to make them feel how they'd grown and changed.

Murray would have disputed him; he would have shown Charlie other reasons for his pleasure. He would have talked about Charlie's need, always, to be in the center of things and in control. He would have said that Charlie had gone to the library and looked through the papers because he'd been feeling low and had wanted to raise his self-image by summoning up a time in which he'd been like a king, with others worshiping him. The desire, then, to take everybody back with him to that time would have become, in Murray's theory, Charlie's act of aggression—the proof of his resentment at the actual progress others had made, while Charlie really felt, deep down, that he had made none. Unmarried, without a son, and without—oh how Murray would have loved to go into the meaning of that part of it!—the visible signs of aging, Charlie really doubted everything about his life, especially those things others envied in him.

Charlie heard the questions Murray would have asked: Why can't you simply enjoy one of your experiences by yourself? Why the compulsion to bring the rest of us in always? Do you feel incomplete without us? Do you believe you're responsible for us not still living together? And Murray would have finished with the question he always asked —Why must you feel guilty toward us? But Charlie realized that he now had an answer which would have left Murray speechless—Because it was my block that killed you.

He shook his head and told himself he was crazy, imagining a dialogue like that. It only led—he laughed to himself at the words—to a dead end. The train stopped, and over the public address system the conductor announced that there would be a delay of a few minutes. Through the dusty windows Charlie saw that another train was stopped parallel to the one he was in, and in it, two Puerto Rican boys were dancing. One of the boys did a running cartwheel and a split. A third boy—not Puerto Rican—walked around with a beret in his palm, trying to collect money. The boys moved to the next car, out of sight, and Charlie wondered if they had parents, and if not, where they stayed at night when winter came.

When the other train seemed to be moving away from Charlie, backward, he knew it was his train that was moving forward. He got out at Nevins Street, went to his bank, opened his safe-deposit box, and removed several long-term savings certificates. From his safe-deposit box he took a mint Lifesaver, sucked on it, and smiled, imagining Danny with him, discovering that he kept a roll of Lifesavers there.

He took the certificates to a bank officer and told him that he wanted to transform them so that the account, to a total of $25,000, would be a joint one, payable in the event of death to either survivor. Charlie's name would remain as one of the owners. The man checked through forms and asked for the name and address of the co-depositor. "Daniel Ginsberg," Charlie said. "Same address as me."

But Charlie could not give the man the other information about Danny, and he took two cards for Danny to fill out and sign. The bank was already closed, so that a guard unlocked the front door to let Charlie out. Charlie stared at the man's gun. In the street he looked both ways, expecting, for a moment, to see Sol. Would Sol have congratulated him?

There had been a time—before he'd gone to work with Mittleman—when he had often daydreamed about the reading of Sol's last will and testament. He had wondered if Sol had left his money directly to the Home, or whether he had named individual boys. Charlie had once believed—if Sol had left him enough money—that he would have taken up Sol's work, spending his life traveling around the country and visiting his boys. He had imagined himself taking an interest in the boys still in the Home, and he had seen himself discovering a great young athlete and training him to break all of his own records.

Charlie saw that the car window was shattered, and he wasn't surprised. Without Danny, he said to himself, his luck was gone.

He opened the glove compartment and saw that the *tsumin* box had been taken. He drove off. If they didn't melt it down, the police would be able to trace it easily enough, it was such an unusual item, but how would he explain having had it in his car? And what if Anita notified the New Jersey police and they sent a routine inquiry over the bridge? Charlie knew of several shops that specialized in Jewish ritual items, and one—on Mott Street—that dealt especially in silver and antiques.

He met with the man from the city and listened to him talk about timetables on the factory construction. When the man asked him where his boy was, Charlie thought, *Maybe it's Danny who's following me! Maybe he took the box.*

He walked around the neighborhood in which he'd been born and thought again how amazing it was—each store and building in the city was actually owned by somebody, and once a month each tenant had to pay rent to the owner. He had once thought that apartment building owners were the kings in real estate, but Max had taught him otherwise. Max rarely bought an old apartment house, unless it could be knocked down and a new one built. Land might increase in value, but there was no depreciation on land.

In their declining years, Max had taught him, apartment houses were dumps of garbage: depreciation was nil, potential for proceeds of sale low, everything in need of repair and replacement. Cash flow was high and disappeared into maintenance.

Charlie came to the building in which he'd been born, an aged red-brick structure six stories high, with fire escapes on the street side. He did not know which rooms inside the building had belonged to his mother and father. He knew none of the tenants in the building.

He drove to Ocean Parkway, to Irving's building. A moving van was parked in front. Inside the building the elevator door was open and the elevator itself was submerged halfway below floor level. Two men stood on top of the elevator cab, steadying an enormous purple couch on its end. They worked the elevator by its pulleys.

He sat in Irving's living room and told him the truth about his search for Danny, about the Home being closed, about the policeman, and about Danny's name not being listed in the records of the Home. Irving assured Charlie that he had in fact seen Danny—at the game, at the funeral, and at Anita's house. "He was strange, I thought," Irving said. "He made me uncomfortable, and I usually like bright kids."

Irving's wife pressed Charlie to stay for dinner, and when she did he realized that he had completely forgotten about football practice at the school. He had been in the subway at the time it would have started. He walked to the door and

Irving stood with him, his arm in Charlie's. He urged Charlie to call him more often—every day if he wanted to.

They walked down the stairs into the lobby, their arms linked. Charlie asked Irving to call Anita and tell her he'd forgotten about practice but that she shouldn't worry about him. Charlie told Irving that he shouldn't worry either.

"I never do," Irving said. "Murray was the one I always worried about. You'll live to be a hundred—everybody knows that."

"Me and you," Charlie said.

Irving patted his stomach. "I eat too much."

Charlie got into his car and Irving talked to him across the shattered window, without commenting on it. Irving laughed. "In all the books I teach it's usually the son who goes off in search of a father, but with you things are opposite, aren't they?" He made Charlie roll the broken window down and he reached in and took Charlie's right hand in both of his. "You're all right, Charlie. No matter what happened, we all love you, do you understand?"

Charlie drove off and watched Irving, like a small child, lift an arm and wave good-bye by wiggling his fingers.

When Charlie arrived at Dr. Fogel's house the streetlights were already on, though the sky was not yet black. A sign was planted in the lawn, stating that the house was for sale. There was an envelope scotch-taped to the door, with his name on it.

The note was printed, in block letters:

DEAR CHAIM
YOUR YOUNG FRIEND DANIEL GINSBERG
TELEPHONED AND ASKED ME TO TELL YOU
THAT HE IS IN GOOD HEALTH. YOU NEED
NOT WORRY ABOUT HIM. AS FOR MYSELF I
AM VISITING RELATIVES IN FAR ROCKAWAY
FOR SEVERAL DAYS. WON'T YOU CALL ME
NEXT WEEK SO THAT WE MAY TALK WITH
EACH OTHER? YOU ARE VERY MUCH IN MY

THOUGHTS THESE DAYS. HOW IS YOUR UNCLE SOL FEELING? HE DID NOT APPEAR WELL TO ME. PLEASE COME AND TALK WITH ME SOON.

(DR.) ELIEZER FOGEL

Going home, on the New Jersey side of the bridge, under the bright lights of a gas station, Charlie saw two beautiful girls standing next to suitcases, hitchhiking. They seemed to be about Sandy's age. He slowed down, and the one closer to him smiled at him with such openness that he felt himself grow hard at once. He pulled to the side of the road, they waved at him with delight, picked up their suitcases, and then he panicked, pressed down full on the accelerator, and drove away.

He had, slowing for them, he realized, been imagining them in his car, one with her thigh pressed against him, the other breathing on his neck from behind. The one next to him would have held the gun against his ribs. His shirt was drenched in sweat. In his imagination he saw the girls making him drive to a motel where they would have registered together, and where, having taken his money, they would have ordered him to strip off his clothes. Hey listen, he heard himself say. You got the wrong guy. I was for women's liberation before there were women.

He parked on the side of the road and closed his eyes. He considered going back and picking them up—to prove to himself how insane his thoughts were. They were probably as sweet as they looked, heading back for their prep schools or colleges after a weekend in the city visiting friends.

In his rear-view mirror he saw a spinning red flasher moving upon him quickly. He sat up straight, wiped his face with his handkerchief. The red flasher went by—a tow truck hauling a smashed-up Cadillac. He moved his car back into traffic. There was no point in going back just to prove to himself that he could. They'd have been picked up by now anyway, he knew.

195

When Charlie entered the house, Mr. and Mrs. Mittleman were sitting in the living room, watching home movies. He walked through, to the kitchen, to fix himself supper, but Mrs. Mittleman made him sit in the living room while she prepared a plate for him. She told him that he looked very hungry.

On the screen in front of him he saw himself walking toward himself, growing larger. Danny was walking beside him. The boy looked younger than Charlie had remembered him being. Charlie's head and shoulders now filled most of the screen. "I decided, with the boy here, that I should try to capture some of our life together on film," Mr. Mittleman said. "Since we're like a family."

The images on the screen were blurred. Then, in color, Charlie saw himself and Danny in the park, tossing a football to one another.

Mr. Mittleman spoke to Charlie, his cigar between his teeth. "I thought you'd like to have a print of this so I made an extra one for later on," he said, "so you can remember what things were like now when you two were young and happy together."

Seven

I saw him again today for the 1st time in 40 days. He walked by me 3 times and didn't see me. He walked 3 steps ahead of Dr. Fogel, knocking branches aside. Dr. Fogel looked very happy. He kept stopping and closing his eyes and breathing in the fresh air through his nostrils. He looked younger than he did since I remember him.

What surprised me: how old Charlie looked in comparison! Steam came out of his mouth when he breathed and talked. He wore a blue wool hat pulled down over his ears like a Canadian lumberman and his black curls stuck out on his forehead. His eyes were moving fast, and he was excited by what he was seeing but I could still tell how much he had changed. He didn't look like a young man anymore. I felt so bad for him that I wanted to cry out to him to take care of himself, but I stayed where I was on the ground, covered with leaves.

I could see how much he missed me by the worry in his brow and this is what I thought: IF I CAN'T HAVE HIM THEN NOBODY ELSE WILL.

I wanted to laugh out loud at that idea!

I followed them from a long distance. Charlie had a rolled up map in his hand but I knew he was thinking of me and wondering whether or not I exist. These are the places he might guess he'd find me in: the deserted Home,

Dr. Fogel's house, the basement of Murray's School, the woods around Anita's house, the basement or empty apartment of 1 of Mr. Mittleman's buildings, here on Dr. Fogel's land.

I couldn't hear anything they said to each other and I liked it better that way. He must see that my plan worked even more successfully than I'd hoped for and that now I have no identity or existence at all. My fate is truly in his hands, if he wants me.

While I followed them I had fun imagining myself telling him about what I'd thought and how I imagined the future. I know how scared he is of dying young. I saw myself telling him that nothing would happen to me if I murdered him because I didn't exist. I would tell the judge and jury what I told myself, that if I couldn't have him nobody else could. My defense would be this: How can you convict a boy who was so abandoned that even a Jewish orphanage tried to destroy him?

They would ask me: Why did Charlie Sapistein take you in? And I would tell them that he wasn't there to give an answer.

An old joke that Sol told me: "Chutzpa" is when a boy murders his mother and father and asks for mercy from the court because he's an orphan.

What would Dr. Fogel and Sol feel toward one another if they met at Charlie's funeral?

They went to the area where the old cabins are and Charlie made a motion with his hand which showed he would level all of them. They looked into the cabin where I stayed last night but I leave no traces. I have everything I need in my sack and pockets: my Tephillin and Talis and prayer book and PIRKAY AVOS and money and an extra shirt and set of underwear and candy bars for energy and the package for Anita.

I didn't go into the clearing where the cabins are when they went inside for fear one of them would look out a window and see me. I sat on a stump and tried to imagine Dr. Fogel's father and his settlement living here 50 years ago. There are no traces of their existence in any of the buildings. There are no books or carvings on walls or pieces of newspaper.

After they left I walked into town and mailed the stopwatch to Anita. Then I went into a supermarket and bought food for supper. It's more difficult being Kosher because I can't eat meat and I have to check the canned foods and the packages to make sure they're all right. I look for things with eggs in them, for protein. I eat a lot of cheese and canned mackerel and day-old bread.

At night I take out the lantern I bought from under the cabin floor and light it and I'm alone. I'm hundreds of yards from any road so nobody can see the light through the woods. The lantern is a blue camping lantern with a gas cartridge and a piece of mesh nylon called a mantel which has phosphorous dust on it and gives off a strong white light for me to read by. I do no cooking because I don't want the odors to attract animals. In the mornings I carry my garbage out to the road.

What I believe: If he came once he'll come again! If Dr. Fogel came with him that must mean Charlie started putting on Tephillin in the morning or praying. I have enough money for another 3 weeks, the way I live. The less I eat the smaller my stomach and intestines become and the less food I need to survive on. I looked at my reflection in a mirror in the supermarket and I'm thinner, but not that much to worry about myself.

I look better than he does. I have lots of sayings saved up for him, for us to listen to together. Here's one, to explain why it's all right for his friends from the Home to treat him the way they do: "A man's gifts make room for him."

A question to think about: If I knew the end of the world were coming tomorrow would I want to stay here alone or be with him?

My answer now, when I'm alone: I would want to stay alone. But would my answer be the same if I didn't see him come for me today and if I didn't know he'll be back?

Things he could do with the land if he buys it from Dr. Fogel: sell it to the state or government for conservation. Build a planned community for people who want to flee the city. Sell it to an organization like a charity or religious group to get income for himself every year after

40. Make a deal with Mr. Mittleman and divide it into lots for subdevelopments.

A better idea: Buy some expensive land near the property and build garden apartments so that this land's value increases, and then sell this land!

To tell Dr. Fogel: This is what the Rabbis taught: "God, the people of Israel, and the land of Israel are one."

I said Minchah in the afternoon and Maariv when the sun went down. I wash before I eat and after I eat. I say a prayer after I eat and after I go to the bathroom. Indoors I wear a Yamulka at all times. I put on my Tephillin in the mornings just in case Mr. Mittleman is right about my age.

Will I ever know the truth about how old I really am?

Will I ever stop wanting to know? Can any other human being understand how much it presses against my life for me to feel I'll never never know! Even if someone should read this would that someone understand what I feel?

Charlie would tell me not to worry about it. He'd want to protect me.

What would he think if he knew I lied to him. I HAVE NO MOTHER AND NO MEMORY OF ANY MOTHER.

I like sleeping on the wood floor. I sleep better without any kind of artificial heat. I sleep on top of the winter coat he bought for me which has an insulated lining with half of it on top of me.

What I wonder about: If we really couldn't be together and if I really meant what I said and if I crept up on him 1 night in his bed while he was sleeping and if his eyes opened at the last moment and were staring into my eyes, would I have the courage to do it?

This is what I would say to him: In Hebrew my name means "God is my Judge."

THURSDAY

It rained all day today and I stayed inside the cabin. I had to read standing up so I could look out the window in case I saw them coming, but they never came.

I wrote a letter to Ephraim and told him what I

imagined I would do to Charlie, but I tore it up when I was done.

If Hannah knew I was here I bet she would run away and try to live with me, that's how young and foolish she is.

It was raining too hard to walk through the woods and get new food. I collected rainwater in an empty can. I kept thinking I was going to get hungrier, but I never did. I made a sandwich out of 2 pieces of bread, bits of apple, and peanuts.

I was too worried to do a lot of reading or memorizing. I'm learning how to let my mind do nothing when it wants to.

FRIDAY

The rain ended in the middle of last night and I heard it stop and I never fell back to sleep. I started to walk out of the woods even before the sun came up and I was in town before the stores were open. I went into an all-night diner and ordered hot chocolate and toasted English muffins with jam. The odor of frying bacon and eggs and griddle cakes was VERY tempting. The eggs and griddle cakes would not be Kosher because they would be fried in the same pan and on the same griddle that was used for "Trayf."

A package store was open when I finished my hot chocolate and muffins and I went in and bought cheese, apples, grapes, a can of tuna fish, and a small head of lettuce. I have to be sure I don't get weak. The man asked me if I wanted to work in his store after school and I said no. I didn't like the way he looked at me and after I walked out I went around to the side and peered through the window to see if he was telephoning anyone but he wasn't.

I put on my Tephillin and prayed and then I had breakfast with myself. The food tasted wonderful. I asked God to forgive me for having the hot chocolate and muffins before I prayed, but I could justify that on the grounds of health. In the Jewish religion health comes before everything else! I smiled at my reasoning.

I took a walk after breakfast through the woods and

201

I found a small pond, about 80 feet wide and 30 feet across. I sat on a rock and this is the passage I decided to memorize: "IF YOU ARE ABOUT TO PLANT A TREE AND SOMEONE TELLS YOU THAT THE MESSIAH HAS COME, FINISH YOUR WORK AND THEN GO FORTH TO MEET THE MESSIAH."

The ground was wet everywhere, so I lay my coat across the rock and slept there, in the sun. When I woke up the wool fuzz was sticking to my lips from sweating and I remember I was scared for a second, not knowing where I was.

Then I walked back, following the trail I'd made before by breaking branches and it was very strange, because just as I was thinking to myself that if he were to catch me unawares I would say to him, "Well hi Charlie, and how do you like your boy scout?" I saw him coming toward me, and behind him was Dr. Fogel . . . and behind Dr. Fogel was Mr. Mittleman puffing on a cigar!

I was scared but I decided to take my chances and not move rather than attract attention by stirring up noises. I took 2 steps and pressed myself against a tree. God was with me! They veered off to the right, away from me.

I waited and followed them. Mr. Mittleman looked funny, waddling behind. I thought of calling to him, "Hey Max—where's your movie camera?" But I didn't. I realized I never saw him in a coat before or outside at all. His face looked bloodless. He was even shorter than Dr. Fogel. He didn't say anything to them.

They looked at the clearing where the cabins were and I was afraid they would go into mine again even though I left it clean and bare, but they didn't. They were gone before I had a chance to make a decision. I didn't want Charlie to see me the 1st time with Mr. Mittleman there. But that was a mistake, not to show myself.

The important thing now is to make sure Charlie gets the land for himself, without Mr. Mittleman's money or help! If he really has all the money he told Anita he did, that should be enough.

Will Charlie spend Shabbos with Dr. Fogel?

Also: Where is his beloved Uncle Sol, and what happened at their meeting??

It's almost sundown now. I promised to wash myself for Shabbos and change into my other set of underwear and clean shirt. If I wash the clothes I'm wearing and put them out to dry before Shabbos I'll be safe because Dr. Fogel and Charlie won't ride here on Shabbos.

I'll make a blessing over the grapes, for the wine.

SATURDAY NIGHT

Today I observed Shabbos by doing no work: no writing or carrying or cooking or lighting matches or buying or thinking about money. I left my money out of my pocket all day on a board next to the front door and I never touched it.

After I ate bread and grapes I prayed all morning, doing the entire service except for the part of taking out the Torah. I sang the prayers out loud and my voice sounded nice inside the cabin. It's not like a girl's voice anymore. When my praying was over I spread 3 napkins out in the middle of the floor and made lunch. I made Kiddush over the grapes again, washed my hands, and made a Motzi over the bread and when I was done eating I washed my fingertips and said the blessings after meals. Then I took a nap and I didn't dream.

When I woke up I studied the way old men study Talmud in Orthodox synagogues on Saturday afternoons and I tried to see how many points of view I could give on the same question.

This is the question I asked: CAN A JEW BE A JEW ALONE?

I gave Murray's answer and Dr. Fogel's answer and Sol's answer and Ephraim's answer and Charlie's answer and Mr. Mittleman's answer and Rabbi Akiba's answer and Maimonides's answer and Danny Ginsberg's answer.

Guess whose answer was best? *Danny Ginsberg's!*

MURRAY's answer was yes, a Jew can be a Jew alone but he's a better Jew when he's part of the Jewish people.

203

DR. FOGEL quoted God's promise to Abraham, saying "I will establish my covenant between me and thee and thy seed after thee in their generations for an everlasting covenant, to be a God unto thee, and to thy seed after thee." Dr. Fogel asked: Why would God say "everlasting" if He didn't mean it?

SOL said he learned that God promised the Jews that the Messiah would come 1 day and His people would be there. But if there were 1 Jew left that would mean there would be an end to all Jews and that would mean the Messiah's time had come. Then God's promise to His people would *not* have been fulfilled. All Jews should be proud of their heritage! he added.

EPHRAIM said a Jew could be a Jew alone because his father had been a Jew alone. He said the word "alone" shouldn't be taken literally. He said he thought I meant it to represent the way you felt about being Jewish.

CHARLIE said he believed that a Jew could not be a Jew alone, but he said he didn't have to give reasons for his feeling.

MR. MITTLEMAN said my question was Anti-Semitic and that an Anti-Semite is somebody who hates Jews more than is necessary.

RABBI AKIBA said no.

MAIMONIDES said yes.

DANNY GINSBERG said a Jew could be a Jew alone because Abraham had been a Jew alone. Everybody had to agree with me, because it was in the Torah.

Then we talked about whether a 2nd Jew alone would know if he were a 2nd Abraham. How would God talk to a man if he wanted to in today's world? (Mr. Mittleman said he would come through on an answering service!) What are His signs? If there were no Jews would there still be a Sabbath? Is there any place in the Bible where it definitely says the Messiah will come, or did Sol make that part up? If Dr. Fogel doesn't believe in Israel and does believe in the Bible coming from God, how does he explain God's promise to Abraham to give him the land of Canaan for an everlasting possession?

Also: If God gave the Torah to Moses on Mount Sinai, how did Dr. Fogel explain who wrote the last 8 parts, after Moses dies?

I asked Charlie why he didn't want to give reasons for his feeling and he got angry with me and told me not to feel so proud because I knew how to use words. He surprised me and quoted the saying about God being concerned above all with what is in a man's heart.

This is what he asked me: Where in the Bible does it say that Abraham knew how to read and write?

Mr. Mittleman said that God was too smart to have ever put his promise in writing.

Sol said, God bless the state of Israel!

Then it was time for Minchah and Maariv. When I finished praying I went outside and when I saw 3 stars I went back inside and I lit the lanterns for Havdalah and sniffed salt and pepper from the palm of my hand. I kissed the backs of both my hands and wished myself a good week.

I sat on the step of the cabin making myself think of nothing until it became chilly, when I came back inside and had supper.

If I had enough food and money, could I go on forever like this, filling my days with nothing but prayer and study and eating and washing and sleeping?

The answer is no.

SUNDAY

It's the middle of the afternoon now and here I am, sitting next to my own pond and thinking how lucky I was to have thought to come here instead of staying in the city. I wonder if Dr. Fogel sat here when he was a boy and his father was the leader of the colony.

I just gave myself my 1st music lesson on the Tonette, learning to read notes and how to blow to get a good pure tone. I bought one in a drugstore this morning.

My promise: to practice music one hour every day. This will give me a start for when I come out and can take up a real instrument. I think the sweet fragrance of the Sabbath is going to stay with me all week long, because when I realized this morning that Charlie was not going to come today it didn't make me unhappy. Sunday is his big day for selling houses.

Charlie's fatal trouble: He's too good. If he had the ability to reject me he wouldn't be worried the way he is now and I wouldn't be able to make him do what I want. Mr. Mittleman would agree with me. This is what he would say: If you want to get ahead, learn to be bad! Too many people like Charlie, even after what he did to Murray, whether by accident or not.

My question: Why is he so good? If he were less good, would I have seen that in his eyes also, even in the photos, and would that have kept me from trying to find him? And if I hadn't wanted to find him and if everything hadn't happened the way it had and if I hadn't just thought what I thought about him being too good, would that have made him something else, and would anybody else ever have thought the same about him?

If I think the thought he will too!

Does that mean there's hope?

A fact: THE JEWISH PEOPLE ARE LESS THAN ⅓ OF 1% OF THE WORLD'S POPULATION, INCLUDING CHILDREN.

To do: list the great contributions of the Jews to civilization, including not only those of people everybody knows like Einstein and Spinoza and Freud, but also others. In America, for example, find out if Jews really run the publishing industry and garment industry and movie industry and diamond industry and Democratic party and radio and TV and universities.

Some examples I remember of things even Jews don't know about famous Jews: Emil Berliner invented the gramophone and the microphone. A Jew discovered petroleum in Galicia in 1853. The International Postal Union was invented by Joseph Michaelson. The telephone was really invented by Philip Reiss in 1864. Nahum Salamon was the 1st man to manufacture bicycles. Bubonic plague serum and typhus fever serum were invented by Jews. The repeating rifle was invented by a Jew. In 1854 in Germany a Jew made and drove the 1st electric automobile. (Look up names I forgot!)

The question: What would happen if the whole world were Jewish?

The answer: There would be a shortage of Rabbis.

If I'm feeling so good now, is Charlie feeling the opposite?

Things that are not in my notebook: what I dream about when I dream. What each person I meet looks like. What I think between the time when I finish writing in my notebook until I go to sleep on that day. What I eat at every meal and/or between meals.

Also: I don't put down every single detail of what people look like, or everything they say, or what rooms I'm in are like. I don't put down what kinds of shoes people wear or what color the pants and shoes and socks and underwear and shirt I'm wearing now are. I don't put down how each thing I eat tastes and every time I drink water or go to the bathroom.

I don't put down only the important things either. Sometimes I forget the important things.

How different am I when I write things down from when I do the things I'm writing about?

I don't put down the stories I see all the time when I think of how people's lives, like Charlie's or Dr. Fogel's or Hannah's, would be so different with small changes and when I follow their lives along different lines, coming from them saying things or making decisions or having things happen to them that are different from the way things are.

When I imagine how their lives might become different lives from the ones they have I always see them in my head as if they're walking away from me on a path covered with leaves and I'm seeing them from behind. Then I see them come to places where there are several directions they can go in, including straight ahead. I imagine what lies ahead on each road. Each road has new turning points and I see them making choices or being forced on to paths and I see them in the future with different lives being led right there on the paths, and when I look from behind I can see 8 or 10 or 12 or more different lives being acted out by them at stopping points on the road, as if on theater stages. Sometimes I see all the lives being led at the same time and I can see which ones would have been the best choices. But sometimes a good choice at 1 point leads to a bad choice later and vice versa. And sometimes the paths intersect and the people shake hands with themselves and kiss themselves in delight at meeting themselves.

Now I'm going to do what I mean, in an opposite way, going backward.

Do I really know everything my mind went through during the instant in which I had the idea to do what I'm going to do and during which it sped backward in time even while it was writing in time right now and saw everything that happened in time back then and which I'll now put down?

What did my mind do with all the years in between??

Without further ado, Danny Ginsberg presents:

THE STORY OF NEW ZION

a story by

Daniel Ginsberg

One bright day in the 3rd quarter of the century in which we now live, a young boy of indeterminate age chanced to be walking through a deserted section of some woods in upstate New York, where he had been sojourning, on his way to freedom (for the boy was an orphan who had run away from the orphanage which had held him—and in those days there were still orphans, though they were forgotten by the public at large), when he spied a tree trunk that attracted his attention by the strange light flickering from it. Upon closer examination the boy discovered that the strange light came from sunbeams dancing upon the filaments of an intricate spider web, which web covered a hollow in the old tree, and below which web the boy saw what it was that was causing the marvelous light to glisten at him.

He stuck his fingers through the sticky web and took out the box. It was made of highly polished metal, and though the boy could tell that it was very old, it still shone as if it were new. Upon the lid of the box was a Star of David, and the initials, in Hebrew אנ.

The brass hasp of the box gave way easily to the pressure of the boy's fingers, and inside he found an envelope addressed as follows:

> A LETTER TO MY JEWISH AMERICAN GRANDCHILDREN LIVING IN ZIONAMERICA

The boy, looking around stealthily to be sure he was not being spied upon, for he was fearful of having his whereabouts detected before he could establish a new existence for himself (he had, upon quitting the orphanage which had held him in bondage, made sure to destroy all records of himself, including fingerprints and photographs, so that, when he had come to some new town which was not hostile to children like himself, he would be able to start anew), then made his way to a bold rock beside a pond, where he sat himself down.

As he was wondering whether or not he had the right to look within the letter, a shaft of bright light seemed to fall upon his hand where he held the letter, and the boy was so transfixed by the nature of the curious light that he did not even realize for a while that it was burning his knuckles. When he released the letter with a cry of pain, it floated to the ground, but though it fell upon mud, when the boy lifted it, it showed no signs of dirt, and his hand too had no mark from the burn.

Was the boy religious? Did he believe in signs from above? Did he believe that the same light which had attracted him first to the tree was now offering him the letter as his own?

Alas, dear reader, we shall never know what went on inside him! All we know is that, without any seeming thought, he did in fact reach inside the envelope and from it he plucked the letter.

The paper was remarkably well preserved, and showed no signs of aging, not even at the corners. The script was quite legible, the boy was pleased to see, and he looked around once more, to assure himself of his privacy amidst Nature (did a frog croak? did birds twitter above him? if they did, would he even have noticed, so lost was he in contemplation of his treasure?) and then he read:

MY DEAREST GRANDCHILDREN,

As I write this letter, who can know if you exist or if you do not because how do I know if my son who has long ago deserted me will have married, and if he married, will have had children? Remember what the Talmud said (I'm telling you this in English because who knows if anyone will speak Hebrew anymore in the time in which you will be living?): "The unmarried person lives without joy, without blessing, and without good. He is not a man in the full sense of the term." Which shows that He wanted us to have children, also from when it says that a man may divorce his wife if she is barren for 10 years and a wife may divorce her husband if he is impotent.

So if you are there somewhere reading me and hearing my voice I want you to know about how I came to America and founded my colony of New Zion and how it all ended so maybe you will not repeat my mistakes and will have a better life as Jews than I or your father, who calls himself, so I am told by those who see him, "Doctor" Fogel.

Was I to blame? In the Talmud the Rabbis blame the evil nature of Absalom who revolted against David the King on David himself, who brought him up with too much freedom, but who could say that of me?

Listen for a minute, my grandchildren. This is a voice from the past and even from the Old Country, as it is called, telling you to be good Jews and to remember Israel, for does it not say that it is an inheritance unto you?

Remember this: GOD, THE PEOPLE OF ISRAEL, AND THE LAND OF ISRAEL ARE ONE. If you are born a Jew, you remain a Jew always, and a stranger in all lands but your own. And I Eliezer Fogel know this better than any man, for I tried to establish God's land here in America and my end is that I end alone, without my wife or my son or my followers, so that I am condemned never to have the blessing even of praying in a Minyan, or of knowing if my children and grandchildren will follow after me and redeem my life for me!

I am hoping you understand what these words mean, coming to you now, across the years. This is what you should remember if you are a Jew: Trust Nobody, not even other Jews. I trusted in man, and was paid in kind!

What was my life like in the Old Country, where I was a student in the Cheder of the great Riminova Rebbe, may his name be blessed? I might have become his prize pupil and a wise man myself but I was too eager. This is what Eliezer Fogel says: "Don't be so eager!" In my village we were taught to honor the stranger and when he came into our midst and stayed with us for Shabbos and told me of the land of Palestine and of the people who were going there to make it a Homeland for the Jewish People, I trusted in him.

May the worms feast on his flesh!

And what was my life like in our Shtetl in Europe before I left it? Now I have beautiful memories of a community devoted to God and Torah and one's fellow Jew, but the truth is, my grandchildren, the Shtetl had a smell like rotting onions! It stank like poverty stinks and sickness stinks and sadness stinks!

You should study what life was like for Jews in the Shtetl and through the centuries, wherever they were, unless they catered to the Goyim, and then you will see that the great miracle is our survival and that you are alive and still a Jew despite everything!

This is what we said: "If God lived in the Shtetl His windows would be broken."

But more than His windows broke. Didn't His heart break to see our suffering? Or was the Rebbe right, that Suffering was our lot, that it showed we were His people, and that the New Doctrine of Zionism was trying to take from God what was His, who had to work through His time and in His way?

My son left me when he told me this was so, but what did he ever know of sorrow and hardship, having been born here in America?

I declare this: God wanted us to regain the land of Israel, of our forefathers Abraham, Isaac, and Jacob, whenever we could, for why else did He choose us to be a blessing to the nations, and how could we be a blessing to the nations in these terrible times if we have no nation of our own, no land which is our own, where we can be safe from Destruction? Remember this: "If there is no bread there is no study."

On our Holiest day, Yom Kippur, God himself cannot forgive us all our sins. We must ask our fellow men for forgiveness. Do you understand me? We Jews are a people of this world!

Here for you is another way of seeing what I mean. The Rabbis say "If a person who withholds himself from wine is called a sinner, how much more so is one a sinner who withdraws from all of life's enjoyments."

I believed this when I was a young man, and so I trusted the stranger who stayed with us and I gave him my money so that he would buy me passage to the border and onto a ship bound for Palestine, to join with the Knights of Zion in building our Homeland.

So, my dear grandchildren, bound to me in the blood of the children of Israel, I wish you long life and happiness! But how can a Jew enjoy life if he is not part of His people? For in the study of Torah is the highest happiness. Remember what we sing each Shabbos when we open the Holy Ark—OUT OF ZION SHALL GO FORTH TORAH!

And so I came to America. The voyage across the ocean stank. There was an epidemic and half the ship died. Jews were thrown overboard into the sea. Did they believe they were going to the Promised

212

Land? I arrived in New York, with no money and in ill health.

If you want to know the rest you should ask your father. I became a man of the world. I studied money. I made my fortune and I bought land and I left Gomorrah and moved here to the country to build a colony which would train Jews and prepare them for a future life in the land of Israel. I had many followers in my time, don't ask me how many. We had cabins full of Jews who spoke all languages, but with each other Yiddish.

We built our homes with my money. I continued to study money. I married and had only one son and I saw my duty in life as preparing others for the journey I never made. Did I believe it was God's will to stay here, or did I really love the land I was in also? Who can tell.

We argued about everything: Should a mother nurse and bring up her own children or should she put them in the care of others? Were children private property or communal? Should we speak in Hebrew or Yiddish? We farmed the land and we built furniture to sell and we prayed and we had children. We sent settlers to Palestine and many died and half of those who didn't die came back to New York.

You should look up and study about all the things we argued about: Marxism and Socialism and practical Zionism and synthetic Zionism and cultural Zionism and political Zionism. Some of us followed Herzl and some of us followed Jabotinsky and some of us followed Weizmann and some of us followed Gordon.

Look up the history of Palestine before and after the Mandate!

Chaim Weizmann said this: "Memory is right."

On several hundred acres, at our height, we were like Babel itself. Answer me this: Why did God give us so much brains if he wanted us to be One people? Without poverty, nothing joined us except our different theories. We became our own enemy.

The Colony of New Zion has been dead for 20

years. I have lived here alone since its death studying Torah and finding only questions. Maybe, wherever he is, my son has answers. My followers forsook me for the temptation of America. Why should they suffer the hard winters of our colony and the harder life in Palestine? Hadn't they left the Old Country to abandon Suffering?

Many of them forsook God, so that they lost both ways, in this world and in the next one too!

Many of them died and we buried them.

My son, your father, wanted them to stay and, like Akiba, he warned them against corruption and assimilation, but when they fled, he fled also. He had my blood.

Without land a man is nothing. Without God a man is nothing.

I left my land to my son, and I left myself only enough money to travel to Palestine, where I hope to die and be buried soon after my arrival there.

Finally, I leave you the words of Rabbi Akiba, "Whoever is buried in Palestine is as though he were buried underneath the altar, for all Palestine is fit for the altar."

The choice is yours!

The boy was about to return the letter to its envelope when a thin slip of a paper fluttered out of it. He caught it in the air as if it were a frail butterfly. On it was 1 sentence, in the same handwriting as that on the letter, except that the script was very shaky as if it had been written by a much older man than the one who had written the letter. Trembling, the boy read: "If my grandchildren are not in the world, I pray that you will use this letter with your mind and with your heart, so that you, my dear friend Daniel, can tell the generations of the Story of New Zion!"

Amen. Selah.

What I learned today from writing a story: Not to be fooled by the deceptive power of my own imagination.

Even if I could write things like this forever, filling myself with myself, the answer is still no.

If I created enough people like Dr. Fogel's father, from the way I see people the way I described today, would they be able to keep each other busy and happy after a certain point, or would they still need me?

Remember this: There were no Jews before Abraham.

Also: Never never show this to Dr. Fogel.

Why did I love my story while I was writing it and despise it now that it's finished?

My decision: If Charlie comes tomorrow I'll reveal myself!

MONDAY

This morning I found a tree that had a hollow and a spider web over the hollow and I wondered if I ever saw it before I wrote my story or if writing my story made me notice it. I don't know enough about Nature to know how long the spider's web could have been there, or if he could have spun it overnight.

Once when King Saul was chasing David with his soldiers to kill him, David hid in the hollow of a tree and a spider spun a web over the hollow so that David's life was saved.

I stuck my hand through the web and inside the tree trunk was nothing but pieces of wood like sponge.

I woke up feeling better and I walked in some new directions on the property but didn't find any artifacts of the old settlement or any traces that anyone ever lived in any other part. There were some flat stretches that might have been farming land.

If Charlie marries Anita and I go to live with them, what will happen between Hannah and myself, living in the same house? What do brothers and sisters who are close to the same age feel toward each other and if they think unhealthy thoughts, what do they do about them?

I practiced music for an hour this morning, before lunch.

After lunch I walked outside on the roads all around the property, to make sure there are no other ways of getting inside, so that I won't miss him if he comes again.

While I was walking outside and looking in across the fence at the trees I saw the 2nd story I'm going to write down now. I knew football practice started by then and that he wouldn't be coming today. I was imagining horses and wagons of Jews going in and out of the property and speaking to each other and to their horses in Yiddish and Polish and Russian and Hebrew when something made my mind see an opposite scene, from the future, and this is what it was:

THE EPILOGUE

A Story Projected from Real Life

by

Daniel Ginsberg

Twenty years had passed from the time when the 2 friends had last seen one another. The visitor, a tall blond man in his early thirties, with strangely restful hazel eyes, was passing through the town in which he had once spent several crucial months of his life, and out of curiosity he had driven along the road he knew to see if the house he had once known so well was still there.

He had walked up to the door, and, seeing that the name was the same as that of his childhood friend, he had knocked.

When the door opened, the visitor and his friend needed to look at each other for only the briefest instant before the flash of recognition entered their mutual eyes and all of the changes of the 20 years which had passed were obliterated.

They embraced like brothers and held one another tightly and then stood back.

"I don't believe it," said the tall handsome man in the doorway, who was as dark as his friend was fair. "It is too good to be true!"

"No," said the visitor. "It is true!"

"You're Daniel Ginsberg!"

"And you are," said Daniel, "by the nameplate on your door, Ephraim Mendelsohn!"

They now shook hands, somewhat awkwardly, since

they had grown used to covering up their strongest emotions in their regular lives, and Ephraim invited his dear friend to come into his house.

Daniel looked around the kitchen, once so familiar to him, and it seemed that it had been only yesterday that he had been sitting there and that the 2 of them had been boys, each lost in his own world. How much, really, had they known of one another's inner thoughts back then? And yet, how close they had been, in a way that could never be repeated!

"The kitchen is the same," Daniel said, and then, without warning, he felt a rush of tears flood his eyes and he was holding his friend by both shoulders and staring into his warm eyes and saying, "Oh Ephraim—there's so much I want to know, don't you see? There are so many questions, so many thoughts!"

"I know how you feel," Ephraim said, and he too was crying, from a mixture of joy and sadness. "I have questions also, though for the moment it seems enough to have you here with me."

"I thought the same thing," Daniel said. "And even if I should turn around now and leave, without talking with you or ever seeing you again, the moment that has just passed would be enough, wouldn't it?"

"Yes!" Ephraim said, and he took his friend by the arm. "But come," he said. "Let me offer you a drink, or some nourishment."

Daniel had walked to an old cabinet and opened the glass doors without asking his friend's leave. He took out a beautiful antique Tsumin box and held it in his hands and shook it gently so that the bells tinkled. "When did you recover this?" he asked. "It is the same one—the one which was lost 20 years ago, in the week in which your father died, is it not?"

Ephraim looked down for a brief second, and then looked up and smiled, and Daniel wondered about the shadow which had flickered across his friend's eyes, in the moment before he spoke. "It was an accident. I was purchasing a Talis for my son Moshe—"

"A son?" Daniel exclaimed. "How wonderful!"

"I have 3 sons," Ephraim said. "But let me continue."

"Please do."

"I was purchasing a Talis for my son Moshe, named after my father, as I know you must realize, for his coming Bar Mitzvah—this was less than 10 days ago—when, in the store of the old Jew from whom I often buy objects of Jewish interest, I saw it in the corner of a shelf behind him, and I recognized it at once!"

"How curious," Daniel said. "That you should find it in the same week in which I should be passing through!"

The 2 friends laughed, and Ephraim asked Daniel if he would write down the coincidental experience in his diary, but Daniel only sighed. "I have long since given up such foolishness," he said. "I think it was my way back then of keeping myself from having to live in the real world and communicating with real people."

"I thought so at the time," Ephraim said. "But I didn't dare say so, for I knew how much it meant to you!"

Daniel nodded and a dark look came across his brow. "In a way, it was my writing things down that sustained me, you know. I'm not sure I would have survived without it."

"Of course you would," Ephraim said, and he clapped his friend on the back. "Why, just look at you now!"

The 2 friends talked like this for a long while and then they retreated to Ephraim's living room and talked to one another about their lives and their families and all the intervening years and books they'd read and people they had known and what had become of them.

Ephraim was now a widower whose wife had died 4 years before, after giving birth to their 3rd son. Ephraim did not think he would ever remarry, so intimate had he and his wife been to one another! But Daniel had to wonder secretly as to the real reason, for he remembered how affected his friend had been when his friend's father had died and his mother had cared for the family of 4 brothers and 2 sisters by herself. All this happened many years ago.

Daniel thought of a saying from Rabbi Akiba which he loved very much: "When a husband and wife have merit, God's presence may be found in their midst. When they lack merit, a fire consumes them."

Ephraim showed his friend the laboratory he had built in his basement and the hothouses he had added on to the house in back, where he did his botanical research, for he had become a highly successful consultant to scientific firms. "By working at home," he explained, "I am able to be with the children more—and that is the most important thing."

Daniel, walking through the hothouses and admiring the plants, said laughingly, "Murray the Mower."

Ephraim puffed on his pipe and laughed also. "I know," he said. "It's very strange, isn't it, how these things work themselves out in life? But now, Daniel, tell me about yourself."

Daniel and his friend adjourned to Ephraim's office and, smiling at the coincidence, Daniel told his friend that he too was a research scientist, and about his work in Biomedical Engineering. Daniel also revealed that, under the pseudonym of Charles Fogelstein, which name Ephraim at once recognized, he was also a highly successful writer of science-fiction books for children.

"Why, I read them to my sons all the time!" Ephraim exclaimed. "And in all the years I never thought to see anything special in the name of the author!"

As the afternoon wore on and was subdued into dusk, the friends talked as if time had had a stop.

This is what Daniel learned:

Ephraim's sister, Hannah, had become a lawyer, and was married to a Jewish lawyer and lived in New York City and had 2 lovely children of her own.

Dov had moved to California, where he was a highly regarded brain surgeon, and went on camping trips with his family of a wife and 4 children.

Rivka lived in Washington, D.C. and was married to a Congressman whose name Daniel recognized. She had 3 beautiful children.

Eli had emigrated to Israel at the age of 16, and at the age of 17 he had been killed in a guerrilla attack on his border settlement.

The youngest child, Murray, whom Daniel had never seen, was a student at Harvard University.

"Just think," Daniel said, "of all the things I would feel if I were to meet him, and of how he would not understand. Isn't that the difference, my friend?"

Ephraim's mother, Anita, had moved to Florida, where she was an educational consultant and was receiving continual offers of marriage, though she had never accepted any. "Please give them all my love when you see them," Daniel said.

"They'll be so happy to know about how your life has turned out," Ephraim said. "We have talked about you often through the years." Then Ephraim paused meaningfully. "You heard about Charlie, didn't you?"

Daniel said he had, though he did not explain how. Charlie had died of a malignant brain tumor, just before his 40th birthday.

"I used to think," Daniel said, "that if I had not left him, he would not have become ill. That was the way my mind worked in those days, though I see how foolish such thoughts were."

Ephraim, who vividly remembered visiting the man in question in the hospital before his death, did not tell his friend that Charlie had asked for Daniel frequently, up until the end!

Dr. Fogel, who had been a teacher to both Murray and Charlie, and to Daniel also, had died, and according to his wishes, his body had been transported to Israel for burial.

Mr. Mittleman had died, but Mrs. Mittleman was still alive, and quite a wealthy woman. She was living in a retirement village in Florida. Anita visited her several times a year and the 2 women shared much, strange to say.

Ephraim did not know what had happened to Charlie's wife or beautiful daughter. They had moved away from Brooklyn and no one had heard from them again. Some of Charlie and Murray's old friends, for they had grown up in the same orphanage in which Daniel himself had been raised, still kept in touch with Ephraim, though a few of them had died.

Irving and Jerry and Herman had died. The others had not.

The 2 friends laughed together, remembering experiences they had shared, but they did not make any promises about seeing one another again, for to do so would have ruined the magic of the afternoon.

"Will you stay and eat with us?" Ephraim asked.

"I fear not," Daniel said, and Ephraim understood.

The friends were at the door when a car drove up and 3 children bounded out of it. "Your boys!" Daniel said.

"They're just returning from Hebrew School," Ephraim said. "We have a synagogue in our town now, and quite a nice community of Jews."

"Would Dr. Fogel approve of them?" Daniel asked, and the 2 friends laughed at the joke.

Then Ephraim, after mentioning to Daniel that he had for many years feared that his friend was long since dead, introduced his boys to Daniel and they each gave him their names. The oldest, 12 years old, was named Moshe, and the middle son, 9 years old, was named Chaim, and the youngest boy, who was 4 years old, was named Daniel!

THE END

This is what I believe: True friends lie to one another, the way Ephraim did to Daniel when they were boys.

A puzzle Ephraim showed me in a book:

> All sentences
> within this box
> are false.

My diary is the box and my story is the sentence.

What I know nothing about: what it's really like to study Torah. What would a truly wise man do to me if he saw my thoughts written down?

In Murray's study once I looked into one of his volumes of the Talmud and I couldn't understand anything except a few words. The Talmud is written mostly in Aramaic. There is a Babylonian Talmud and a Jerusalem Talmud but I couldn't even tell which one I was looking at.

When I think of all the things I would have to learn, first just to be able to read and understand the letters and words themselves, and then to know how to follow the arguments between the Rabbis and understand them and interpret them, I get sick inside!

I don't even know what any boy my age who goes to a regular Yeshiva knows. My memorizing is no substitute.

Can a dedicated man learn as much between the ages of 55 and 65 as he does between the ages of 5 and 15? Why should there be such a difference?

Oh how far I am from God, whatever my real age may be!!

TUESDAY

It rained all day today and I didn't go outside. I stood at the window but he never came. Have I miscalculated?

Asking myself that question makes me especially calm and I don't know why. I made up no stories today. I stood at the window and prayed and waited. I tried to ask myself what we really have in common, other than our origins, and why, really, I ever expected him to take me in.

I was outside just before because the rain stopped. There was a full moon in the sky and the clouds floating in front of it like vapors made it look like a sliver of dry ice with steam coming off. I felt very close to it, as if I could touch it and burn my fingers!

There are special prayers for the new moon and the new month in Hebrew but I don't know what they are. The Jewish calendar goes according to the changes of the moon, not the sun, and I don't know why that is either, or whether it was always that way.

In the time of Rabbi Akiba some Jewish men had a dangerous operation performed on themselves to conceal their circumcisions against the Romans.

How much do I know about all the exact persecutions Jews suffered throughout History?

I found some empty cartridge shells in back of one of the other cabins, but I haven't heard gunshots or seen tracks of any hunters.

Is Charlie with Anita now, and are either of them thinking of me at this moment?

Sometimes I'm an idiot!

I woke in the middle of the night and heard them, across the way, in another cabin. At first I was scared, but then I listened for a while and I could tell they were just teenagers making out. They were laughing and struggling with each other and throwing beer cans against the walls.

I walked across the clearing and listened at the wall to their cabin. I heard a girl giggle and say, "Don't you 2 do anything we wouldn't do!"

I heard a guy's voice and he sounded drunk. I couldn't make out his words, except that he kept saying, "C'mon, huh? C'mon, huh? C'mon, huh?"

I heard another girl giggle and tell somebody to stop, but she didn't mean it. I wondered what she looked like. Her voice was very refined, as if she took speech lessons. She sounded much older than the others and I wondered what she was doing there. I wondered what her face would look like in the morning when she faces her mother across the breakfast table.

This is what one of the guys shouted that made the 3 others laugh: "Because it's my birthday!"

Then I acted like an idiot, I don't know why. I just kicked the door open and yelled in at them, "THEN HAPPY BIRTHDAY, GANG!" and then I ran!

The girls screamed but I didn't wait to see what any of them looked like. I ran into the woods behind the clearing through the wet leaves and the slosh and I didn't stop until I thought I was far enough away. The girls were still screeching and I heard the guys cursing and yelling at them to shut up.

They probably thought I was just somebody from their school who followed them but I can't take any chances.

It doesn't matter why I did, even if it was just for fun, because it told me what I must have wanted to tell myself anyway: that I shouldn't stay here anymore. Charlie

223

might come back again, and then again he might not. There's no reason to wait any longer. The best thing is to admit that I miscalculated and to go forth.

What the words "go forth" remind me of: the Rabbi's speech at Murray's funeral.

In the woods, thinking of them hopping around with their pants caught around their ankles, I had a good laugh. I thought of the guys at the Home and how I would have been a hero to them if I could have told them a story like that about myself! I could have added things about seeing the girls naked and it wouldn't have mattered if anyone believed me or not.

I sat on the ground with my back against a tree and didn't think about anything except how I must have scared them to death and about what a child I was not to have been able to control myself when he said it was his birthday.

What I forgot to do: wish him a "mazel tov."

Even if I hadn't barged in on them, how can I sleep in the cabin tonight wondering if they'll be coming back? If I sleep outside I'll surely catch a terrible chill. Just from sitting on the ground for less than an hour with my jacket under me I'm sniffling this morning.

When everything was silent for a long time I walked back to the clearing. The sky was filled with millions of stars and I thought of God's promise to Abraham.

There were 9 empty beer cans in their cabin and some leftover potato chips and a damp army blanket they left behind. I took it to my cabin and I lay on the floor with it under me and that way I couldn't feel the dampness under my coat. I was afraid to go to sleep for fear they'd return but I rested well until sunup.

Then I said my prayers and had a farewell breakfast of potato chips, warm beer, bread, and lettuce. I'll get something warm to drink in town at the bus station before I leave.

Will I ever see this land again? If I hadn't come here to wait for him, in how many different directions might my life have gone? But since I did come here, even though it was a temporary mistake, it was a necessary step for me so that I might realize how foolish my planning was, for I was really waiting on him to do something instead of relying on myself to create my own fate.

That was what my foolish act last night showed me, so that I revise my earlier statement about you being an idiot, Daniel Ginsberg. For if you had not acted the fool you might have erred in waiting here even longer!

Charlie will be surprised when he sees me to find such a new look in my eye! He'll see that even though I have to make plans and decisions concerning my future, I'm not as much in need of him as even I thought I was a few days ago.

My name is Daniel Ginsberg and I come from the Home and I can save myself, thank you.

שמע ישראל יי אלהינו יי אחד

Hear O Israel the Lord Our God the Lord is One!

Eight

Danny sat at a table in a corner of the small cafeteria, sipping from his glass of tea. As disappointed as he had been at not finding Dr. Fogel at home, he was surprised at how good it felt nonetheless simply to be in Brooklyn again. He had been foolish in those thoughts also: imagining himself living in the country all the time with Charlie.

He had even, during his walks around Dr. Fogel's property, sometimes imagined an entire colony of orphans there, living new lives. In Danny's dreams Charlie had, of course, been the director of the colony, one that contained hundreds of Jewish boys, including refugees from all over the world. There had been classes and workshops and teams, good meals and singing and parties and dances. On Saturday nights, busloads of beautiful young girls had been brought in (blindfolded, so they could not return on their own), and Danny had fallen in love with one of them. . . .

Danny felt comfortable in the cafeteria, among old Jewish men. Next to the counter two bearded men were playing chess, and two others, looking like their twins, sat behind them, watching the moves. This, Danny thought, remembering Charlie's phrase, was probably their home away from home.

Through the window Danny watched a Puerto Rican family moving their possessions. The father had ropes around his chest and, as he pulled a dolly loaded high with boxes and clothing and furniture, he strained forward like a work-horse, steam billowing from his nose. At the very top, a large green stuffed easy chair was turned upside down. A boy wearing sneakers pushed the load from behind, one hand stretched high, on the leg of the green chair, to keep it from toppling. The mother walked behind the boy, push-ing an enormous black baby carriage that overflowed with pots and clothing and clothes hangers and plastic dish drain-ers and toys. She carried an infant in a pack on her back. A small girl in a red flowered coat walked at her side, suck-ing her thumb and pulling a wagon filled with shoes.

Danny had intended to pay Dr. Fogel for his room and board. In his situation, the best thing would be to keep all arrangements aboveboard; he did not want anything for nothing. What he did want—and what he had intended to explain to Dr. Fogel—was to live in an Orthodox Jewish home during the weeks preceding his Bar Mitzvah. Dr. Fogel was the only person he knew who had a home that was both kosher and located near a synagogue.

If Dr. Fogel had been unwilling to take him in he would have asked to be sent somewhere else—another Jewish home, a Yeshiva that had sleep-in facilities, a hotel or room-ing house that catered to Orthodox Jewish men. Whatever else Dr. Fogel might have been capable of, Danny had reasoned, he could not have knowingly kept another Jew from the performance of a *mitzvah*.

Danny warmed his hands on the outside of the glass of tea and bent over it to sniff in the steam. He'd had the passage ready for him, should he have needed it. Had not Simeon the Righteous said that the continuance of the Jewish peo-ple depended on three things—the study and practice of Torah, religious ritual, and acts of loving-kindness?

Danny took out his notebook. None of the men in the cafeteria seemed to question his presence. He wondered what they would say were he to go to each of them and tell them his life story and then ask for theirs. He would stand in the

227

middle of the room and ask who would be the first to teach him Yiddish, and who would be the first to tell him about his childhood, and who could remember a story his father's father had told him when he had been a child. . . .

*

I'm in Brooklyn again and I'm sitting in a room called Skulsky's Dairy Cafeteria with 8 other Jewish men, and I know I made the right decision in leaving. They're old men and I could probably make them happy by telling them about myself and making them tell me about themselves, but the best thing is to do nothing.

I have no obligation to bring joy into the lives of others at every moment of my life. I still believe in Simeon the Righteous's doctrine of Torah, ritual, and acts of loving-kindness, but the important thing for Danny Ginsberg right now is to consider his situation and to make New Plans!

That's what the Rabbis mean when they say "There is no Torah without bread."

Despite all my setbacks, what surprises me is how good I still feel, as if I'm ready for any experience which may befall me!

There was a sign on Dr. Fogel's front lawn saying his house was sold. I looked in his windows and all the rooms were bare. Even the curtains and venetian blinds were gone. The Mezuzah was gone from the front doorpost.

But this is what I thought: Even if he flew to Israel to spend the rest of his life on a Zionist kibbutz, my life would stay the same! If night becomes day and day becomes night, my fate still remains in my own hands.

What I still have to do, no matter what: find a place to stay until I can face Charlie and say to him: "THIS IS WHO I AM AND THIS IS WHAT I WANT TO DO WITH MY LIFE AND THESE ARE THE THINGS YOU CAN HELP ME WITH IF YOU WANT TO."

It's all right for Ephraim to live in the country because he was born there, but if Charlie asked me I would tell him he should come back to the city so he can be in touch with his early life.

Also: It would be all right with me if Sol lived with us too, since he's so old already.

*

Danny put a teaspoonful of strawberry jam into his tea, as he had seen one of the old men do. The sweetness caused him to close his eyes and sigh with pleasure. If Charlie should refuse him, he wanted to be able to allow that to make no difference either. If there were no records of him anywhere, then he wanted to be ready to demand that new ones be created. He wanted to be ready to go to whomever he had to go to—whatever civil liberties groups or legal aid groups or Jewish groups—in order to receive a true accounting of his origins: the names of his mother and father, and of their mothers and fathers; his real date of birth; and his rights, under law, concerning his future.

But until such a moment arrived he had to be careful. He could not, for example, as he had considered doing, spend his nights in bus terminals or on the subways, for if a policeman were to question him, and if someone else were to discover that he had no actual identity before he himself demanded that his identity be returned to him, then he would lose control. They would be able to do with him whatever they wanted to.

His secret wish—not so secret, really, since he had been prepared to discuss it with Dr. Fogel—was that he be sent to a Yeshiva where students lived in, if such a Yeshiva existed. In Yeshivas, he knew, students spent half the day studying Jewish subjects and learning Hebrew, and half the day studying what students in regular schools studied. So long as the Home had been alive, he supposed there had been technical reasons for keeping him there—but if there was no one place any longer into which a Jewish orphan had to be placed, and if he could demonstrate to them his potential for becoming a contributing member of the adult Jewish community when he would reach that age, he did not see how or why they could deny him. To do so, he told himself, would be to deny all of Jewish history and practice.

*

What I am: a good investment. If somebody were to support me now, he would be paid back many times over in the future.

I don't depreciate and my expenses are still deductible.

To remember: Don't be shy about my talents and brains and what I know.

What I need to do more of: Decide which talents to cultivate. There must be boys and girls my age somewhere who already practice musical instruments or study mathematics or science or Torah 5 or 6 or 7 hours every day. If you do anything that much every day you will eventually know things nobody else knows.

But I can't become like that until I have 1 place to be living in.

Is Dr. Fogel a happy man?

Like the men who are sitting around me right now he has observed ritual and studied Torah all his life and knows no other way of living. His devotion to the Home must be counted an act of loving-kindness no matter what his reasons were, even if rituals are to him like water to a fish!

But the Rabbis say this also: SUFFERING IS A GIFT FROM GOD.

What interests me as soon as I write down what the Rabbis say more than why they say it is this: Why, sitting here at this moment of my life, did the question about Dr. Fogel come into my head? If I didn't write it down, would the rest of my life be different than what it's going to be?

My conclusion: If I followed all my thoughts forever, to the ends and beginnings of their trails, I would never have time for living!

Coming into the city on the bus I saw what would have happened if I stayed on the land: I would have caught a chill. Each night I would have slept half-awake, worrying. My head would have become heavy with fluid and I would have been afraid to go to a doctor for fear he would have to know who I was or send me to a hospital and then they would have disposed of me through some agency that would have placed me with morons and delinquents and retards and retreads.

I looked at my reflection in the window of the bus coming here and I saw a scene with myself stumbling into a synagogue. People stared at me as if I was an old dwarf. I was shouting to them that it was my Bar Mitzvah. I saw clean-shaven men in Yamulkas and suits coming down the aisles to carry me away. I saw myself screaming that I was Jewish and that it was my Bar Mitzvah day and that I was in the House of God. I began chanting my Haftorah even as they carried me down the aisle above their heads. My nose was dripping and my eyelids were stuck together with phlegm. My ears were stopped up. Yet my voice, when I heard myself singing, was pure and sweet like a child's!

Outside in the lobby of the synagogue they laid me on the marble floor, which was made of large black and white squares. They wrapped me in an army blanket and telephoned the police but I rolled away from them out the door, down the steps and into the street, and I got up and ran deliriously until I found another Synagogue! I went inside and saw that the Ark was open and they were taking out the Torah. The Cantor and Rabbi wore long black robes and the Torah glistened with its silver breastplate and silver crowns. I smelled cloves. I hid behind the back row where nobody could see me and when it was time for the Bar Mitzvah boy to be called to the Torah I marched down the aisle, my eyes on the Eternal Light, and summoned myself to the Bimah. I could smell my own foul odors as if my flesh was already rotting! I had the army blanket wrapped around me to cover my body where it showed through the slashes in my clothing.

I stopped, realizing that I could not in summoning myself for the Aliyah give the name of my father. A thick crowd of men in black suits was blocking my way to the Bimah.

The real Bar Mitzvah boy was holding his mother's hand and giggling and pointing at me. I demanded that the men let me through but they pushed me backward and walked over me. Then they lifted me above their heads again and I floated out of the sanctuary. The Rabbi stood above me, and when my blanket was torn away, he looked at me and then said, with disgust, just like Dr. Fogel: "Do you call yourself a Jew?"

Here's a beautiful new one I memorized from PIRKAY AVOS on the bus: "If love depends on some selfish end, when the end fails then love fails. But if it does not depend on a selfish end, it will never fail."

This is why: If you love a woman because she's beautiful and she becomes sick and loses her beauty, then the love is gone too. But where love is for the sake of God, as when a disciple loves his master in order to learn, then the love never vanishes because the cause endures forever!

*

Danny went to the counter, bought a cheese Danish, and asked that his glass of tea be refilled. The old man who served him looked past Danny and said, as if to no one, "It's snowing."

Danny sat at his table and watched the large white flakes fall. He saw himself, on the ground, with flakes falling on his own cheeks and covering him. He saw Charlie and Dr. Fogel finding him there, on the forest floor, hard and cold, and he saw the tears in Charlie's eyes—and then, what thrilled him more, the anger.

He saw Charlie raise his fists to the sky and curse God. Dr. Fogel walked away, into the woods. I'll be with you soon, Charlie, Danny said to himself as he sipped his tea. We'll be together again. He saw Charlie walking into a strange synagogue. Charlie sat, without praying, for hours —through an entire service—until the time came to say the Kaddish. Then he rose. *Yisgadal v'yiskadash* . . . Would Dr. Fogel have stopped him if he were sitting in the same *shul?* If Danny had no blood relative living after him, who would the Rabbis say would be allowed to say *Kaddish* for him? What was the Law?

He saw Charlie sitting on a tree stump, his head in his hands, snow resting like a fine net on his black curls, and then he saw his own body rise from its mound of snow, shake the flakes away, and he heard himself shout: "Surprise!"

*

Each error I make leads me closer to the truth, for I know better the things I cannot do! I could not stay with Charlie without any definite arrangement, but I did not have to leave him the way I did. That was an error. But once I left him and forced him to make a decision I could not simply return and say I made a mistake because that would have made him think I was too weak a person for him to want to live with permanently!

The question now is how can we continue to live together if he'll have me if my official identity has been destroyed? I have to know how old I really am! I have to be Bar Mitzvahed because of what I believe about being Jewish!

I can't live in fear from day to day that at any moment I can be taken away from him.

What I'm doing about it: I'm narrowing my "options." I can't stay with Charlie for the above reasons and I can't stay with Anita because he would know and because they might think I was trying to come between them if they have plans, and I can't stay on Dr. Fogel's land because of the people who come there and because I might become ill, and I can't stay with Dr. Fogel because I don't know where he is. I have $13 left and some change but I can't go to a YMHA because they might demand identification even if they believe the age I give them.

A question: How normal do I really want to be?

*

Danny looked up and saw, through the window, a tall boy in a green silk shirt and black silk pants striding along, no

233

more than five feet away. The boy wore a wide-brimmed white hat, had a silver toothpick in his mouth, and was surrounded by a circle of Puerto Rican teenagers, who kept pace with him. Around the boy's neck, on a heavy chain, was an enormous silver Star of David, with what looked like a diamond in its center. Danny exhaled in awe and looked into the boy's face: it was Larry Silverberg!

He saw Larry look toward the cafeteria—right at him— but he didn't know if Larry could see more than his own reflection. Danny found himself rising from his chair and waving at Larry to come in, but Larry was already gone.

Should he follow him? Danny sat and tried to know what the right thing to do was. He didn't trust his feelings. His head filled with questions. Why was Larry wearing a Jewish star? Had he changed? How had he been released from jail so soon? Where was he living? Danny wondered, for an instant, if Larry had in some way been sent to lead him to safety, but as soon as he thought such a thought, he laughed to himself: why would God bother to joke with him in such a way?

He saw himself inviting Larry to sit at the table with him in the cafeteria, and he heard them talking to each other. Larry would slap Danny's back and say something like "Fancy meeting you here!" and Danny would tell him how good he looked.

"So tell me, Danny," he heard Larry say, fingering his Jewish star and sighing, "how've you been?"

"Not bad," Danny would reply. "And yourself?"

"Can't complain," Larry would say.

Danny saw Larry inviting him home, so that they could live together. He heard them reminiscing about the Home, and he heard Larry praising him for having run away.

*

Just a moment ago, while I was wondering where I would spend the night, LARRY SILVERBERG walked by right outside the window, almost close enough for me to

234

reach out and touch him and I wondered for an instant if he had been sent as my Deliverance!

I saw so many things at the same time!

I saw us talking about old times at the Home like Charlie and Murray and Irving, and I heard Larry asking me if I remembered the time they let a boy stay with us for a few days before they realized he was in the wrong place and should have been sent to a different place, with other Mongolian children. The boy was Jewish. Samstag was his name but I remembered his nose was so pushed in like an Irishman's that we called him O'Hara.

This is what I heard Larry say to me: I wouldn't want to be like that. If I had a kid born like that I'd flush him down the toilet first thing and tell them they couldn't do nothing to me without the evidence. You see people walking in the streets sometimes with idiot kids who are 50 years old and what good does it do for anybody?

What surprised me: He wore an enormous Jewish star on his chest with a sparkling diamond in its center. He said that O'Hara had bad blood and tried to kill Heshy with a pair of pliers by pulling his teeth from his head but that he caught him and beat him up. I told him I never heard the whole story.

I imagined us living together and me helping him in his work. This is what I made up that he does: He sells welfare documents and social security cards. He caters to a Puerto Rican trade and he told me he could get passports and draft cards and driver's licenses and he said he would get me a new birth certificate in the name of Charles Fogelstein but I said I wanted my real birth certificate in the name of Daniel Ginsberg, so I can know when my Bar Mitzvah is.

He said he couldn't get real birth certificates.

I was too confused when he passed by in front of me to do anything except stand and wave at him when he was almost gone from sight. But he didn't see me, or if he saw me he didn't recognize me from the Home. He wore a white hat like a cowboy.

I feel very relieved that I didn't see him because if I went to live with him, what would my life turn out to be like? Also: Why did he wear the Jewish Star? What happened to him after he left the Home and was in jail? Was he the only Jew there? Did they do to him what he did to others, or worse things?

This is what worries me about the way my mind works sometimes: that I can see myself living with him and becoming his slave! He would make love to me the way he did to the boys at the Home and I would be too weak to stop him and too grateful to run away!

This is what he would say to me: Let's face it, Danny, who ever gave a shit about us, right? So if we don't give a shit about each other where will we end up?

This would be my answer: Dead!

Can I put living with another orphan I knew from the Home on my list of solutions that won't work even though I didn't think of it before, and then cross it off my list the way Charlie does?

If Larry did see me but didn't show it because of the boys who walked in a circle around him, will he come back later to find me? What will he want of me? If he comes back later to try to find me, how will I refuse him without being able to tell him where I'm living and what I'm doing?

*

Danny glanced up and found himself looking into the eyes of a policeman, two tables away. Even though the policeman was sitting down, Danny could tell at once that he was the same height as Charlie. The policeman wore his blue winter coat, open, and his hat. A slender pink scar that ran diagonally from the man's lip to his chin was moist and seemed to shimmer. Danny felt his own right hand move, wanting to touch the delicate line. The policeman glanced at an old man who was snoring, and he winked at Danny. Danny nodded, smiled, and told himself to move slowly so as not to arouse suspicion.

Being in a Jewish cafeteria and wearing a *yamulka* helped him, he knew. With all the Negroes and Puerto Ricans and winos in the neighborhood, why would the policeman be interested in him? Danny tried to look at the policeman in a

236

way that would make him feel nothing. The policeman was eating a sandwich and drinking from a cup of coffee. Danny did not want to have to answer any questions. He closed his notebook and watched the policeman bite a chunk from a pickle.

So that he would appear not to be panicking, or fleeing, Danny opened his notebook again.

*

A policeman is looking at me now from another table and I'm writing so he'll think I'm doing some kind of homework or special studying. None of the old men talk to him. He's Charlie's age and size but his eyes are bloodshot and they look like Larry Silverberg's eyes will look like in 20 years.

Larry Silverberg wants to go to Israel and be a machine gunner in the Israeli Air Force so he can fly low in planes and see the faces on Arabs when he strafes them.

Was the diamond real and if he said it was would he let me bring it to Mr. Plaut to check? If we sold it how long could we live on the money?

Rabbi Akiba said that suffering is good for it can lead to repentance and repentance can lead to God.

Value equals the present worth of future benefits.

To memorize: the Song of Solomon. One passage I remember: "His locks are curled and black as a raven."

What Dr. Fogel would believe: That when it said God chose the people of Israel it meant He chose us for Suffering, if we must suffer to serve him.

What Danny Ginsberg believes: That doesn't make it easier to believe in God and in being a member of His Chosen People when you think of the 6 million who died the way they did!

What this makes me think: How small my own suffering is.

What Charlie would say if I said that: Everything helps, if you want to let it.

I want to come to him and say to him: Now I'm a man! Was he ever Bar Mitzvahed? He never said. Could he memorize enough Hebrew when he was 13, and did he do the Haftorah or just the blessings before the Haftorah, or nothing?

What I just realized: In the Epilogue that Daniel Ginsberg wrote on his last full day on Dr. Fogel's land, he left out what happened to Sol!

The answer is he died and nobody knew who he was or who to telephone. He had no family and no permanent address and no money and nothing in his wallet said he was Jewish so they buried him in a public grave in a small town in Ohio where no Jews live and none of his boys ever learned of his death.

Did I imagine that or did Charlie?

The policeman is eating a piece of noodle pudding now. I'm looking at him and thinking that if I had to I would say something to him like this: "I like the pieces with raisins in them best, don't you? I like any kind of pudding if it has lots of soft raisins in it."

I would be telling the truth if I said that and that way he would not see things in my eyes that I'm hiding.

*

Danny dipped his fingertips in his glass of water and said his prayers silently, his lips moving so that the policeman would see what he was doing. Then he stood, picked up his sack, and walked from the cafeteria. The policeman did not seem to pay attention.

When Danny arrived at the synagogue he was surprised, for a moment, to see teenage boys playing basketball in its schoolyard. They wore *yamulkas* that were pinned to their hair with bobby pins and he could see the fringes of their *tsitsis* flapping from under their shirts.

He felt better. Beyond the players, where there was an indentation in the building, he saw two couples, back to back, necking. Both girls had their hands in the boys' hair, below their *yamulkas*. Danny smiled. A small boy, smaller

238

than Danny, sat under the basket next to the fence, a cigarette dangling from the center of his mouth. He waved slightly to Danny, with two fingers, as if he knew him.

It seemed impossible to Danny—miraculous—that all these boys, boys who had never tasted pork or lobster or bacon in their lives, boys who had never eaten milk with meat, boys who had never worked or traveled by car or written or telephoned on the Sabbath, boys who prayed three times a day and recited blessings each time they ate or washed or went to the bathroom—that all of them should look like normal American boys. It made him see how much of a dreamworld he had, until now, been living in—how foolishly, in his imagination, his life had been led. It was as if, he thought to himself, everything that had happened to him until his return to Brooklyn had been the dream, and his real life were about to begin.

He walked toward the boy who had waved to him and stopped when he was standing above him. He slipped his fingers through the wires of the fence.

"Shalom," Danny said.

The boy rolled his eyes.

"My name is Danny."

"I got nexts," the boy said, without looking at him.

"It's all right," Danny said. "I mean, I don't really know how to play. . . ."

The boy said nothing. Danny watched a player drive for the basket, grunt, stop suddenly, and leap high in the air banking a shot off the metal backboard. "Match that shit!" the player yelled to the boy who had been guarding him. He fixed his *yamulka* with his right hand, to keep it from falling. "You match that and I'll eat crud."

Danny laughed, but the boy below him only sucked in on his cigarette. "I'm Jewish," Danny said.

"Big fucking deal," the boy said, and got up and walked away, toward the two couples who were necking. He tapped one of the boys on the shoulder and the boy let go of the girl and stepped aside. The boy Danny had been speaking to, six inches shorter than the girl, flipped his cigarette to the side, put his arms around the girl's waist, and she bent down and pressed her lips against his.

Danny entered the synagogue. The lobby was dark and odorless. The sanctuary was empty and Danny stood at the back, imagining himself on the *bimah* chanting his *Haftorah*. He had never actually prayed in a real synagogue, with other Jewish men. The sanctuary was dark, with blackened wood benches, a set of wine-red velvet drapes covering the Holy Ark, and small stained-glass windows set into the walls at the sides, near the ceiling. Directly above Danny's head there was a balcony, with a curtain in front of the first row, and Danny assumed that the women sat there, so that the men would not see them while they prayed.

Danny walked along dark corridors, looking for the rabbi's study. He saw a lighted room in front of him, with one woman sitting in it. His decision was made.

"I'd like to see the rabbi," he said.

The woman looked up from her typing. "I'm sorry, darling, but he's at a funeral—is there something I can do for you?"

Danny tried again: "Can I wait for him? Can I see him later today?"

The woman rolled the page up in her typewriter, erased something, then looked at Danny again. "You're not from our Yeshiva, are you? I don't recognize you."

"No," Danny said. He spoke quickly. "I'm not from your Yeshiva, but I'm Jewish—I'm Jewish and I want to be Bar Mitzvahed."

"Well, that's very nice, dear, but you should be Bar Mitzvahed in your own *shul*."

"I don't have a *shul*," Danny said. "I'm an orphan."

The woman sighed, as if she had been through the experience a thousand times before. "I really don't see what we can do for you, then." She brushed her erasures from the page. "You know, we get many parents with children like yourself who are unaffiliated with any synagogue and who reach Bar Mitzvah age and suddenly discover they're

Jewish. But what do you expect us to do? We're not your local supermarket, you know, that you come to us when you need something and forget about us when you don't. Believe me, darling, being Jewish should be a full-time occupation."

She began typing again.

"I want to see the rabbi," Danny said. "Please give me an appointment."

"Well. Today he's at a funeral, tomorrow he has a meeting in the city, and then it's *Shabbos,* isn't it?" She glanced at a desk calendar. "I really don't see when—but why am I even looking?" She glared at Danny and suddenly he saw Mrs. Mittleman's face. He closed his eyes to make the image go away. "I'm really very busy, and I'm sorry, but I believe I've given you enough time. . . ."

"But you're not *listening* to me," Danny said. "I told you I don't have parents. I'm an orphan. The Torah says . . ." He felt dizzy from the heat inside the building, and he found that he could not look into the woman's eyes. "I just remembered something . . ." he began.

"You seem like such a nice boy. I'd like to help you, believe me, but my hands are tied, don't you see?"

He looked at her hands and saw bright red nailpolish. "I just remembered why it is I came to your *shul* and not another."

"Yes?"

"I know Dr. Fogel. He taught me my *Haftorah* and *Maftir* at the Maimonides Home for Jewish Boys. But they closed the Home."

The woman smiled. "Oh yes," she said. "Who didn't know Dr. Fogel? We're all so sorry he moved away. Such a happy man!" Her smile vanished. "I've listened to everything you said."

"Then you'll let me see the rabbi?"

She took his hand in hers. "Don't you think I'd like to help you if I could? But what you're asking I don't have to give. We're booked up solid for almost two years ahead with Bar Mitzvahs, and we're still growing." She sighed.

"When I first came here we didn't even have a Yeshiva, and now we have over four hundred students in the elementary school alone. Don't you think that's wonderful?"

"I want to see the rabbi."

"But how would we fit you in, darling? Can we ask one of our regular members to have his son share his Bar Mitzvah with a stranger—?"

Danny thought of the passages he knew, from the Torah, about honoring the stranger and caring for the widowed and orphaned, but he saw no point in sharing them with her. He thought his head was clear. He was eliminating another option. He spoke firmly: "I'm asking you for the last time and giving you your last chance—will you please let me see the rabbi?"

She pushed her chair back and reached for the telephone. "You're doing what, young man?"

"The sin will be on your hands then," he said, and, to his delight, he saw her look at her hands. He turned and walked away.

"Wait!" she called, and he stopped, saw that she had picked up the telephone receiver and had begun dialing. Her face was pale. "I'll telephone the rabbi for you," she said. Danny smiled—she didn't fool him. He kept walking. She called after him: "What did you say your name was, darling? Just give me your name—!"

Danny turned and gave her his best smile. "Adolf Hitler!" he cried, and then he ran down the hall and out of the building, as fast as he could, his sack swinging at his side.

*

LATER

I'm sitting on the floor of the dormitory right where my own bed used to be, writing by candlelight. I stopped in a store and bought candles and Kosher baloney, potato chips, and a sour pickle for supper. I'm wearing my extra shirt and underwear for warmth in case it gets very cold.

What surprised me: how easily I climbed the wall where Larry and the others used to do it!

While I was walking around the empty building before I could hear Larry Silverberg talking to me about the 2 of us living in Israel together when I would be a doctor there (he remembered that) and about the things we would do together to girls from the Israeli Army. He said they didn't care who they slept around with. Things are very loose in Israel.

This is the thought that came to me then: I CAN ASK CHARLIE TO SELL ALL HIS BELONGINGS AND TAKE ME TO ISRAEL WITH HIM!

What ties does he have, to land or family, that have to keep him here?

This afternoon I went to Dr. Fogel's Shul to see the Rabbi and ask him to let me be Bar Mitzvahed but he wasn't there and his secretary told me what I think I knew before I went: that it was hopeless.

She was scared of me, from what I said to her. I wish Charlie could have seen her face when she refused me and wanted my name so she could give it to the police and I told her it was Adolf Hitler. She'll never be able to explain me to herself.

Why I had no choice: If I want to become Bar Mitzvahed I have to go to a synagogue and tell a Rabbi. If I want to see a Rabbi I have to see his secretary and speak to her if she's there when I arrive. If she asks me why I want to see the Rabbi I have to tell her or she'll become suspicious. If I state my case and she refuses me the way she did today then I can never return to the same synagogue again because they might be ready for me the 2nd time.

I'll try another synagogue tomorrow and if they won't have me, I'll know for certain that that option is gone also, and that means I'll have to do what I didn't want to do: Ask Charlie to help me become Bar Mitzvahed.

But he'll have to account for me also, to whatever synagogue he goes to, which shows why I should come to him with my situation all planned out.

If I couldn't have come here, where could I have gone?

This is what my mind has been thinking: that when all my options are gone, only my true choice will be left and the way will be clear!

Do I really believe that?

The answer is that I believe it when I write it but not when I'm doing things like eating in a cafeteria or talking to the secretary.

A story I thought of writing: about Charlie when he was a boy, before he came to the Home and was living with his grandmother. She didn't speak English. He didn't understand her when she talked to him in Yiddish. Is this why he couldn't learn to read? I saw her with a red scarf on her head and no teeth. Remember to ask him if what I imagined was so. Did he lie to me about his mother the way I lied to him about mine?

If I can't become his son, can I become his brother?

Could he do that more easily by law than making me his son?

If I become his brother and he marries Anita, then I become an uncle to Hannah! Would she love me more or less in that situation?

The answer: Let's find out!

A conclusion: If I have no identity and no money and no food and no clothes I'll still have my imagination. I could invent stories and live in them, the way I did with Dr. Fogel's father, and with Ephraim and the Epilogue.

But the truth is this too: that would just be playing with words!

This is what I really believe: that if I concentrate and think hard enough I can always find a choice and a solution I didn't think of before.

That's how I have 2 more new options: 1. becoming Charlie's brother instead of his son. 2. emigrating to Israel with him.

What I hear Charlie saying: Stop imagining me! I'm still here!

Sometimes I forget exactly what he looks like. I saw the dark square on the wall downstairs where the picture of him I liked most used to be. Is it more terrible to live through an experience or to imagine living through it?

How easy and short my 5 years of life in the Home now seem!

If I can't figure out the solution to my life maybe others can.

Guess what? The instant I wrote down that sentence they all started to talk inside my head, sitting around the cabin and searching for solutions. I'll know what each of them said when I write their words down. That way I can discover the truth at the same moment each of them does!

Here he is again, folks, your favorite storyteller, bringing you a new story about your favorite Jewish orphan:

> THE FINAL SOLUTION
>
> A Most Surprising Sequel by
>
> ✡ Daniel Ginsberg ✡

When last we encountered our young hero he had become reunited for a brief and wonderful afternoon with his dear friend from childhood, Ephraim Mendelsohn, who was himself the son of an orphan who had, a generation earlier, been raised in the very same Home for Jewish orphans as our hero Daniel Ginsberg!

But now let us journey back in time, dear reader, to an afternoon many years earlier, and to a day which Daniel Ginsberg often reflected upon, for when he considered the course of his brief life and the man he had become, he knew that the afternoon we are about to describe for you was the turning point of his existence!

If he did not hear what he heard on that afternoon and decided what he decided he might never have become the man he is, and millions of children would have been without the opportunity of reading those magical works of science fiction which he now writes under the name of Charles Fogelstein.

Knowing his true identity, we, of course, can see where the hero and heroine of so many of his tales come from—those homeless wanderers, Abra-X and Sara-Y, who, in order to save the planet Earth, dare to enter the unknown anti-universe through a black hole of space. But the ways in which they use their Imagination and Knowledge to transform those they meet, both the good and the evil, the beautiful and the horrifying, the remembered and the unexpected—especially the unexpected!—are doubtless well known to many of you, and we leave it to your discretion to interpret his tales in the light of what we are about to tell you about his life.

For there was a time when, like the hero and heroine of his tales, he too had lost his way in life, despite his numerous talents and his awesome ingenuity. There was a time when, forced to run away from the Home in which he had been raised as a Jewish Orphan, he became confused and distressed. To whom did he belong? When and where had he really been born? What would become of him if he became a ward of the state?

These were the questions which vexed him, and which moved him to set forth from the city for a sojourn in the country, during which sojourn, as you have already seen, he chanced to discover the curious document written by the father of one of Daniel's most influential teachers, Dr. Fogel.

What immediate effect did reading this document have on our young man, lost and confused as he was?

This is the answer: He imagined Epilogues to his own life, one of which you have already had the pleasure of reading. And he imagined himself at the end of his own life, and an old man living alone in the woods and looking back over a life wasted. Even his precious Torah and study no longer satisfied him! For what had he done with his life? He recited his favorite saying from PIRKAY AVOS to himself: WHO IS THE RIGHTEOUS MAN? HE WHO DOETH RIGHTEOUS DEEDS!

He saw himself writing in a notebook just as he did when a boy, and he saw that all his thoughts and study had merely been the exercise of his own vanity!

Vanity of vanities, he chanted to himself, during his last days on earth. All is vanity and a torture under the sun, and my vanity was to have believed in the reality of my own mind!

When I am gone, he said to himself, who will ever know that my mind existed and contained what I believe it contained?

Truly, he concluded, thinking back over a lifetime of thoughts, when I contemplated my own words I was like the worm in horseradish who thinks the horseradish sweet!

Where oh where, he asked, are the other lives I have not led?

Being a good Jew, and not believing in any real afterlife, he realized how futile his lonely existence had been, and even as he scoured the pages of his mind for sayings from the Rabbis, his heart was breaking in 2.

Like Jerusalem, he confessed at last, he too was lost because he had adhered too strictly to the law.

Thus, kind reader, would your young hero muse, considering his future life. Oh how unhappy he was as he walked back to his cabin from his favorite pond, for he saw how few choices in life truly lay open to him!

For if there was 1 thing that was certain about our young hero, it was that HE LOVED LIFE! Despite his harsh upbringing and the plight he found himself in, despite the sufferings he had undergone (which he knew were as nothing compared to the sufferings of others, especially of Jews throughout History!) our hero continued to love life! He wanted to live! He wanted to have those things he desired only so that new desires would take the place of the old! He wanted to explore as many of those possible lives which he had previously imagined for himself as life would allow him to! Though he had been living a strange life, apart from the ordinary world of normal boys, yet still he hungered to bring private joy and hope into the lives of others, more and less fortunate than he in these very early years had been.

Did his strength lie in his imagination or in his foolishness?

But listen now to what happened: He was thinking thoughts such as these and approaching his cabin when he heard the unmistakable sound of voices. At first, like a small animal suddenly face to face with a hunter, he was startled and afraid. But then he recognized the tones of some of the voices and his heart grew warm. He walked on silent padded toes to the cabin wall and pressed his ear against the winter wood.

Inside, he soon discovered, those people whom he had

loved most in life until this moment were gathered in a circle and were discussing him, wondering what had become of him, and debating what to do with him, should they find him.

He crawled under the cabin, so as not to be caught should one of them have gone to the door or window, and he listened to them through the floor.

DR. FOGEL, his former teacher in the Orphanage from which he had come, said that he could find a position for him in a Yeshiva. In exchange for cleaning rooms and making beds and such tasks, Daniel would receive a full scholarship. Dr. Fogel believed that the boy had the brains and inclination to become a great Talmudic scholar.

UNCLE SOL, an old man who had been a benefactor to the Home and the lifelong enemy of Dr. Fogel due to a conflict about how Jewish the Home should be, which fascinating story we shall tell to you presently, disagreed violently. Uncle Sol did not see why the boy, as he referred to him, should receive such special treatment. He believed that young Daniel should 1st return to the Home from which he had run away, a Home which had produced over the years some of the most distinguished doctors and lawyers and businessmen in America. Uncle Sol believed that the boy needed to be forced to face reality, however harsh it was.

MR. MITTLEMAN, a highly successful realtor in whose home Daniel had lived for a brief time, then spoke. He said they should do nothing until they were forced to. "In what way are we responsible for him?" he asked.

Dr. Fogel retorted in Hebrew, reciting the Rabbinical saying כל ישראל ערבים זה בזה, which meant: "All Israel is responsible for one another."

Then Uncle Sol said, "If you believe that, why don't you believe in the state of Israel?"

Dr. Fogel replied that the state of Israel was material and would pass away. What lived on was God's word and commandments!

IRVING, a Professor and a former orphan in the Home with which all these individuals were associated, agreed with Dr. Fogel. He said that he and his wife had been to Israel on a tour and had found it to be terribly

248

vulgar and materialistic. "All people care about there is clothes, property, and money," he said. "They're worse than Americans."

"God bless the state of Israel!" replied Uncle Sol, and he spoke about the Second World War and of how the nations of the world, before and after, refused to allow Jews to come upon their shores. If the Jews had a Homeland before 1940 and did not have to rely on others, millions of them would have been spared the gas chamber! He challenged Dr. Fogel to prove why it was a good thing that, homeless, the Jews should be forced to wander and be massacred forever. Didn't God command His children to love life? "Never again!" he proclaimed.

Then, before Dr. Fogel could reply, Daniel heard the voice he had been hoping to hear, that of his dear friend, CHARLES SAPISTEIN, himself a former orphan from the Home and a man who was different from all other men in ways which they did not perceive. "Why don't you just let the kid live with me?" he asked, simply.

There was a silence for several seconds, during which Daniel heard the sounds of chairs moving, and of his own excited heartbeat.

When the other men did not answer him, Charles spoke again. "Come on," he said. "Talk to me. It's my life, isn't it? It was given to me to do with what I want, right? So why can't I let him stay with me?"

"Oh Charlie," came the sound of a female voice, that of Ephraim's mother, ANITA MENDELSOHN, who was then, just recently widowed, an attractive young mother whom Daniel suspected of wanting to marry Charles. "You're such a sucker, aren't you, Charlie?" she asked.

Then Charles laughed. "Me? Why should you think that? You don't understand anything. I've lived with the boy already and do you know what? I like having him with me. You think I'm doing it just to be noble and to pay back some invisible thing for what was done for me once upon a time by the Home and Uncle Sol and everybody, but it's not that at all!"

"What is it then?" Anita questioned.

"You have to be willing to take chances," Charles retorted. "To step into people's lives if you have to!"

249

"I don't see why," said Anita.

Daniel's heart fell when he heard what it was that Charles next said: "What would you propose then?" Charles asked.

Daniel felt true despair! "Why don't we pool our money—you certainly have enough—and send him to Israel, since he loves Jewish things so much," said Anita Mendelsohn. "On the Kibbutzim lots of children grow up without real mothers and fathers. He'd be quite happy there. I've looked into the matter."

"But that's the easy way out for all of us," he heard Charles say. "Don't you see that?"

Daniel had to fight to hold himself back, to keep from crawling out from under the building and bursting into the room, but even as he heard them argue with Charles he sensed that the solution was in sight. "Where there's a will there's a way, right?" he heard Charles say to them, and he sensed how important this was for the completion of Charles's own most strange and interesting life. He believed that his friends above him were becoming angry, for he heard the sounds of much scraping, and then the slow steady sound of something quite heavy, like iron beating steadily against wood, which he at first believed

*

Danny stopped writing and listened; the sound he had been writing about in his story was coming up the metal staircase to the dormitory. *No!* he cried to himself. *Not yet! I'm not ready!*

He pressed his fingers against the inside corners of his eyes, to make his dizziness go away. Then he blew out the candles, stuffed his notebook into his sack, and rose from the floor. The sound was louder. He stood rigid in the middle of the room, his fists clenched, his body trembling. He was so angry he didn't know what to do. Why was somebody coming *now?*

He heard steps clicking along the hallway, toward him. For the briefest instant his anger flowed down and out of him and his heart suddenly flared; he saw the door open, with Charlie standing there, his arms spread wide for him to run to. . . .

His imagination did not fool him. He picked up his sack and moved quickly across the floor, opened the door at the end that led to the game room, ran through the empty chamber and then down the stairs at the far end of the wing. The footsteps followed him.

Outside, in the moonlight, the courtyard was white. Danny stood in a doorway. The snow had stopped falling and had not stuck to the ground. He felt cold. He thought of Larry's hideout, but remembered that they had never given him a key.

"Stop where you are."

Danny turned but saw no one.

"This is a policeman talking to you. In the name of the law I'm ordering you to stop where you are, drop what you have, and put your hands over your head."

Danny smiled and ducked back inside the building, running as fast as he could, feeling a strength in his legs he had never suspected was there. He pushed through swinging doors and ran down the corridor in which the photos and trophies had been, and he felt as if he were in one of his own dreams, when, running fast, he would suddenly find himself taking off and flying above the heads of the other boys from the Home.

He plunged down a staircase, into the kitchen. The stoves and sinks were already gone. He passed through the kitchen to the laundry room, and from the laundry room into the boiler room. He heard steps, slow and steady, walking from the kitchen into the laundry room, and he couldn't understand how the policeman, without even running, was staying so close behind him.

A beam of light shone in under the door. "I'm giving you your last chance. Come out now with your hands up. This is a warning."

Danny burst through the door and up the stairs. *The shul!* If he could make it there, even though he himself might not be saved, his notebooks would. He could leave them in the *Genizah,* wrapped in a *talis.* Even if the building were torn down, Danny knew, the Federation would never allow holy books to be destroyed, not only because it would be a sin, but because the old books were probably worth money and could be sold to some Yeshiva or library.

Going up, he took the stairs two at a time, thrilled by his anger and the ability it gave him to move so swiftly in the dark. The courtyard was beautiful and peaceful in the moonlight, but he knew that he hated it. He hated the courtyard and the buildings and the Home and his years in it and the people he'd lived with, and he wished only—to make the experience complete—to see his face in a mirror, to see what he looked like when he was smiling with hatred.

He walked to the *shul,* down the steps, and entered. The room, without chairs or the table in front, seemed larger than he had remembered it. The ark, built into the east wall, had been stripped of its worn velvet curtain. Across the courtyard a door closed, but Danny did not hear footsteps.

The *Genizah* was locked. Did Dr. Fogel still have the key? Did he have Danny's receipt? Danny saw that he might be able to use the *tephillin* and receipt someday as evidence, if necessary, to prove he had existed and had been a boy in the Home.

A shaft of moonlight shone through the door. Danny smiled, remembering the shaft of light that had led to Dr. Fogel's father's letter, and as he stared at the fluttering motes of dust he saw that the light was shining on a small scrap of paper, no larger than the palm of his own hand. It lay folded, in a sitting position, half on the floor, half against a side wall.

Danny picked it up and before he had read the words he recognized the handwriting—it was a piece from one of Charlie's lists! Then Charlie *had* come for him! He read: "check Fed of JP again/ buy T notes/ Call Zond/Lil/Fgl/ Gtlmn/cityman/ buy sh crm blds/ 25 G for DG/ oil chang cr/ mk new list."

Danny slipped the piece of paper into his pocket and

climbed up and into the ark, sliding the doors closed behind him but leaving a slight opening so he could peer out. He felt calm. The inside of the ark was smaller than he had expected it to be, and in it he could neither stand nor sit. His nose itched.

A few seconds later he saw the policeman standing in the doorway, silhouetted by moonlight, and without seeing his face, Danny knew it was the same man he had seen in the cafeteria.

He saw the long silver cylinder of the policeman's gun barrel, raised in the air. He thought he smelled parchment. A tiny spider crawled across his left shoe and out the crack between the doors. The policeman yawned, stretched, and sat down in the doorway, facing the courtyard. Below ground level, he would not have been seen by anyone in front of him.

"I can wait as long as you can," the policeman said. "I can wait forever. Your best chance is to come forward now."

Danny let his body dip backward slowly, so that the right side of his head rested against the back wall of the ark. He was amazed at how easy it was becoming, second by second, for him to stay still in such an awkward position—his neck crooked to one side, his knees slightly bent, one foot directly in front of the other, his back hunched over, the knuckles of his left hand pressed between his left cheek and the door.

The spider's underside passed in front of him, going from one door to the other, then back again. He remembered when Charlie had told him about how in this room, as a boy, and before anyone had known of his reading problem, Dr. Fogel had picked him up in his arms every Saturday morning when the Torah was taken from the ark so that Charlie could kiss it with his lips. We kiss the Torah and we dance with it and we decorate it with beautiful velvet covers embroidered with gold and silver thread, Danny thought. We hang silver jewelry on it and put silver crowns and bells upon it and we kiss the fringes of our *talises* where they have touched its words.

Why?

Danny's left eye bulged, looking through the crack. He saw silk lines glistening—the spider was actually spinning a web across the opening and Danny could hardly believe it. He stared, hypnotized, as the insect trailed a moonlit thread back and forth, and he tried to imagine the pattern of that part of the web which he could not see. He smiled and felt his cheek rub wood.

The policeman approached the ark and stood directly in front of it, watching the spider. Danny held his breath and could not, in the shadows, see the policeman's eyes.

He tried to imagine endings to his life. He saw Charlie finding him, asleep in the ark, and carrying him across the courtyard in his arms, out the gate, and into his car. On the way to the hospital, Charlie driving recklessly and turning toward the rear to curse at Danny for having played the fool, the car swerved and crashed. Charlie was dead.

If the policeman went out and locked the door to the *shul*, what would Danny do then?

The policeman had his gun raised above his shoulder, the barrel in his right fist. Danny closed his eyes and, as the gun butt came crashing down against the ark, just below Danny's nose, he held his breath.

"Got 'im."

Danny's mouth was open but he was not screaming because he knew that if he did the policeman might fire at him. He was pleased with his ability to control his body and his mind—to stay awake without moving and to continue to see epilogues in his head, even with his eyes open.

He saw Charlie and Dr. Fogel and Mr. Mittleman and Mrs. Mittleman and Sol and Ephraim and Hannah and Larry and Anita and Mr. Gitelman walking away from the cabin and getting into cars. Their faces were drawn. He followed them along highways and over bridges until they came to the hospital and walked up the stairs and stood around Danny's bed, to see how well his bullet wound was healing. The policeman was there also, his hat in his hand, telling Danny that he had only been doing his job. He said he admired the Jews because they had finally learned to fight back.

The policeman and Sol talked about great Jewish boxers they'd seen—Benny Leonard and Barney Ross and Abe Attel and Gus Lesnevich and Jackie "Kid" Berg, and Danny watched them go out through the hospital door with Sol's arm around the policeman's shoulder.

"If you come forward now I won't hurt you," the policeman called. "After this I shoot first and ask questions second. I got a wife and five kids. You got three minutes."

To keep himself awake Danny thought of the evil great men from the Bible had committed. Moses had murdered an Egyptian overseer and David had had Bathsheba's husband killed and Saul had tried to have David killed and Cain had killed Abel and Abraham had been willing to kill Isaac and had sent Ishmael into the desert and Joseph's brothers had sold him into slavery and Esau had been robbed of his birthright by Jacob and Noah had slept with his daughters. . . .

He heard a clicking sound and knew it was the gun. He believed the man, about waiting, and about shooting. If the man killed him, he wondered how anyone would ever know it had happened, or who he was. If the policeman examined his notebooks and discovered the truth—if he knew what to believe and what not to believe—he would realize the complications, and the publicity that would come for having shot a defenseless child who was also an orphan and a Jew.

Danny saw that he had no choice left, but he didn't understand why this was so. Where had he gone wrong? What had he done to cause the policeman to follow him? And did what he was about to do mean that he should never have run away from the Home in the first place?

He couldn't believe that. For what, he asked, would his life have become had he stayed there and never known Charlie?

He breathed in, as lightly as possible, through his nose, and decided to stop trying to imagine any life other than the one he had lived. He didn't question the choices he had made, or even the mistakes, for they still didn't seem to him, despite where he was now, to have been wrong choices.

He was not responsible for the policeman, he concluded, just as he was not responsible for being an orphan. The thought pleased him, but at the same time he saw that he was liable, at any instant, to move or to make noise or to fall asleep, and that if he did . . .

"All right," he said, sliding open the doors to the ark. "I'll come peacefully, Officer. I have no choice. Please don't shoot. I'm only a boy. My name is . . ."

Nine

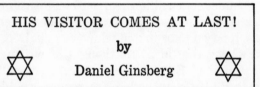

This is today's true story.

> HIS VISITOR COMES AT LAST!
>
> by
>
> Daniel Ginsberg

Charlie came to visit Danny today but Danny never said anything out loud to him, even when Charlie spoke about them being together again after they send Danny back to Brooklyn. Danny gets more things he wants from being quiet than from talking. He wrote a note to the Director when he first came here and told him about what they were going to do to the Home one day in changing it into a halfway house for Jewish mental patients and other Jewish boys with Special Problems and the Director thinks that maybe it can be arranged and that's what Danny wrote out in a note today to Charlie. That way he can be safe here until they renovate the Home and then he can go there again.

Danny wrote down for Charlie that he's the only Jew in the place and that they won't give him Kosher food. He told Charlie that a man has to stay with him in the mornings when he puts his Tephillin on because of the straps. They won't force Danny to eat meat unless he starts los-

257

ing weight or his blood tests show he's ill. Charlie said he'd speak to somebody from the Federation about speaking to somebody from the state about having frozen food sent in for Danny the way they do for Jews on airplanes!

A question for whoever is reading this: If you were a Jew on a plane and Arab hijackers asked all Jews to stand up, what would you do?

Charlie and Danny would stay in their seats!

Under the Romans Rabbi Akiba said a Jew can forsake some rituals if his survival is at stake. But he can never forsake the study of Torah!

Also: The Rabbis say that God saved the Children of Israel from Egypt because EVEN UNDER SLAVERY THEY KEPT THEIR HEBREW NAMES.

What Danny was imagining when Charlie was with him: that they were 2 Rabbis reciting things they memorized to each other and that when it was time for Charlie to leave the aides listened to them debating each other very Talmudically and nobody could remember which one of them was supposed to be in and which one out!

Danny loves that idea! He thought of writing it down for his dear friend Ephraim as a story to be called THE TWO MAD RABBIS in which the reader would have to guess which one really was and which one wasn't, but he decided Charlie would think it was too strange if Charlie was able to read any of it.

This is why Danny lets them read his notebooks now even though he hardly ever writes in them anymore, except to make lists or to put down the unimportant thoughts he has: because if he didn't let them they would anyway! They read to him out loud from his notebooks and say things like "That's very interesting" and then they wait and expect him to say something back, but he says Nothing.

They can never know what parts of his notebooks he wrote before the events occurred and what parts he wrote after and what parts he made up because he writes this down every time:

DANNY THE ORPHAN SAYS,
"ALL ORPHANS ARE LIARS."

A spider spins a web for 1 of 2 reasons: to trap other insects for food, or to lure his mate!

Danny never told Charlie about his plan to ask Charlie to take them both to Israel, but he believes that's still 1 option that's left, as long as Israel still exists.

What Danny thinks when he considers that sentence: But Israel won't exist for the Jews forever! The Torah will. (Dr. Fogel was right all the time!)

Danny is quite content where he lives now, having all the time he wants. He's in a place with boys nobody knows what to do with yet. Everything is temporary, even the buildings they're in and the people who work in them. They can all be transferred at any moment if the state says so. They call the boys "a mixed bag." People pass through the place where Danny lives going from 1 institution to another, or from 1 institution to the real world and vice versa.

Here are some places they go to and come from: foster homes, mental hospitals, reformatories, state orphanages, religious orphanages, courtrooms, halfway houses, religious organizations, welfare offices, real families, places for the retarded, places for the emotionally disturbed, places for the handicapped.

Danny's the oldest boy here! He's good at helping new boys when they 1st come in because they appreciate his silence. He doesn't show any reaction to the things they do and say and after a while they just seem to be attracted toward him. Most of the day most of the boys sleep and watch TV.

Danny didn't say anything to Charlie because he said to himself: As long as you're out there and I'm in here, what do we really have in common? You can always come here if you want but I can't go there. That's the difference!

While Charlie was talking an 11 year old boy named Michael took off all his clothes and went to the bathroom on the floor. Danny showed Charlie his friend Jimmy by glancing at Jimmy with his eyes. Jimmy is 7 years old and goes back and forth in front of the window all day long like an upside down pendulum.

They don't know where some of the boys here come

from or what their names are. Some boys who come in at one end of the ward and go out the other are normal boys and they stay less than a week and Danny knows he'll never see them again.

Danny thinks they'll keep him as long as he wants them to because most of their cases don't interest them the way he does, even if they read what he's writing down right now! The 1st thing Danny ever said when the policeman brought him to the station was "I DON'T EXIST" and he discovered that he can repeat that out loud or in writing and it always gets people interested in him.

He showed his notebook to Charlie, offering him the chance to read what he writes now, but Charlie wasn't interested. Charlie said he's been studying with Dr. Fogel but when Danny didn't ask him any questions Charlie didn't tell him what he was learning. Charlie said that he and Dr. Fogel and Sol and Anita and Mr. Mittleman all talked about Danny after he ran away and here's a list of their ideas:

1. SOL told Charlie to adopt Danny as a son until he was 21.

2. MR. MITTLEMAN offered to pay all costs to send Danny to Israel to live on a Kibbutz.

3. ANITA said Danny could live with her family and go to her school.

4. DR. FOGEL said Danny's fate should be left in his own hands.

But when Danny showed no reaction to their ideas Charlie laughed and tried to brush his hair with his hand but Danny pulled away. "Oh Danny, Danny," Charlie said. "What do you want from my life?"

And that was when Charlie informed him that if he got well after they send him back to Brooklyn, Charlie would be willing to let Danny live with him. He talked with people at the Federation of Jewish Philanthropies and they were going to work things out. Charlie said he wanted Danny to have his own room and that he thought Mr. and Mrs. Mittleman would let Charlie pay to have one built on to the house.

He also told Danny that Anita sent a Thank You for
the stopwatch. He said she was having a lot of fun with
it. He said she was getting very big and very beautiful
and was still in charge of the school and that he saw her
almost every night.

Danny showed nothing in his face to his old friend.
He didn't trust him and he didn't *not* trust him. That's
what life is teaching him!

Charlie said Anita wanted him to stay with her and
her family for a while so they could see how things would
work out and he asked Danny what he thought of that
idea, but Danny just stared back into Charlie's eyes. Charlie said he wasn't going to do it, but not because of Danny.
"There are lots of things you don't understand," Charlie
said. "As smart as you are."

Danny thought then of asking Charlie if he and his
old friends were going to have a memorial touch football
game in Brooklyn once a year for Murray but he didn't.

Charlie talked about the other people they shared in
common and this is what happened to all of them:

1. DR. FOGEL has gone to live with his older sister and
her husband in an Orthodox section of Far Rockaway. He
decided not to sell his land to Charlie.

2. SOL is living in a senior citizen city in California and
selling real estate. Charlie left Danny one of Sol's cards for
a joke and told him to put it in his storybook, and this is
what it was like:

PIONEER ESTATES
Pioneer City, California 94300
California's Finest Resort-Retirement Community
"Peripheral Privacy Guaranteed"

Condominiums	"Uncle" Sol Kantor
Homes	Licensed Real Estate Salesman
Rentals	(415) 586-3732

---

3. MR. MITTLEMAN had a stroke and is in the hospital.
The left side of his face and body is paralyzed and his brain

261

isn't what it used to be. When he comes home he'll never work again. Charlie and Charlie's accountant have searched through his files but they can't find books explaining his finances. Now they're working from other documents but Charlie says it's all a mess.

4. THE MAN FROM THE CITY is in jail and all that money is lost.

5. LILLIAN wants Charlie to send money for SANDY to go to college.

Charlie's eyes were clear and he looked better than he did when Danny saw him in the country, and this is what Danny saw: that Charlie thrives most when other people need him!

Who needs him now? Anita and her children. Lillian and Sandy. Mr. and Mrs. Mittleman. Sol and Dr. Fogel. And DANNY GINSBERG!

Danny listened to his friend talk about different things and he thought to himself, Even though Charlie had the life he had from the time he was brought to the Home, he's just a normal man. Charlie didn't seem very large to Danny and it was hard for Danny to remember how they used to talk to each other so much.

Danny missed his memories.

Danny pictured himself on the hill overlooking the school with Charlie down below yelling at the boys while they practiced and he saw himself waving good-bye to Charlie. But Charlie didn't look up and see him.

Danny wondered if Charlie was imagining what it would be like for them to meet in 20 or 30 or 40 years and what they would look like and if they would be old and stooped over. He felt that Charlie's being with him and talking and Danny's being with Charlie and not talking was like something he could have imagined before today ever took place!

Nothing surprises Danny anymore.

Charlie said a man told him they'll let Danny use the library next week but Danny didn't tell Charlie that he doesn't memorize sayings anymore. His head got too full of them and he needs to make room now because his next project is to memorize the entire Torah! He knows he can do it because what he's memorized up until now would be almost twice as long written out as the whole Torah is. There are less than 9,000 basic Hebrew words in the Torah altogether.

Why Danny's doing this: because he sees more than ever that Dr. Fogel is right not to believe in a mere nation such as Israel. THE ONLY THING THAT LIFE AND HISTORY TEACH US THAT IS CERTAIN IS OUR SUFFERING AND OUR TORAH! Those are the things that endure and that can never be taken away from us. Even if they burn our land and destroy our dwellings and take away our possessions and strip us naked, we can still carry His words in our hearts and our minds and they will sustain us!

*

Old age would be best, Charlie told himself as he drove home. He had always believed that. Despite the love and attention he'd received as a boy, for his successes, he remembered even then how he'd longed to be an older man. Old men, he believed, were free because they were farthest from their own childhoods. Charlie could hear all the arguments Murray would have given him, about the strength of emotions engendered in early years, but Charlie didn't see why it had, necessarily, to be that way. When he reached forty he would be on the other side; he could, as it were, start again. When he learned to read and to study he felt he would also learn to lose those desires that now drove him, and that, as they had just proved again with Danny, troubled his life.

He sensed that he and Danny shared this, and the thought pleased him. He knew that, long before he reached Charlie's present age, Danny would have lost the desire to remember his childhood. Charlie felt somewhat reassured to see that he was right: in all their conversations Danny had never—except for a brief mention of his mother—seemed to want

263

to talk about the past. Nor had Charlie ever sensed that the boy made a special effort to deny all the years that had passed before he'd left the Home. They simply didn't interest him.

Was this, then, why he had become so angry at the end of their visit—because he saw that Danny already believed what he was still trying to make himself believe? The boy's silence had driven him crazy. Charlie had tried to stay calm, he'd tried to be kind, yet even while he'd been talking calmly he remembered noticing how hard his hand was squeezing Danny's arm.

"Your trouble is you think too much," he said just before he left. "You need to open up more, Danny. You resist things too much." He was staring at his hand as if it belonged to somebody else. He knew that he was hurting Danny, but the boy wouldn't admit it or cry out. "If you didn't imagine me so much, you'd have done better, don't you see? Come on. Tell me."

Danny nodded his head up and down then, and Charlie saw that he was on the verge of replying. He squeezed harder. "I'm smarter than you give me credit for and I don't just mean with money," Charlie continued. "I'll tell you this now because you'll have plenty of time to think about it, right? Just because you think something doesn't mean it can't occur to somebody else!"

Danny nodded again, as if, Charlie thought, he were saying, *All right. I'll try to think about that is my answer to you,* and Charlie let go of him and stood. "Damn!" he said. "Just forget the whole thing, okay? It's crazy, my talking to you and seeing you but it's like we never even knew each other. I'm glad I came but if you want me to come again you let me know, okay?"

Danny nodded his head to show that he would. They sat next to each other in silence for a while, their backs to the TV set. Nobody seemed to pay attention to them, but Charlie saw, for the first time during the visit, how happy Danny seemed. His anger had pleased the boy. . . .

When Charlie arrived home the house was dark. Mrs. Mittleman had left him a note saying that she was at the hospital visiting Max and that Charlie's supper was warming in a pot on the stove.

Charlie ate at the kitchen table, and, in his head, he saw himself standing with his back to the door of Danny's place, telling Danny that he had begun putting on *tephillin* every morning and that Ephraim wanted to visit Danny also.

He saw Danny's neck grow red as he shook his head from side to side to indicate that he didn't want Ephraim to see him there. Danny gestured to Charlie to stay where he was. He went to one of the aides and the two of them left the room and when they returned Danny had his notebooks with him. He opened one, and, finding the section he wanted, he tore the pages from the notebook and handed them to Charlie. The section was called "The Epilogue." "For Ephraim?" Charlie asked. Danny nodded, and, moving backward into the room, he smiled for the first time. "As a present?" Charlie asked and Danny, still smiling, nodded again. The smile did nothing to comfort Charlie.

*

A LETTER TO CHARLIE FROM DANNY

I just went downstairs to get a candy bar for energy. I have my own private room which used to be a Dr.'s office and I have a desk, but when they give me a pen or pencil a man has to stay in the room with me. The other boys are always exchanging clothes with each other but I still have the coat you bought me.

It was good to stop writing and get out of my own head for a while because it reminded me of what I really wanted to tell you, Charlie, with sincerity, the way I couldn't tell you when you were here, and this is what it is:

I don't feel any bitterness toward you, my dear and loyal friend. You did the best you could and you did love me in your way. But how many people in today's world are capable of a true and full change of heart?

I can see you hanging upside down in the sewer as a boy with Murray holding you by the ankles, and I wonder: Do you exist or did I create you?

My Conclusion: Desire is Creation!

When you were leaving and the man unlocked the steel door I saw that you were tempted to take me around and give me a big hug and a kiss so I shuffled backward and then I smiled for the 1st time to show you that I plan to be getting out of here when the time is right. But this time I want to be exactly sure of where I'm going! If I didn't want to keep to my rule of not talking I would have made a joke about how a member of an endangered species has to be extra careful and then my words would have reunited us in the right way, but I knew that the best thing is to do nothing. I'm still very young, whatever my exact age is. My setbacks are temporary. My whole life is ahead of me! For what do you have to show for your life, and you've lived more than twice as long as I have!

I do not cry unto the Lord! As the olive does not give of its precious oil except under pressure, say the Rabbis, so Israel does not bring forth its highest virtues except through adversity.

AS IT IS WITH ISRAEL SO SHALL IT BE WITH DANIEL GINSBERG!

Things I didn't tell you: that I read about a system in France where you can buy an old person's home from him while he's still living in it. You give the old person the money to use and he can keep the money and still live in the house until he dies. Then it becomes yours. That's a system Mr. Mittleman would have loved!

Also: that I observe the Sabbath here by praying and reading and not carrying or traveling or working or writing.

Also: that I saw you and Dr. Fogel and Mr. Mitleman on Dr. Fogel's land.

Also: that I say Kaddish for Murray every day in silent devotion.

Also: all the other things that happened to me

after I left you. I could write to you and tell you to ask somebody here for the pages for the days I was away but then you would only know about the things I wrote down and not about *everything else* that happened. But you would see at least 3 things in my notebooks that prove that not everything I say happened really did happen, including 1 thing in today's story.

What are they?

You weren't bothered by the other boys who stared at us and did things. One boy kept pulling your sleeve and saying, "My name's Richard and I want a shower. My name's Richard and I want a shower."

Things you forgot: You forgot to tell me about Anita's other children. You forgot to tell me if you started practicing Shabbos. You forgot to tell me how you imagine Sol dying.

What I just realized: Maybe you were just making up all the things you said about praying and about studying with Dr. Fogel and about what all the people we both knew together think should happen to me and what's happened to all of them since I left!

But if you could make all that up, then it was Danny Ginsberg's influence on you that did it!

As soon as I think of him making things up so as to get me to wonder if he did or not I get the feeling inside myself that makes me feel best: that I can write forever even if they never let me out of here and I only have my memories!

This is what I wanted to say to him to make us both laugh: Life has mountains and life has valleys.

AND HERE IS MY MOST IMPORTANT DIS-COVERY: THAT THE WAY I WAS GOING EVER SINCE I FIRST SAW HIM AND DECIDED TO RUN AWAY FROM THE HOME, THERE WAS *NO SOLUTION* TO MY LIFE!

But at the exact same time I still feel that Charlie and I could be so happy together, and I even saw that I could write a real story about what it would be like for us to be living together and eventually having our own families and sharing a large house, or 2 different houses on the same piece of land, and bringing up our children together and not having to search for our happiness with others! I could send him the story the way I sent "The Epilogue" to Ephraim, but I won't do it because I know that he has to discover what I learned by himself!

In the story I could show what our life would be like *without* each other: I would stay here or run away again or be sent from 1 institution to another and all the while my talents would be drying up because the precious years when such talents are developed most highly were being neglected. *(Remember Murray's beliefs!)* Charlie would continue in his life, struggling to support all the people who need him and wondering always if his life might have been different had he made a different choice.

By showing you that, the story could make you feel that it wasn't just a fairy tale to consider us living together, as strange and without precedent as that might seem at 1st. If he sees that we really could be so happy together in a way most people never are and that his decision will make all problems disappear, then I know that he'll do whatever has to be done and that we'll both look back someday at this period of our life and chuckle over what happened in our early and difficult days! But I won't write the story for him because if he believes that my story deceived him in any way by playing on his feelings, and forced him into believing, it would be just as bad as it was before. I would be living under the fear that it was all temporary again and that things we hadn't foreseen or caused, like the policeman, would always be there threatening to destroy our life together.